TERRY LYNN THOMAS grew up in the San Francisco Bay Area, which explains her love of foggy beaches and Gothic mysteries. When her husband promised to buy Terry a horse and the time to write if she moved to Mississippi with him, she jumped at the chance. Although she had written several novels and screenplays prior to 2006, after she relocated to the South she set out to write in earnest and has never looked back.

Terry Lynn writes the Sarah Bennett Mysteries, set on the California coast during the 1940s, which feature a misunderstood medium in love with a spy. *The Drowned Woman* is a recipient of the IndieBRAG Medallion. She also writes the Cat Carlisle Mysteries, set in Britain during World War II. The first book in this series, *The Silent Woman*, came out in April 2018 and has since become a *USA Today* bestseller. When she's not writing, you can find Terry Lynn riding her horse, walking in the woods with her dogs, or visiting old cemeteries in search of story ideas.

PRAISE FOR TERRY LYNN THOMAS

'I flew through the pages of this well-crafted historical thriller'

'I am hooked on historical fiction, especially women in World War II. This book includes all the intrigue of espionage, secrets, German paperwork – and of course, murder. It was just what I was looking for!'

'*The Silent Woman* will keep you turning pages long into the night, and eagerly awaiting the next instalment of Catherine Carlisle's story'

'I highly recommend this book to both lovers of historical fiction and those that have an interest in pre-war Europe as a whole'

'This one is a page turner. Couldn't put it down! I highly recommend this book, and I can't wait until the next one'

'You are transported to another time and lifestyle in such a way you feel you have lived it'

'Will certainly read the next book with these characters'

'I thoroughly enjoyed this historical novel'

House of Lies

TERRY LYNN THOMAS

ONE PLACE. MANY STORIES

HQ
An imprint of HarperCollins*Publishers* Ltd
1 London Bridge Street
London SE1 9GF

First published in Great Britain by
HQ, an imprint of HarperCollins*Publishers* Ltd 2020

Terry Lynn Thomas asserts the moral right to be
identified as the author of this work.
A catalogue record for this book is
available from the British Library.

ISBN: 9780008331191

MIX
Paper from
responsible sources
FSC™ C007454

Printed by CPI Group (UK) Ltd, Croydon CR0 4YY

This book is dedicated to all the brave souls who made the ultimate sacrifice so we didn't have to. #NeverForget

Prologue

Rivenby, October 1941

The waxing moonlight dappled the path as Cat crept along the trail leading to Thomas's house. Leaves crunched beneath her feet, and her breath curled like dragon fire into the cold night air. The moon, although not yet full, was bright and crisp and stunningly beautiful. Tipping her head back, she allowed herself to get lost in the night sky for a moment, allowed her mind to envision an England not at war, an England with plenty of ham and oranges and unlimited butter and sugar. She said a silent prayer for those who were fighting and dying at this very minute, for those who would never see another moon again. Shivering, she continued on the path, stepping right into Thomas Charles's arms.

'Pay attention,' he whispered in her ear as he pulled her close to him. 'You never know who might be prowling in the woods at night.'

'I was just looking at the moon,' she said.

'Soon we won't have to meet in the woods under the dark of night,' Thomas said.

'I rather like these clandestine trysts. It's exciting.'

He laughed and took her hand. 'Where shall we walk tonight?'

'Back to your house? I'm freezing.'

They walked through the woods, comfortable in the silence.

'You're very good at this, you know,' Cat said.

'At what?'

'Creeping soundlessly through the woods.' She pulled him to a stop. 'You don't make any noise. Do you miss the excitement?'

'What are you talking about?'

'The excitement of spying. Of participating in the war. I know you enjoy working at the constabulary, and god knows DCI Kent is glad to have you. But it's not the same as your old life, is it? I just wondered if you missed the cloak and dagger intrigue and wished you were spying in France or someplace more exciting than Rivenby.'

'No. I'm finished with all that.' He put his hands on her shoulders. The moonlight danced across the planes of his cheeks. A slight wind ruffled his hair, which he wore longer than was fashionable. 'I worry about our friends and find myself thinking of Jacque and Emile.'

'Maybe they got out safely,' Cat said. She thought of the kind French couple who had so graciously hosted them while they were working on their last book. Cat knew full well Thomas's book writing was a guise for the real undercover work he did. He had offered her a job – and the accompanying much-needed sense of purpose – just when her life was at its lowest. The work had saved her.

So many people opened their homes, their family archives and their libraries to Cat and Thomas. They had maintained those relationships until the war broke out, when by necessity they had rushed back to England. Some people had managed to stay in touch, and Thomas, by virtue of his connections, was able to help where he could, connecting this person with that person, who would in turn provide an exit visa or funds where needed. But as the war raged on and communication became more difficult, Cat and Thomas were left to speculate as to the safety of their friends. They wondered and worried, helpless to do anything from their remote village in Northern England. Cat knew Thomas felt guilty at his inability to do much for the war effort, but a serious injury had left him sidelined, at least for now. She suspected at some point he would get involved. How could he not?

Six months ago, Thomas and Cat had agreed to assist Stephen Templeton – a historian who had devoted his life to smuggling artefacts out of the destructive reach of the Reich – by safekeeping various religious relics, documents and other items. They reasoned since Rivenby was tucked away in the northern reaches of England, the relics could be safely stored without too much worry. Thomas's house was secure, so he had readily agreed to help where he could.

'When will the chalice be here?' Cat asked.

'Not quite sure,' Thomas said.

'It's rather exciting, isn't it? Us keeping a medieval relic stolen from a castle in France.'

'Not a castle, love. A small family chapel which is now occupied by the Nazis,' Thomas said.

'You don't think anyone will try to steal it, do you?'

'Unlikely. It will be well protected in the safe. I owe Stephen Templeton a favour, so I'm happy to do this for him.' Thomas pulled Cat close to him just as the outline of his house appeared in shadowy relief against the night sky.

They walked arm in arm up to the front door, careful not to wake Beck and the missus as they crept up the stairs to Thomas's bedroom.

Chapter 1

Scotland, October 1941

Hugh Bettencourt thought how much easier his life would be if his wife was no longer a part of it. He stopped buttoning his pristine white shirt as he imagined his fingers wrapped around Margaret's lily-white throat, squeezing until the life faded from her beautiful face. Passive by nature, on the rare occasions when Hugh's pent-up anger broke through his otherwise calm mien, it was quickly tamped down by centuries of good breeding. Bettencourts did not show emotion. It was simply not done. There would be no murdering Margaret. Not today. Not ever. Hugh had cast his lot with her when he had married her.

'Coward,' he said out loud, his voice full of disgust. The sorry state of his relations with his wife paled when compared to the tricky situation with his finances. To make matters worse, his mother had finagled a weekend invitation to the party. Now she waited for him, ready to scold and issue ultimatums. He and Margaret, his errant wife, had been commanded to come to Hugh's mother's suite for a little chat.

He turned away from the window, with its stunning view of the Scottish Highlands, and finished buttoning his shirt. While he buttoned the gold cufflinks, which had belonged to his father and his grandfather before him, Hugh forced his thoughts to his current situation. Surely his mother would see that Margaret's relentless need for money had brought about his financial situation. When she laid eyes on Margaret, Lady Rosalind would realise just how out of control her daughter-in-law had become. As if the overdraft didn't speak for itself. Hugh wondered if his wife was taking drugs, opium or even heroin. He remembered horror stories of fellow soldiers becoming addicted, and knew that drug use was fashionable in some circles.

Hugh wanted a divorce. It would be so much easier if he had his mother's backing. If he couldn't divorce Margaret, he could at least lock her up in an asylum. He laughed out loud at that thought, taking pleasure in the image of Margaret being carted away, kicking and screaming all the while.

Hugh put on his dinner jacket, remembering the days when he had a valet to tend to his dressing and ironing, remembering when he didn't have to worry about his own meals. What he wouldn't give for a simple life, with a simple wife who loved him. Alas, that was not to be. Hugh girded himself for battle. Time to face Lady Rosalind.

The sun slipped down into the cold Scottish night as he made his way down the corridor to the suite of rooms that the Shorehams provided for his mother. Lady Rosalind Thackery Bettencourt required a corner suite, with plenty of firewood and comfortable arrangements for her own maid, the elderly Bettina, who should have retired long ago. Hugh paused outside his mother's door, took a deep breath and knocked gently.

'Come.' There was no mistaking the icy intention in his mother's tone.

Hugh pushed open the door and stepped inside. For a moment, he was taken aback by the spacious splendour. Although he had spent summers at the Shorehams' house as a child and had been a guest more than once over the years, never had he stayed in this particular room, which, if his recollection served, had belonged to Martin's

6

parents while they were alive. A good three times the size of Hugh's tiny room, this suite was warmed by a blazing fire with chairs arranged around it, thick rugs, newer curtains and a high four-poster bed with two eiderdowns on top. His mother moved towards him, her beringed hands extended, a forced smile on her face.

'Hugh, thank you for honouring me with your presence.' They went through the motions of air-kissing each other's cheeks. His mother was tall and had a patrician nose, piercing blue eyes and a no-nonsense manner that either put you off or made you love her. Hugh had always loved her. Lady Rosalind had rallied around Hugh when his brother James had died and he was forced to take on the mantle of his family responsibility, a job for which Hugh was ill-suited. And heaven knew, Lady Rosalind had done her best to forge a relationship with Margaret. A wave of sadness washed over him. What a disappointment he had been to his family.

'Where's Margaret?'

Hugh sighed. 'I haven't seen her all day.' In truth, Hugh and Margaret had probably spent a total of two nights together in the past six months. Margaret always had a string of lovers, who were beguiled by Margaret's beauty and undeniable sexual prowess in the beginning. As time wore on and the men realised the woman they had so desired was unhinged and possibly on drugs, they sent her packing. When Margaret threw the inevitable tantrum and threatened to tell wives of the affair, a generous cheque and a bauble of fine jewellery would quiet her. At this time, Margaret would then slink home and try to seduce Hugh with promises of renewed devotion. For years he had believed her, had taken her back each time she crawled home, full of false remorse. Things would be good between them until Margaret got bored again, until she found a new lover to please her. Then Hugh would be left alone, stupidly wondering how he allowed himself to be played like a piano and hating himself for it.

'Hugh? Are you listening to me? I said go find her. I must speak to you both at once,' Lady Rosalind said.

Just then Margaret stepped into the room in a cloud of perfume and alcohol, wearing a backless, form-fitting blue dress better suited for a jazz club than an elegant dinner in a country house. *What was she thinking?*

'Where've you been?' Hugh snapped.

'Stop it, Hugh. I'm not going to be called to heel like an obedient herding dog. I'm here and I'm only three minutes late.' She walked towards Hugh's mother. 'Lady Rosalind. You're looking well.'

'Nonsense. I'm looking every second of my years, thanks to you two.' She turned her attention to Hugh. 'Were you going to tell me you dipped into the money your father left you? You know full well the terms of your father's will. That money was to provide you an income for life. You can't just spend your capital, Hugh.'

Out of the corner of his eye, Hugh saw Margaret fidget with her necklace, a diamond and sapphire affair that he had never seen before.

'What are you talking about, mother? I know there's an overdraft, but I certainly don't know anything about using Father's money.' A recollection of a morning last August popped into his mind. He had met Margaret coming out of the bank. She had been in such a hurry she almost didn't see him. When he'd called her name, she had jumped, startled at his sudden appearance, and had surprised him with kind words and an invitation to lunch. Her actions were so out of character, he should have been suspicious. Now he saw the error of his ways in not demanding an explanation – for there was no reason in the world for Margaret to visit Hugh's banker. He turned on her and snapped, 'What have you done?'

'Don't you dare take that tone with me,' Margaret shouted. Hugh flinched, wondering if anyone else in the household was eavesdropping on this very embarrassing family row.

Before Hugh could fire back, Lady Rosalind interrupted. 'She forged your name, Hugh.' Lady Rosalind sat down and beckoned to the two chairs across from her. Hugh and Margaret remained standing. 'She spent what you had and then some. When the bank wouldn't extend the overdraft, she forged your name and accessed the money your father left you. I'm not going to ask what she's done with the money.' She ran her eyes over Margaret's body, before she stared hard at Margaret's face. 'Are you on drugs?'

'How dare you,' Margaret hissed. But she hesitated before she spoke, and Hugh noticed the startled flicker of shame. 'You've no business involving yourself in our marriage, Lady Rosalind. You go too far.'

'Since I'm supporting you both financially, I've every right.'

Lady Rosalind sat back and surveyed Hugh and Margaret like they were errant schoolchildren. A cramp of fear formed in Hugh's belly, as a sense of impending doom curled around him. He swallowed the lump that had formed in his throat. He hadn't felt like this since the war, when he had spent months in the trenches waiting to die.

Lady Rosalind addressed Margaret. 'I hired an inquiry agent. I've been having you followed for months, Margaret. I am fully aware of your licentious ways, the men, the drugs, the parties. It seems your husband is unable to control you. I, on the other hand, am not so easily thwarted.'

'I'm leaving. I don't care what you've done or who you've hired. You've no right to speak to me that way.' Margaret turned and headed to the door.

'I could prosecute.' Lady Rosalind's words hung in the air.

Margaret stopped and slowly turned around to face Hugh's mother.

'You wouldn't dare.'

Lady Rosalind plastered a condescending smile on her face.

'Of course I would. Surely you know how vindictive I can be, Margaret. Nothing would give me more pleasure than to see you held accountable for your immorality and criminal activity. After all, forgery is a crime. Lucky for you both, I'm feeling generous. I have an alternative proposition for both of you.' Once again, she beckoned to the chairs across from her. 'Now sit.'

Margaret turned on Hugh, fury flashing in her eyes. 'Are you

9

ever going to stand up to her? Don't you ever get tired of being beaten down by Mummy?'

Defeated, Hugh sat down.

'You're both headed for trouble so deep I'm afraid even I won't be able to get you out.' Lady Rosalind sat back, crossed her legs and studied Hugh and Margaret with that inscrutable look that had brought stronger men than Hugh to their knees. 'I know you rarely live together, and that Margaret is off doing god knows what with her friends while you stay at the flat in Edinburgh. I know that your creditors are tired of lending you money, and that Margaret has committed an offence that could land her in prison.'

'Mother, what are you trying to say? Get to the point,' Hugh said.

'Thank you, darling,' Margaret said. She reached for Hugh's hand, but he pushed it away. The gesture wasn't lost on Lady Rosalind.

'Very well. Let's not beat around the bush. Hugh has done a miserable job at managing our family's finances. If it weren't for Mr Williams and his expertise in these matters, we would likely be ruined. As of now, Hugh is no longer at the helm, for lack of a better word. Mr Williams is going to manage the Bettencourt interests, with my close supervision, of course.'

'Of course,' Margaret said.

Lady Rosalind continued. 'In addition to paying your overdraft, I will give you both a very generous allowance.'

'And what do we do in return?' Margaret gave words to Hugh's thoughts.

'Simple. You will move to the family home and live as husband and wife. You, Margaret, will act like the wife of a Bettencourt. No more parties, no more leaving your husband alone for months on end.' She turned towards Hugh. 'And you, my son, will get your life and your house in order.'

'And if we say no?' Hugh asked.

'I'll give you a stipend for rent and food, but as for any other money, you'll be on your own. Margaret will have to rely on your charity. That's my offer.'

Hugh stood, relieved at the lifeline his mother had tossed him. He wanted out of the marriage and would be grateful for his stipend, but he clung to his last shred of dignity as he faced his mother. 'Thank you. I'll think about it.' He turned and walked out of the room, leaving Margaret and his mother staring after him.

Taking the servants' staircase, he went out the back door and walked the familiar trail around the Shorehams' house, through the rose garden, the kitchen garden and back towards the front door. The cold night air knocked some sense into him. There was a small cottage near his mother's house. His old nanny had lived there until her death a year ago. It stood empty now. He could fix it up and live there. Maybe grow vegetables, settle down to a simple life free of Margaret.

A blast of warm air greeted him as he entered through the front door and followed the murmur of voices and the sound of ice cubes against crystal glasses. Pausing for a moment, he stood in the doorway of Martin Shoreham's drawing room, surveying the well-heeled crowd, knowing there would be no more fancy drinks parties or opulent dinners. Hugh would be a social outcast. He didn't care. God, he was tired. Tired of his mother, of Margaret, of trying to cope with responsibilities he was so clearly unable to handle.

The Shorehams' house had been full of guests since Friday. The weekend thus far had consisted of fine meals, good wine and bracing outdoor activities during the day. October was Hugh's favourite time to be in Scotland. In another two months, the region would be covered with snow. Those who remained would be housebound. Here, in the bosom of his old friends, the war, the threat of bombs and the rationing seemed a long way away. For a moment, he wondered how Martin managed to ply his guests with a never-ending run of food and wine, even sweet desserts – just when sugar and everything else seemed to be at a premium. As far as he knew, no one had been asked for their ration card. He certainly hadn't.

Margaret had joined the party in Hugh's absence. She stood in the corner with Hugh's childhood friend and their host for the weekend, Martin Shoreham. Her dark hair fell in tresses down her back, still thick and full despite her age. Through the diligent use of expensive make-ups and potions, her skin retained the glow of someone twenty years younger. There was no denying, when Margaret Bettencourt walked in a room all heads turned. Hugh had been beguiled by her from the very beginning, but their twenty-four-year marriage had been more than tumultuous. It had started out reckless and full of gay weekends, dances, parties and ski trips to Switzerland. Now he could barely stand to look at her as she leaned towards Martin, giggled, and whispered something in his ear. What the devil was she up to?

Hugh stepped into the room as Martin's wife, Hermione, weaved her way through the crowd. Martin, Hermione and Hugh had been friends since childhood. Although he and Martin had jokingly vied for Hermione's love, there was no denying Martin and Hermione were made for each other. They had married young and still treated each other with love, affection, a deep friendship. Hugh had always been envious of their solid marriage and their easy way with each other, especially in light of his own marriage, which had been its own special hell. God, how he wanted out.

Hermione's eyes found Hugh. She waved as she walked towards him. The years had not been as kind to Hermione as they had to Margaret. Smile lines had formed around her eyes. Her skin had a weathered look to it, from hours spent riding horses and golfing. Her waist had thickened, and she was a wee bit too plump through the hips. But Hermione still had her beautiful blonde hair – the silver that laced through it only added to its shimmering beauty – which she now wore piled high on her head. Physical attributes aside, all one had to do was look into Hermione's eyes to see the innate kindness there. She was the woman to turn to in times of trouble, the solid foundation to be leaned on. Hugh couldn't count how many times he had come running to Hermione when Margaret had been gallivanting in London with her friends, doing god only knew what.

They met at the drinks trolley. Filling two crystal glasses with ice and pouring just the right amount of Scotch, he handed one to Hermione just as she reached him. She took it and raised her glass to him in a silent toast.

'Another successful house party,' Hugh said.

Hermione gave him a tired smile as she wove her free arm through his. 'We've just about depleted the wine cellar. We've made a deal with the butcher. Every three months he gets a case of our fine claret, and we in turn get fresh beef. I don't know how long the arrangement will continue. When the wine's gone, we'll be eating tinned beans like everyone else. I'm afraid this will be the last party for us.'

The two of them stood shoulder to shoulder surveying the crowd. Hugh was grateful for the weekend house party; at least he knew he and Margaret would be fed, have a roof over their head and a bed to sleep in. Despite his utter failure as a husband, he still felt responsible to provide Margaret these basic necessities.

Tongues loosened and the laughter got louder as more alcohol was consumed. The lights had been dimmed and silver candelabras had been placed strategically around the room, casting the guests in warm flickering light, their voices hushed by the thick carpets and opulent velvet curtains. For a moment, Hugh pretended that the world was right again. That there was no war. No threat of invasion. But even those thoughts couldn't overcome the feeling of ruination that settled over him. Hugh's eyes lit on Margaret and Martin, who were still engaged in conversation. Margaret leaned over to Martin, talking to him in that certain way of hers, gesturing with her hands. Margaret had a knack for making you feel like you were the only person in the world. That was her special charm, the facet of her personality that allowed her to manipulate so completely. Margaret was doing all of the talking, while Martin stood by, his expression running the gamut of attentive, serious, concerned, and – finally – upset. When he wobbled on his feet, placing a hand against the wall as though to steady himself, Hugh became concerned. But Martin recovered, his waxy pale cheeks mottling red with anger. He said something to Margaret before he turned and left the room. Ever relentless, Margaret hurried after him.

Hugh set down his glass and started after Martin, but Hermione placed a hand on his arm.

'Wait. I need to talk to you.'

He turned to face her, startled by the look of concern in her eyes. 'What's wrong?'

'Nothing's wrong with me. I'm worried about you. You've been skulking around this house, hardly speaking to anyone and avoiding your wife. I know you and Margaret have drifted apart over the years. God knows, she's got the energy of a twenty-year-old – just being around her exhausts me. But there's more to it. What's going on, Hugh? Margaret's been hell for leather to get Martin alone since you two arrived. He's been avoiding her – until now. Something's wrong, dear friend. I can see it in your eyes.' She turned away from Hugh, tactfully giving him time to compose himself as she freshened their drinks. Handing Hugh his glass, she asked, 'What's happened?'

'Between my mother and my wife, I'm at my wits' end. Turns out my wife has managed to saddle me with a monumental overdraft. When the bank wouldn't give her any more money, she forged my name and helped herself to a chunk of my capital.'

'Dear god,' Hermione said.

'Oh, it gets worse. You see, I'm so out of touch with Margaret, I had no idea of the forgery. Would you like to know how I found out?' Hugh didn't wait for a response. 'My mother told me. Seems she'd hired an investigator to keep an eye on Margaret.' Hugh downed his drink. 'Just now, Mother sat us both down and issued an ultimatum. We're to move home and behave like a normal married couple.'

'And if you don't?' Hermione asked.

'I'm to receive a stipend to live on and will otherwise be disinherited. And you know what, Hermione? I don't care. I am going to divorce my wife and retire to Nanny's cottage. God

14

knows, I'm ready to live a quiet life.' Hugh sighed. 'Just saying those words gives me relief.'

'You poor dear,' Hermione said.

'How's Martin? I haven't had a moment alone with him all week.'

'I'm not sure. He's been distant of late, but I assume he's worried about the business and the war, like we all are. We don't talk like we used to.' She sighed. 'But we've been married a long time and things can't stay perfect forever.'

Across the room, the Shorehams' housekeeper beckoned Hermione with a wave.

Hermione set her drink down. 'If you'll excuse me. It seems I'm needed.' She turned to face Hugh. 'If there's anything I can do for you, I hope you'll ask. You're a dear friend, and Martin and I will always help you. You'd do the same if the circumstances were reversed.'

After giving Hugh's arm a reassuring squeeze, Hermione hurried off to speak to the housekeeper, leaving Hugh alone to wallow in his problems.

***

Alex Bradshaw, also known as Bradley Alexander, Jeffrey Bradford and Ford Jefferson, was born the fourth son of an alcoholic wastrel who squandered his family fortune and beat his children until they systematically left home. An intelligent young man who had a knack for all things mechanical, Alex had suffered a bout of scarlet fever when he was fourteen, which left him homebound and bedridden for nearly a year. During this time he taught himself locksmithing from a book he found in his father's vast and underused library. Practising on every lock in the house, including the various safes scattered around his family home, Alex soon became a master safecracker. When he was eighteen, he started sneaking into other fine homes near his own, practising on the safes and lockboxes of his neighbours. By the time he was twenty-two, there wasn't a lock he couldn't tame.

15

On this October morning, he woke just as the autumn sun shone through his window. His bedsit, on the top floor of a luxury Edinburgh hotel, was just big enough to hold a bed, a desk and a comfortable chair. A small kitchen area provided a kettle for his tea and room to store a tin of biscuits. He smiled as he put the kettle on. Last night's job couldn't have gone better.

A small velvet bag lay on the table beside his bed. He dumped the contents – a strand of pearls, a diamond brooch and a dozen loose stones – on the forest-green counterpane, pleased at the size and quality of the goods he had stolen. The loose diamonds would be easy to sell. It would be days, maybe weeks, before Vanessa Trevelyan realised her precious jewels were no longer in residence. He thought of her as he went through his morning ablutions – imperious, bossy and condescending to all who crossed her path. Alex didn't begrudge the woman her shortcomings. After all, no one was perfect. But she was greedy and cruel, a terrible combination for someone in a position of power.

Alex had stumbled across Vanessa Trevelyan quite by accident, hearing her name mentioned at a cocktail party months before. A quick investigation revealed Vanessa's husband had died with considerable wealth. A generous man by nature, he had left respectable legacies to his loyal servants, along with an even larger chunk of his money to Saint Agnus's Orphanage. Vanessa Trevelyan had been outraged by her husband's generosity and had threatened to contest his will, claiming her husband was not in a fit state of mind to leave so much money to the servants. Word of this got out, and after said servants received their money, they left en masse, leaving Vanessa Trevelyan a huge house to run and no one to help her do so. After trying without success to hire help from the closest village, she went straight to Saint Agnus and offered to care for two sweetly disposed sisters, whose parents tragically died in a car accident. Saint Agnus, always short of funds and grateful for two fewer mouths to feed during this time of rationing, took Vanessa Trevelyan up on her offer. In reality, the girls were no more than slaves. No schooling was provided for them. Alex heard, but hadn't been able to verify, that the girls shared an attic bedroom and were often sent to bed hungry.

He picked up one of the diamonds and held it up to the morning light, where it glistened and glimmered and seemed to grow hot in his hand. Lady Trevelyan would most certainly not be happy when she discovered her diamonds had been stolen. He smiled. *If only I could be there when she discovers her loss.* Now all he had to do was arrange for money to be transferred for the care of the orphans. Maybe a legacy from a long-lost relative? The sisters would receive enough money for an education and room and board. Neither of them would be treated poorly again. Not if Alex had any say in the matter. Timmer Ashcourt, Alex's trusted friend and man of business would see to it.

***

Two hours later, with the diamonds properly disposed of, money in pocket, and assurance the girls would be extricated from Vanessa Trevelyan's care as soon as possible, Alex had ordered breakfast at his favourite café and was just settling in to read the morning paper when an over-dressed gentleman in a camel-hair coat, silk scarf and leather gloves sat down across from him. The waitress hurried over with a smile on her face.

'Can I get you some tea, sir?'

'Only some privacy,' the man growled. Once the waitress scurried away, the man turned his attention to Alex. 'Mr Bradshaw?'

Alex recognised Michael Grenville immediately. A frisson of fear ran down his spine. Michael Grenville was a notorious criminal. A master of theft, murder, arson and any combination of the three, Michael Grenville had never been found guilty of a crime. Witnesses slated to testify against him often turned up dead. The last thing Alex needed was involvement with a man like Grenville.

Unsure how to proceed, Alex pretended to be annoyed and said, 'Yes?'

'Michael Grenville's the name. I have a job for you.'

'Excuse me?'

'I've a well-paying job that demands a certain level of expertise.'

Alex feigned ignorance. 'Forgive me, sir. You must have me confused for someone else.'

The man recited a detailed precis of every single thing Alex had stolen over the past year, including Lady Trevelyan's diamonds, and even knew Alex had attended a dinner party at Martin Shoreham's estate, accepting a last-minute invitation and turning it into a reconnaissance mission. The evening had been fruitful, and Alex had come away with some ideas for future jobs.

'You steal from the rich and give generously to the poor. Lady Trevelyan won't be happy when she discovers her diamonds are missing. Rather embarrassing for you if the police came and arrested you in front of all those fancy people.' The man leaned back in his chair and crossed his legs. 'Do I have your attention now? Very good. Now listen closely.'

The job was rather straightforward: intercept a medieval relic, which had been smuggled out of France and was soon to be transported for safekeeping to a small village.

'You'll impersonate the assigned guard. After the chalice is safely stored, you'll return to the house and extricate it.'

'Why not take it during transport?' Alex asked.

'Because I want you to check out the house and see if there is anything else of value there.'

'You are going to rob a house twice?' He shook his head. *Foolish mistake.*

'No. I am interested in the house's occupant. No need to concern yourself with that. I'll see you have appropriate credentials and explain how I want the job handled.'

'I don't need you to tell me how to do my job,' Alex said.

18

'You'll do as I say and be paid well for it.' Grenville reached into his coat pocket and put a picture of a middle-aged woman on the table between them. 'I want you to be on the lookout for this woman while you're in Rivenby.'

Alex took the picture and studied it. The woman had a thin face, with prominent cheekbones and full lips. She wore a dowdy hat, a frumpy jumper and a tweed skirt with an uneven hem. Her eyes had a beseeching look in them, as though she were trapped and trying to escape.

'Who is she?' Alex asked.

'None of your business. Let's just say I want to find her.'

It would be very easy for Alex to flee from Michael Grenville. He had connections in the underbelly of Edinburgh and London. He could easily placate the man and simply move on, with Michael Grenville none the wiser.

'Don't think about running away, Mr Bradshaw,' Michael Grenville said. 'If you run, I'll find you. That's a promise.'

'How do I know I can trust you? You could be with the police.'

The man reached into his coat pocket and pulled out a thick wad of notes. 'There's twice that much when the job is complete. Get to Rivenby and lie low. I'll be in touch.' Michael Grenville slid out from behind the table, pulled his hat down over his face and walked out the door.

Alex sat for a moment, disconcerted that someone actually knew about his past criminal history. Glancing around the room to make sure no one had been spying on their conversation, he tucked the envelope into his coat pocket.

***

Hugh awoke to a cold grey morning and the sound of rain pinging against his window. Resisting the urge to stay under the warm eiderdown, Hugh placed his feet on the cold floor and dressed hurriedly. Margaret hadn't spoken to him at all the previous evening, and she hadn't come to their bedroom, not that Hugh expected her. With any luck, she'd find a new lover to take care of her. If Lady Fate smiled on him, maybe he would never see Margaret again. It didn't take him long to pack his holdall, as most of his belongings were at his mother's house. In a few hours, he would be well away from Margaret. For the first time in their marriage, he was going to sneak off without a word and leave his wife wondering.

Shutting his holdall with a resolute snap, Hugh glanced around the room one more time to make sure he hadn't left any personal belongings. Martin and Hermione would be upset with him for not saying goodbye, but Hugh needed to leave the Shorehams' before his mother came knocking on his door, ready to enforce her own plans for Hugh. He was ready to walk out the door when Margaret burst into the room. A blood-red stain – probably wine – was splattered across her breast. Her rumpled dress hung unevenly around her ankles. The smell of yesterday's drinks, another man's cologne and sweat assaulted Hugh's senses.

Margaret's eyes darted over Hugh and around the room, coming to rest finally on Hugh's closed holdall. 'What are you doing?'

'Having decided on taking up my mother's offer, I'm off to scurry home with my tail between my legs and live a quiet life in a secluded cottage. You, dear wife, are officially free of me. I'll have my solicitor contact you, so we can get divorced.'

'Quiet secluded life? You? Good god, Hugh, you've no idea what it's like to be without funds. Believe me, darling, you'll hate it.' She moved over to the mirror and fussed with her hair.

'Will you never grow up?'

'Me? Grow up? This from the man who is incapable of earning his way in the world. Face it, darling, you've done a horrid job of providing.'

He picked up his holdall and headed towards the door. 'Good luck, Margaret.'

Margaret moved to block his way. 'What about me?'

'Surely you can get one of your lovers to take care of you. And so there's no misunderstanding between us, if you ever forge my signature again, I shall prosecute.'

Margaret's eyes showed fear for a second, but she recovered, secure in the knowledge there would be no legal proceedings. Neither Hugh nor Lady Rosalind would shame themselves with a court case. She walked over to Hugh and reached out to touch his face. He pushed her hand away.

'Darling, I've actually solved all of our problems.' She reached into the small evening bag she carried with her and pulled out a wad of notes, waving them in front of Hugh before she tucked them into his pocket. 'Soon I'll have more. That's a promise.'

'Where did you get that? My god, Margaret, what have you done?' He took the money out of his pocket and thumbed through the wad of bills. Suspicious of Margaret and disgusted with his own momentary swell of greed, he thrust the money back at her.

She snatched it away and tucked it into her purse. 'You don't want it? Fine. I'm just trying to pay you back.' Kicking off her shoes, she sat on the bed and rubbed her feet. 'I'm trying to help you. Help us. Why don't you trust me?'

'Because you've been lying to me since the day I met you. And god knows I've suffered for it.' He imagined Margaret having sex for money, no better than a common prostitute.

'I assure you this money is rightfully mine. I've a plan to get us situated once and for all, far away from your mother. I've recently discovered I'm entitled to a bit of an inheritance. If you want a divorce, fine. I know I've put you through hell. I'm just asking that you wait a little while, so I can get some money to live on.'

'Why do you need me for that? You seem able to navigate the world without me.'

Margaret looked at him, and for the briefest moment he saw the old Margaret, the beautiful young woman who had ignited his passion so long ago. But that Margaret was a figment of his

21

overzealous imagination. It seemed he'd been waiting a lifetime for that particular side of Margaret to get a foothold in their marriage. It hadn't, and the realisation that he had fallen in love with an affectation stung.

'For security, I suppose. I'm a woman, alone.' She looked at him beseechingly. 'We don't have to live together, but it will give me comfort to know you're there if I need you.'

'I thought you said your family was dead.' Hugh stepped away from Margaret, as if putting distance between them would provide protection.

'I have a brother. I haven't seen him since I ran away. My childhood was horrid, actually. It's something I don't care to dwell on, that's why I told you they were dead. I just vowed to be alone and forget them. In any event, my parents passed away and left me money. I intend to get it.'

Hugh thought Margaret could very well be lying, as he had learned ages ago that the truth changed according to whatever agenda she was manipulating. After years of marriage and thousands of lies, Hugh had learned the best course of action was to play along, as a confrontation would only prove fruitless.

'Who is this brother? Where is he? Was there a will? You can't just show up and demand money. There are legal things you need to do. For one thing, we should get a solicitor —'

'I've arranged a solicitor and I have everything under control. I just need you to be available, Hugh. I don't need you to ask questions or get involved. We don't even need to live together. I'm asking you to be near, nothing more, until I get my money.'

'No,' Hugh said. 'I'm finished. I'm going home.' He adjusted the strap of his holdall on his shoulder. 'This is goodbye, Margaret. Face it, we'll be glad to get away from each other.'

'Wait,' she said, stamping her foot like a petulant child.

She moved close to him and fixed the top button of his shirt. Against his will, the heat of her aroused him, just as she knew it would. 'We've had a good run, Hugh. I know you don't love me anymore, but if we're going to part ways, I'd like to do so as friends.'

Her kind words were so out of character, he should have been suspicious, should have known that she was just being nice to him because she had no lover waiting to provide for her. But her nearness, the physicality of her, evoked a response that took away his reason.

'I'm asking you to trust me this one last time. Allow me to at least repay you some of the money I stole. After I do that, we'll part ways, divorce and you'll never have to see me again. Come with me while I get my inheritance.' She ran her fingers over his lips.

He had to get away from her, before she pulled him in as she had done so many times before.

'Where is your brother?' He couldn't stop himself. He bent close and nuzzled her neck.

She brushed his lips with hers before she stood on tiptoes and whispered in his ear. 'I'm going to get the money to which I am entitled and make things right with you. But you will not get involved. Those are my conditions. You can come with me, do as I say, and recoup your losses. Or we can say goodbye today and you can step out of this home and into your life of dependence on Mummy for your stipend. My rules. Your choice.'

She kissed him, and in a brief moment of weakness, he let himself go. After all the betrayals, he still physically craved her.

'I'll go with you,' he murmured into her hair. God help him, he loved her. And hated himself for it.

'Very good.' Margaret pushed away from him. 'I'll go and change. We'll leave in an hour.'

23

Chapter 2

Cat Carlisle hurried home from Emmeline Hinch-Billings's secretarial school, the large ledger tucked under her arm. Autumn was in the air, along with its accompanying chill. She was so proud of all that Emmeline had accomplished, training the young women who enrolled in courses as bookkeepers, secretaries and shorthand typists, and then securing them good jobs. At first Cat thought participating as a silent partner, with generous cash donations when necessary, would be fulfilling enough. When Emmeline Hinch-Billings needed a bookkeeper, Cat had taken over keeping the ledgers. Numbers didn't lie, and Cat had soon discovered she enjoyed the satisfaction of balancing the books.

Try as she might, going over the ledgers in the tiny office at the school proved difficult today. A handful of the young women had received job offers in Scotland. Their excitement had been contagious, their success an inspiration to the new young women who hoped to acquire the skills necessary to earn a living. While encouraging, the thrum of excitement had proved a distraction, and Cat decided she'd be better off doing the books in the privacy of her office at home. The school had been in operation almost a year, and it was already turning a tidy profit, much to the surprise of the bankers who had refused to give Emmeline Hinch-

24

Billings a loan. Cat had stepped in with the financial backing and was happy to have done so.

As she stepped from the lane onto the path that led to the front door of Saint Monica's, Bede Turner was busy hanging linen pillowcases on the clothesline. When she saw Cat, she picked up her laundry basket and headed in her direction.

'You're finished early,' Bede said.

'Couldn't concentrate at the school, too noisy. I thought I'd work here. How's Mrs Grenville doing?' Cat said.

'Not good. She's been in her room crying a good part of the day. I took her a tray with tea and toast about an hour ago. The poor woman's scared to death. And her face is terribly bruised.'

'Should I get her a doctor?'

'Given her current state of mind, a female nurse would probably be better. She does need medical attention though, Miss Catherine.' Bede shook her head. 'I hope you know what you're doing. These women have violent men in their lives who will eventually come looking for them. Have you given any thought as to what might happen when an angry husband shows up on our doorstep? You can't protect these women alone. Can't you at least ask Mr Charles—'

'Bede, I don't want to talk about this. No one is going to find the women we're sheltering. Their batterers live in other counties far away.'

'And what if they tell them where they are? What if they write to them out of guilt or misplaced loyalty? You don't know what's going on in their heads. Are you going to monitor the post every day?' Bede pulled her jumper tighter around her stout body.

'Why would they tell the men who battered them where they are?'

Bede gave Cat a knowing look. 'Because they feel guilty about leaving. Because maybe they still love their husbands, despite the brutal treatment.'

'But they've taken the first step towards freedom by coming here. Doesn't that count for something?'

'I don't like it. I don't like it one bit. We'd be better off with a man around here. That's all I want to say about it. Oh, and that Lucy Bardwell still hasn't done the breakfast dishes, even though it's her turn. I did as you said and left them for her.'

Cat bit back her irritation. Lucy Bardwell had been nothing but trouble since she came to Saint Monica's. She frequently missed her classes at Emmeline's school and rarely did her chores, leaving the others to take on her share of the work. 'Thanks, Bede. I'll deal with Lucy.'

Bede nodded her approval and hurried back to the clothesline, her laundry basket resting on her hip. Cat watched her go, certain she was doing the right thing for these unfortunate women, despite Bede's misgivings. Currently there were only two women in residence at Saint Monica's. Elaina Masterson had shown up for her first day of secretarial training with a fresh scar down the side of her face. 22 years old and the daughter of a farmer, Elaina had married early at the encouragement of her parents, who were eager to have one less mouth to feed. It didn't take long for Elaina to discover her husband's violent side. Over the course of a few months, the beatings increased to a daily occurrence. Elaina had fled back to her parents, but her father had encouraged her to stay by her husband's side and be a better wife. When she returned to her marital home, her husband, who was so drunk he couldn't stand up straight, cut Elaina's face with a knife. The next day after he'd left for work, Elaina took all the money she had, packed her meagre belongings and bought a one-way bus ticket to Rivenby, secure in the knowledge her husband would never find her there. She had taken a room in Miss Foster's boarding house and immediately enrolled in secretarial school. Cat had taken one look at Elaina and knew she needed help.

Shortly after that, Jennie LaGrange had come along. Jennie kept her story to herself, but she was a kind soul, got on well with everyone in the household and didn't shirk at doing her chores. Jennie and Elaina, along with the women who had come before them, had used the sanctuary of Saint Monica's to recover from their brutal home life. Every day they grew mentally stronger. The courses at Emmeline's school engaged their mind. Bede fed them well and gave them chores around the house, so they could feel useful.

Tomorrow Jennie and Elaina would move to Scotland, where good jobs and a new future awaited them. Lucy Bardwell and Alice Grenville were the newest arrivals. Lucy had been at Saint Monica's for six weeks, while Alice Grenville had only arrived two days ago. Although Cat and Bede were both concerned about Alice, who was frightened of her own shadow, Cat believed with time she would heal and the promise of a fresh start would bolster her, like it had for Jennie and Elaina.

Cat stood inside the front door for a moment, savouring the quiet solitude. She carried her ledgers up the stairs, pausing before Alice Grenville's room. She pressed her ear against the door, glad to hear the soft sounds of Alice's snores. *Thank god. The woman needs a good rest.* Her mind was so preoccupied when she stepped into her own bedroom that it took her a moment to see Lucy Bardwell, who stood before the looking glass, dressed in one of Cat's suits.

'Oh!' Lucy cried out.

'What do you think you're doing?' Cat snapped at the same time. She tossed the ledgers on her writing desk and surveyed the clothes that lay scattered on her bed. 'You'd best explain yourself.'

Lucy sat down on the chaise under the window, buried her face in her hands and burst into tears. Cat stood silently by, not taken in by Lucy's dramatic display.

Cat handed her a handkerchief. 'Here.'

'Thank you,' Lucy said. She dabbed her eyes and wiped her nose. 'I'm so sorry, Mrs Carlisle. I know I shouldn't have come in here.'

'You're right. You've no business going through other people's things.' Cat bit back her anger. 'How do you expect anyone to feel safe here if we can't trust each other?'

'You can trust me!' Lucy said. She jumped up and faced Cat, her cheeks pink with either rage or shame, Cat couldn't tell which. 'I haven't had a new dress for as long as I can remember.'

'Neither has anyone else,' Cat said. 'You're not the only one affected by rationing.'

'It's not the rationing,' Lucy said. 'My brother thinks nice clothes are a waste of money. I've had to buy all my things second-hand.' She ran her hand over the fabric of Cat's suit. 'The first thing I'm going to do when I start working is buy a new suit.' She gave Cat a shy smile. 'I mean brand new, as in never worn by anyone else.'

'Lucy, why won't you let me help you get your money? We could get you a solicitor, at least to look into it.'

'Oh no. You mustn't! Ambrose would be so angry.' Her eyes had a frantic look Cat recognised all too well. 'Please. Promise me you won't speak to Ambrose. And I'm sorry I came in here. I know I shouldn't have.'

'Go and change into your own clothes. And when you've finished, there's a sink full of dishes waiting for you.'

'Yes, ma'am,' Lucy said.

'I don't want to have to discuss missing chores with you again, Lucy. I mean it. Another mishap like this, and you'll have to leave.'

Lucy nodded, not meeting Cat's eyes as she grabbed her clothes and hurried out the door.

Cat sat down and tried to focus on her bookkeeping duties, but her mind kept wandering back to Lucy Bardwell. After finding a room in which to lodge, she had registered for school. Cat had noticed the dark-haired, outspoken woman right away, but had never thought she came from a difficult home, until she'd come to school one day with a black eye and a swollen lip. Emmeline and Cat had taken the young girl into a private room to find out what had happened to her.

'It's my brother,' she'd said. 'I went home to get some money out of my bank account. He got angry. Ambrose doesn't believe women should manage their own money.'

Cat had immediately offered Lucy Bardwell a place in her home and a scholarship for school, thinking Lucy could save her money for her future. But Lucy hadn't saved her money. When she didn't show up at school one day, Cat and Bede Turner became worried her brother had found her and taken her away against her will. They had been in the process of formulating a plan to rescue her, when Lucy returned home, laden with shopping bags.

'Where have you been? We've been worried sick about you,' Cat had said.

'I took the day to do some shopping.'

Cat had opened her mouth to chastise Lucy about being reckless with money, but the girl had interrupted her.

'I only have one suit,' Lucy had said. At least she'd had the grace to look embarrassed. 'I don't have anything to wear when I clean it, so I bought another one. Second-hand, mind you.' Lucy had given them a wan smile and hurried out of the room.

'I don't trust that girl one bit,' Bede had said.

Now Cat stared at the ledger before her. She agreed with Bede. Lucy Bardwell couldn't be trusted. More importantly, Cat's intuition said that Lucy was hiding something. Cat would have to find out what that something was.

Chapter 3

Hugh never said goodbye to his mother, nor had he thanked Martin and Hermione for their hospitality. Instead he had left his mother a note, slipping it under her door and creeping away like a thief in the night The note explained Hugh had decided to go away and sort things out, that he didn't see a future with Margaret, and as such, he would be taking the proffered stipend. Writing the words had caused him shame, but there was nothing to be done about it. He had lived his life in James's shadow. Why had he thought that would change once his beloved brother had died? If anything, James's death had thrown Hugh's shortcomings into stark relief.

And here he was, forty-eight years old and dependent on his mummy for bread money. He'd write Martin a letter explaining everything once he and Margaret were settled. They'd arrived in Much Killham in the early afternoon, after an awkward train ride. Although the day had started out with passion, their lovemaking had quickly turned mechanical and void of emotion. It hadn't taken long for Hugh to realise that Margaret was manipulating him with sex, as she had done hundreds of times in the past. When he pushed her away, feeling used once again, she had become angry with him, deliberately finding fault, while her behaviour escalated by the second.

When she'd started yelling, Hugh had hurried out of the house, opting to walk to the train station alone. During the journey, Margaret was too full of indignation to do anything other than sulk. As such, they barely spoke. For the first time in their marriage Hugh didn't try to fill the silence with senseless babble. Instead, he stared out the window and planned a life free of Margaret's never-ending schemes.

They were the only two people disembarking in Much Killham. Bitter cold wind whipped around them as they stood on the platform, while the train chugged away.

'Oh, I hate this place,' Margaret said.

Hugh surveyed the lush green surroundings, savouring the clean wind, while Margaret gave the attendant instructions about their trunks.

'There's no taxi available. We'll have to walk,' Margaret said.

'It's a perfect day for it,' Hugh said.

She gave him a surly look. 'Oh, do be quiet, Hugh. Save your country gentleman nonsense. It's cold. I am not wearing proper shoes. If you hadn't been in such a hurry the estate agent could have met us here and I wouldn't have to spend another minute in this freezing wind.'

Hugh ignored her. He had studied a map of the area on the train and knew their cottage wasn't too far. In another time he would have offered to go on ahead and find a taxi for his wife, as any gentleman would do. But he was tired of his wife and equally tired of being a gentleman.

'We should stop at the shop for some provisions,' Hugh said.

'Do whatever you want,' Margaret said, waving him away in a familiar dismissive gesture.

'Very well. You go to the cottage. I'll walk to the high street and arrange something to cook for dinner.'

'Surely you don't expect me to put on an apron and act like a housewife. I'll starve first.'

'Suit yourself.' Hugh had turned and headed to the grocer's on the corner, leaving Margaret to fend for herself.

Half an hour later, he stood in the lane and surveyed the grey stone cottage with mullioned windows that would be his home. The cottage was small, with two bedrooms upstairs, the kitchen and a small living area downstairs. The cottage hadn't been occupied, it seemed, for quite some time. The front garden was overgrown, and so was the walkway that led to the faded front door.

'What an eyesore,' Hugh said out loud.

The cottage next door was well maintained. Fashioned out of the same grey stone as Hugh's cottage, this house had a front door and window frames painted a glossy black. The garden around the house was weed-free and well mulched. Six apple trees loaded with red fruit lined the back of the house. A medium-sized barn and chicken coop were tucked into a corner. The place was charming, unpretentious, a perfect example of a small yet contained country cottage.

A woman who Hugh guessed to be in her early fifties had stepped out of the front door. Hugh watched as she stepped into a pair of wellies and hurried towards him, an unbelieving smile on her face.

'Hugh Bettencourt?' Her voice held a question now. And as she came nearer, memories came flooding back. Vera. Vera Mills. Could it be? Hugh smiled and set his groceries down. He hurried over to her, but stopped when he got close.

'Is it you?' She beamed at him.

Her brown eyes still held the same warmth. How long had it been since they had seen each other? How long had it been since he had broken her heart? What would have happened if he had stood up to his mother and married Vera?

'Vera,' he said.

'Don't tell me you've taken the cottage?' Time stopped for a moment. Vera Mills smiled at him, that wide smile filled with simple and unadorned kindness, that smile that opened up her face. Hugh felt the warmth radiating from her and accepted it with gratitude, realising just how churlish and cold he had become over the years. In Vera's presence he suddenly saw himself clearly and realised that his relationship with Margaret had pulled his bad qualities to the surface and frozen them in place. Remorse and regret flooded through him. Vera must have sensed it, for she put a warm hand on his arm.

'Let's don't have any regrets, Hugh. Nothing to be done about them.' She took her hand back and stepped away. 'Am I to assume that stylish brunette is your wife?'

'Not for long,' Hugh blurted out. 'We're divorcing.'

'Oh, I'm sorry to hear that,' Vera said. Her eyes travelled to his shopping bag. 'Do you have enough provisions? I know the shops are short on everything. Let me know if you need me to help you with registering for your ration card. And you'll probably need firewood—' She laughed. 'Forgive me. I'm sure you're perfectly capable of getting yourself sorted.'

'Actually, I've no idea where anything is, so perhaps tomorrow you could tell me where to go?'

'I'd be happy to help. Come by for a cup of tea and we can get caught up.'

Before she turned to walk away, she said, 'I'm glad you're here. Glad we'll be neighbours.'

He watched her walk back to her house, resisting the urge to run after her. There were so many things he wanted to ask her, so many things he wanted to say. Turning back to his own front door, he saw a curtain flutter in one of the upstairs rooms. Margaret had witnessed his conversation. Hugh didn't give a damn.

***

That night, Hugh dreamed of Vera Mills. He dreamed of a time when he and Vera were young and life was full of promise. Dressing hurriedly, he lit the fire and put the kettle on. A sheet of paper lay on the kitchen table. Hugh started a list of the things they needed. Secretly he hoped for a glimpse of Vera. Should he go knock on her door? Take her up on her offer of help? After he poured himself a cup of tea, he moved to the window and watched Vera's house, wondering about her life. He had yet to see a man around her house. Had she married? Did she have children?

Doing a quick calculation, he realised that he hadn't seen Vera in close to twenty-six years. They had met one summer when Hermione and Martin had gone to the sea, leaving Hugh on his own. On a whim, he had gone to a dance by himself, and had found Vera sitting alone while the music played. She was spending the summer with some distant relations who lived in Hugh's village. Since she hadn't known anyone, she was glad of Hugh's company. Reluctantly, she allowed him to lead her onto the dance floor. After that dance, they spent the entire evening sitting outside, talking and getting to know each other, unaware that the party had ended and the band had packed away their instruments and left. They would have talked all night had the host and hostess – an embarrassed expression on their faces – not reminded them that it was two-thirty in the morning. After that, they were together every day. They rode bikes, went swimming, shared their favourite books and music. That summer, his heart was full. He had met the woman he would marry.

Lady Rosalind had been touring the United States while Hugh was busy courting Vera Mills. Had she been home to witness her son's new girlfriend, she would have made quick work of the situation. As it was, she had to find out about Hugh and Vera through the church gossip mill. Lady Rosalind had liked Vera, or at least she had made a pretence of welcoming Vera into the Bettencourt home. But when Hugh asked for his aunt's ring, so he could propose, Lady Rosalind put her foot down, packed Hugh off to the family business in Edinburgh and promised to find him a more suitable wife. Vera took it all in her stride. Hugh had

34

suffered mightily, but he didn't dare defy his mother. His only regret was that he and Vera never had a proper goodbye. Lady Rosalind had seen to that.

**

Hugh had been lucky enough to find firewood in one of the outbuildings. He had built a fire and had just put the kettle on when Vera knocked on the door, carrying a roasted chicken, complete with potatoes and garden vegetables, a bountiful meal in these times of rationing. Hugh had been delighted. Margaret had been terse and standoffish. She hadn't even said thank you. After Vera had left, Margaret had complained that women of Vera's ilk left her bored and in need of a drink.

Hugh sighed. Tossing the last two logs onto the embers, Hugh moved to the kitchen sink, washed his hands and started to prepare breakfast. He had just pulled the frying pan out when Margaret came into the room wearing shoes made for walking and carrying a holdall and the large handbag she used for travel.

'I hope you're not cooking for me,' she said. 'You know I don't usually eat in the morning.'

'Very well. I'll just eat your share.' Deliberately keeping his back to her, Hugh cracked two eggs into the frying pan, sliced two pieces of bread from the loaf Vera had brought over yesterday, and put them under the grill. He refilled his tea, not bothering to ask Margaret if she wanted some. Margaret could take care of herself as far as Hugh was concerned.

'You're leaving?' He nodded at the holdall.

'I'm off to deal with my brother. I've found a place to live near his home, so we don't need to be under the same roof. And you can wipe that self-satisfied smile off your face. I saw the way you looked at the matron next door. Childhood sweetheart? You nearly swooned over the food she brought. Really, Hugh. Sometimes I think you are one of the most foolish men I've ever met. Surely you don't fancy her.' Margaret poured herself tea.

Hugh ignored her.

'Things are going along as planned. Take solace in that. With any luck, I'll have some money and we should be free of each other within a couple of weeks.' She moved next to him at the sink. For a brief moment they stood close to each other, gazing out the window. Smoke curled from Vera's chimney. Hugh imagined her kitchen, warm and smelling of apples and baking bread. Vera, busy working on some project, humming under her breath. A wave of longing washed over him, for Vera and for the welcome hearth and home she represented.

'You're maudlin, Hugh. I'm leaving. I'll write if I need you.'

'No,' he said, turning on Margaret, angry at being treated like a puppet. 'I'm going to stay here for one month. Then I'm going to Scotland. I'm not going to chase you down to say goodbye.'

With a sly smile on her face that told Hugh she didn't believe him, Margaret grabbed her handbag and hurried out of the house. Once she had gone and the house had fallen silent, save the fire as it crackled in the grate, Hugh sighed with relief. Life was so much easier when Margaret wasn't around. As for going to Scotland, that was a lie. Hugh wouldn't be going anywhere. Not as long as Vera was next door.

Chapter 4

Lucy Bardwell slipped into the cover of the woods behind Saint Monica's before the sun rose. Careful not to catch Mrs Carlisle's fine blue suit on the brambles, she stepped over a patch of nettles and headed towards the trail that led to the bus stop. Lucy had lingered as Mrs Carlisle tucked the suit back into her wardrobe, where Lucy knew it would be promptly forgotten. That night no one had to ask Lucy to wash up the dinner dishes. When everyone was listening to the wireless, she had sneaked back up to Cat's bedroom and stolen the suit, not feeling the least bit guilty for her transgression. In fact, she felt certain Mrs Carlisle wouldn't even notice the suit was missing. Honestly, Lucy had never seen so many beautiful clothes in one place, all of them made of fine fabric, cut in classic styles that would remain fashionable for years. She glanced down at the skirt and the silk stockings on her long legs – also stolen from Mrs Carlisle's room – and admired what she saw.

When she reached the wide trail, she slipped off her wellies and donned her good city shoes. Tucking the boots behind a shrub, she made a mental note of where she had hidden them for easy retrieval later. She pulled a mirror out of her pocket, checked her lipstick and fiddled with her hat. Once certain she looked her best, she slipped on her grey leather gloves, and hurried to the bus stop before she changed her mind. She didn't think about her actions, didn't question if she was making a mistake, until she had boarded the bus and paid her fare, the gesture a commitment in its own right.

The minute she handed her coins to the driver, doubt settled in. Her love trysts had been conducted in secret, often at a hotel room that Lucy paid for with her own money. She had been so wrapped up in her own life, her schooling, her responsibilities at Saint Monica's and the dance parties that she went to every Wednesday night, she hadn't given much thought to her lover. In Lucy's mind, the secretive nature of their relationship had been her doing. But as she thought over the past few months, she wondered why her lover hadn't been more insistent about spending time with her. He'd never asked about her family or her situation. So preoccupied had she been with her own life, she hadn't given his life, and how he spent his time when he was away from her, much thought.

He loved her. He would love their baby. Surely he would do the right thing and marry her. They could find a nice house, maybe get a nanny to help. Life was so much easier with someone to share its burdens. Lucy wanted to stay active and busy after the baby was born. Often after having a child, a woman would let herself go. Lucy refused to be one of those women. She would be a devoted mother, but she vowed to put just as much effort into being a good wife. When her husband came home at the end of his workday, he would find Lucy waiting for him, looking pretty.

The bus lurched. Waves of nausea interrupted her domestic fantasy. Her stomach rumbled. She took a small piece of bread out of her handbag and ate it slowly. After she forced herself to eat every last bite of it, she leaned back in her seat and closed her eyes, waiting for her stomach to settle. The uncertainty of her situation had been eating away at her since she'd missed her monthly course and ultimately discovered she was pregnant. Once she had explained about the baby, and once plans were made, the knot of tension would fade. Cat Carlisle – in her overzealous need to rescue women in need – would probably be disappointed in Lucy. Lucy liked Cat, admired her and wanted to be like her, but circumstances had changed. Lucy needed a husband, needed a father for the baby she carried. Lucy couldn't worry about Cat Carlisle's approval. Not now. She had other things to tend to.

Thank god she wasn't alone. Their baby would be well loved and cared for. That was all that mattered. Wasn't it? Doubt and insecurity crept into a corner of Lucy's mind, threatening to take control. She needed her lover's tender care right now. Tears welled in her eyes.

Thirty minutes later, the bus pulled to a stop before a large village green. Lucy stood for a moment, taking in the gently curving road, the row of businesses, followed by flats. Deciding it wouldn't do for her to show up feeling peckish, she looked for a café. A cup of tea and a spot of breakfast would serve her well. Nestled between a dressmaker and a clock repair shop, Tea and Biscuits held – by Lucy's count – ten tables covered in blue-and-white checked cloths. A white-haired woman wearing an apron moved nimbly between the tables, taking away dirty dishes and returning from the kitchen with plates filled with breakfast. The smell of the food took Lucy by surprise. Dizzy all of a sudden, she sought a place to sit as her stomach roiled.

'Are you quite all right, dear? You look a bit pale.' The white-haired lady wiped off an empty table and pulled a chair out for Lucy. 'Please, sit down. I'll get you some tea, love. You just sit and rest.'

Lucy's childhood had been a bumpy one. A boating accident had killed her parents when Lucy was just 13 years old. Consequently, she had grown up craving the influence of a mother figure. Her brother, bless his heart, had tried his best to see Lucy got an education and learned comportment. There had been various women over the years – usually women who were rich and beautiful – whom Lucy had tried to emulate. As such, she never really had a well-developed sense of self. When she saw Cat Carlisle at the school, impeccably dressed and so very sophisticated, she knew in an instant she wanted to be like her. Although Lucy had never been a terribly good student, she was an astute observer and had made a practice of studying Cat Carlisle's ways. Before long, she had started to mimic Cat's voice and her sophisticated manners.

When Lucy had met her lover, she had pretended to be as sophisticated as Cat. Her acting was successful. Her lover thought he had found someone well-to-do, educated and influential. Men were so gullible at times. Lucy had giggled about it afterwards, and had joked with her friends about how easy it was to convince the poor sod she was an heiress. The charade had been carried off without a glimmer of guilt on Lucy's part. She imitated Cat Carlisle, pretending to be something far beyond her station in life. It only stood to reason she would attract a lover of that same ilk. Now she had to tell the truth. And she and her lover would need to marry.

She asked herself, *What would Cat Carlisle do?* And when the kindly woman brought her tea, she said, 'Thank you,' with an affected upper-class accent, removed her gloves and waited for the woman to pour for her.

The tea, along with a plate of toast and eggs, went down well and gave Lucy strength.

After thanking the woman who had been so kind to her, Lucy set out, relieved things were going as planned.

A group of boys were playing some sort of a game with sticks and rubbish bin lids. One of the boys – clearly the leader if size were any indication – stood before the group and raised his stick, holding it like a sword. 'We've got dragons to slay, mates. Who's game?' Off they ran, shouting warrior cries, chasing their imaginary dragons. Lucy smiled as she walked past them up the lane, following the instructions given to her by the lady in the café. If she had a little boy, she hoped he would have an imagination and a gang of lads to play with.

Lucy had found her lover's address after snooping through his wallet when he was in the shower. Later she had looked the address up on a map and memorised the directions, writing them down and then repeating them over and over in her head, until she knew them backwards and forwards. Turning down a narrow, wooded lane, she saw three cottages on either side of the street, situated far enough away from the road to provide ample privacy. All were made of the same grey stones and had a myriad of hedges and green lawn surrounding them. All the houses were well maintained, but her lover's stood out. Several beds of rich dark soil were on the far side of the yard. Lucy recognised rows of cabbages, and a few other plants and shrubs. An old oak tree, its leaves an autumn burst of oranges and reds, was laden with acorns. As Lucy approached, two squirrels shimmied up the trunk. Gathering her courage, she stood at the end of the path and braced herself. This conversation was not going to be an easy one.

Just as Lucy was about to step onto the pathway leading to the house, the front door of the cottage opened. Some unknown force made Lucy duck out of sight and move behind a box hedge. Peering between the branches, she watched as a woman stepped into the yard carrying a basket under arm. The woman's hair had once been blonde, but was now laced through with silver strands of grey. She wore an old tattered apron over a boring tweed skirt and a linen shirt and jumper.

Lucy watched as the woman strode across the lawn to the chicken coop, right towards Lucy's hiding place. She held her breath, as the knowing exploded in her belly, threatening a fresh wave of nausea. Oh, how she would have loved to explain away this woman's presence, a housekeeper or a sister, living in her lover's house. But there was no mistaking the thick gold band around the woman's finger. The hot salty tears ran down Lucy's cheeks. She didn't bother about sopping them up with her handkerchief, didn't spend a minute worrying about her make-up. Now she knew why her lover hadn't insisted on knowing more about her. His distance had been deliberate. Her lover, it seemed, had secrets too.

Chapter 5

Once Margaret had left the house, Hugh felt like a dark cloud had floated by, leaving him in the cleansing sunlight. After spending the morning dealing with domestic chores, namely washing the dishes, ironing his shirts – he only scorched one – and sweeping the floors, he decided to spend the rest of the day working outdoors. Earlier, he had seen a pile of logs in the dilapidated shed on the property. If he could find an axe, he could attempt to split them for firewood. Grabbing his coat, he headed outside, but instead of heading to the shed, he headed to Vera's. Her back door stood open, as if inviting him to call on her. Surely there was no harm in saying good morning.

He found Vera on her hands and knees, a bucket of bubbles near her and a brush in her hand. He watched for a moment as she worked industriously on the floor, scrubbing like a washerwoman.

'Hello?' She flinched when he called out, nearly knocking the bucket over. Jumping to her knees with a spry nimbleness that surprised him, she said, 'Good morning. You're up early.'

'I like the mornings. I just wanted to thank you for the food last night. I'm afraid my wife wasn't terribly hospitable.'

'That's all right. Maybe I shouldn't have dropped over without an invitation.'

42

'An invitation is hereby extended. You're welcome anytime. What are you up to today? Other than housework.'

'Almost finished scrubbing the kitchen floor, then I need to pick the rest of my apples.'

Hugh found himself staring at Vera's lips as she spoke, remembering their stolen kisses so very long ago.

'Would you like to help? I can make you lunch in exchange for labour. There are ladders and bags in the shed back there. I'll be with you in just a second.'

It took them two hours to clean the apples off the tree. They worked side by side, enjoying the fresh air and the sounds of the birds. When the apples had been picked, they sat down to bowls of fresh vegetable soup and big cups of tea. They ate in companionable silence, until Vera brought apple pie to the table and cut them each a large piece.

'I still love apples,' Vera said.

'I remember your father's orchard.'

'He liked you,' Vera said.

'Have you lived here long?'

Vera nodded. 'This was my grandmother's house. She left it to me when she passed.'

Hugh leaned back in his chair, appreciative of the home-cooked meal and Vera's easygoing manner.

She tossed her napkin on the table and leaned back. 'With the exception of that summer in Scotland when I met you, most of my holidays were spent here. I was grateful to inherit this place and have come to think of Much Killham as my home. My husband hates it here. Wants to move someplace warmer.'

'Surely you're not leaving.'

'No. I'm staying put. But I don't want to talk about George and me. Tell me about yourself, Hugh. Have you had a good life?'

Vera's direct question took Hugh aback. Had he had a good life? She poured tea for them and fussed around the kitchen, giving him time to contemplate the years that had passed.

'Not really,' he said. 'I've been blessed with the things I need to survive, but my marriage is loveless, and as I sit here and think about your question, I realise that my life has never been my own. I've served, it seems, at the whim of my mother and my wife. Both of them have judged me, and both have found me wanting.' He slapped his knee. 'But I'm finished with them. And I'm vowing, Vera, with you as a witness, that I'm going to start living my life the way I want. Hang everyone else.'

He hadn't realised that his words had moved her, until one lone tear spilled over onto her cheek. Without thinking, Hugh reached out and took her hand. They sat quietly for a moment, until Vera gently took her hand away and dabbed at her eyes with her handkerchief.

'Mine hasn't been so good either,' she said, her voice tremulous. She tucked the handkerchief into the sleeve of her blouse. 'I also am in a loveless marriage. George and I grew up together, knew each other since we were bairns. I didn't have the same passion with him that I had with you, but we married right before he signed up. I'll never forget that day in 1915 when he left on the train. Or the day he came home, for that matter. He was different. So many of them were. Oh, god, the nightmares were horrible. But I stuck by him, hoping it would get better.' She gave Hugh a wistful glance. 'It never did.'

'Vera, I'm so sorry,' Hugh said.

'Don't be. It doesn't matter.'

'He's a fool,' Hugh said. 'I'd give my eye teeth to have a wife like you.'

'Thank you,' Vera whispered. She turned to face him, her eyes soft, her face full of warmth and friendship. 'Enough sentimentality. I've got some things for you to take home. If you could reach that basket for me.' She nodded to a tall set of shelves against the wall. Hugh took down a basket and waited while Vera packed it full. She wrapped newspaper around glass jars of apple butter, added a cabbage, four eggs, two jars of peas and half a loaf of bread.

44

'Thank you,' Hugh said.

Vera laughed. 'You're the one who deserves thanks. I'd still be up on the ladder picking away if it weren't for you. We'll call it a trade,' she said.

Surprised to see it was nearly three o'clock, Hugh thanked her again, took the basket, and headed back to his own empty cottage. The chill in the air reminded him of the firewood he would need to get through the evening. He hurried to the shed and got busy, chopping until his arms ached.

Hugh discovered the news of Martin Shoreham's suicide quite by accident. It wasn't until early evening, just as the sun went down, that Hugh unpacked Vera's basket. He unwrapped the newspaper from the jars of apple butter and was so focused on putting things away, he nearly missed Martin's picture. The photo was an old one, taken at Christmas about five years ago. The original photo had been of Martin, Hermione and their three boys. Hugh knew this because he had taken the picture himself. Curious, he flattened the paper and read the headline. 'Prominent Industrialist Commits Suicide.' He grabbed the counter, holding himself upright with a white-knuckled grip. The paper was a day old, which meant Martin had killed himself right after Hugh and Margaret had left.

Martin. Dead.

He opened his last bottle of good Scotch and took a long drink, right from the bottle, letting it numb the feeling of worry that had taken hold. What had Margaret and Martin been discussing so earnestly at the party? Whatever she said had distressed him. Had Martin given her that money? Taking the stairs two at a time, Hugh stood in the threshold of Margaret's room.

He pulled her big trunk away from the wall and opened the lid, rifling through the clothing that wouldn't fit in the wardrobe. Turning to the small writing desk, he opened the only drawer. There wasn't anything there. He tried to push it shut, but something was caught. Taking the drawer out, he felt around until his fingers landed on a batch of what felt like crumpled papers, but was actually a regular-sized envelope. He tore a chunk of the corner while extricating the envelope from the drawer. Heart pounding, he took the envelope downstairs and sat down on the couch to read the letter written in Martin Shoreham's familiar handwriting.

Margaret,

I see you've found my family. You know full well that if Hermione were to discover that I kept another woman and that we had children together, she would be destroyed. I also know that you've never been one to consider the feelings of others, especially when you stand to gain financially. If it weren't for Hugh, I would take your letter to the police. Blackmail is a crime, but I would never subject Hugh to the embarrassment of your actions. You should be ashamed of yourself. Please know that I have no intention of giving you any more money. You know that I have a mistress. You know that we have a child. I have already paid you handsomely for your silence, but if you choose to disregard our agreement, you may proceed as you wish. But know this. If you ever come near me or my family again, I will report you to the police and use my not insignificant influence to see you ruined legally, financially and socially.

A bitter taste flooded Hugh's mouth. He hurried to the sink and vomited there, heaving until he was empty. His thoughts turned to Hermione. If Hugh told her what Margaret had done, Martin's betrayal would come to light. When it did, Hermione would be devastated. She would be forced to deal with the embarrassment, the anger and the betrayal on her own. There would be no chance to confront Martin, no chance for healing and forgiveness, no chance to honour all the years they had before Martin betrayed her.

What if he took the letter to the police and reported Margaret's blackmail? Blackmail was a criminal offence, wasn't it? But better judgement prevailed. No police. At least not now. He would deal with Margaret himself. The time for reckoning had come.

46

Chapter 6

Thomas Charles walked home from the Rivenby Constabulary, enjoying the cool night air. The moon was getting fuller, and as Thomas walked he recalled childhood tales of the October moon and its mystical power. Funny that the fond memories of his grandmother telling ghost stories about the October moon should creep into his mind now. He stepped into the welcoming cover of the woods that circled his house, Heart's Desire, taking the shortcut home. The sun had gone down ages ago, but his eyes had adjusted to the dark, and the moon cast dappled shadows on the path before him. Stilling his breath, he listened for any unnatural night noises. In the distance an owl hooted. He stopped, straining his ears for the sounds of rustling in the bushes near him. Nothing. Exhaling slowly, he chided himself for being paranoid and continued on his path.

There was no denying Thomas had been tense of late. Beck and the missus, the married couple who served as his valet and cook, had noticed it. Even Cat had noticed it. In fact, Cat and her current venture to protect battered women lay at the root of his anxiety. How could he not worry for her safety? While he admired what she had accomplished – taking the vast inheritance she'd received from her late husband and establishing a refuge for women – there was no denying the inherent danger. But her efforts had paid off and every woman who had sought help had been trained at Emmeline Hinch-Billings's school and sent off to start a new life of independence, a life free from abuse. Of course, in a fine example of her stubbornness, Cat had refused any outside security, especially if it were to be provided by men. Thomas knew it was only a matter of time before some angry husband came calling. But Cat wouldn't listen to reason, and Thomas knew better than to argue. Pushing those thoughts away, he hurried towards his house, the lights warm and welcoming through the window.

A rare medieval chalice had been smuggled out of occupied France and was now en route to Thomas for safekeeping. According to Stephen Templeton, one of the chalices had been stolen right out from under the guards, and after a harrowing chase, had arrived safely in England. Given this was the first item of value Stephen had received for safekeeping, extra security measures would be taken.

Stepping out of the woods and into the clearing, Thomas strode across the well-groomed lawn and reached the front door just as a car pulled up the long drive.

Beck and the missus opened the front door and stepped outside, a halo of light from the house behind them. The missus stood next to her husband, hands clasped in front of her. Beck, who seemed to enjoy the intrigue around the chalice, carried one of his many guns.

'We're ready, sir,' Beck said.

'I can see that,' Thomas said.

'And I've got tea ready. If you ask me, Mr Templeton is too old for this nonsense,' the missus muttered under her breath.

'Why don't you set it up in the dining room? I think that would be most comfortable for Mr Templeton,' Thomas said.

The missus nodded and headed back into the house as the car rolled to a stop. The driver, a tall man with a thatch of dark hair and broad shoulders got out of the car. Thomas was struck by the man's quiet strength, and wondered how Stephen came to find him. When the man moved to the passenger door, Thomas saw the gun holstered under his suit coat. He also noticed the ankle holster and the knife sheathed in the man's suit pocket.

Thomas approached the car and spoke to the driver. 'Welcome. If you'd like to take the chalice and follow Beck, I'll see to Mr Templeton.'

The man nodded at Thomas as he took a leather satchel out of the boot of the car and followed Beck into the house.

'Hello, Stephen,' Thomas said. He held out his hand to the old man.

'Tom.' Stephen held on to Thomas as he hoisted himself out of the car, not letting go until he was steady on his feet. 'I'll be glad to get this chalice out of my house. I haven't slept in a week. Keep expecting the Nazis to break down my doors.'

'I see you've taken proper security measures,' Thomas said.

'I am probably overreacting, but better safe than sorry. That's my motto. That's Evan Fletcher, my guard. Evan's a bit of a brute, but he is good at his job.' He held onto Thomas's arm, as they made their way to the house. Thomas hadn't seen Stephen Templeton in six months or so and was surprised at the change in his friend. His clothes hung from his body. His cheeks had become gaunt, his eyes sunken.

'I'm not dying, lad,' Stephen said. 'I've been ill with influenza. I'll be right as rain in a few months. Just need to rest and put some meat on my old bones.'

'Good to hear,' Thomas said. Once in the bright lights of the house, Stephen let go of Thomas's arm. The men moved into the study, where Evan Fletcher and Beck stood waiting, the leather satchel on Thomas's desk.

'Go ahead and open it, Tom. Let's have a last look at it before you lock it away. I'll just sit down, if you don't mind.'

Beck moved through the room, closing the curtains, enjoying every minute of the intrigue. When the room was safe from prying eyes, Thomas unzipped the satchel and pulled out the chalice, which was wrapped in a velvet cloth. The missus moved over to the desk, watching quietly as Thomas removed the wrapping to reveal the treasure he had agreed to safeguard for the foreseeable future.

'Bless my soul,' the missus said. 'I believe this is the most beautiful thing I've ever seen.' She stepped closer and studied the artefact. 'Shouldn't this be in a museum?'

The chalice was short and squat, made of gold so pure it shone even in the dim light. Chunks of amethysts, garnets, peridots and tourmaline were set around the edge, adding to the chalice's luminescence. Thomas had never seen anything so unique and beautiful. The piece shimmered with something beyond its riches, as though all those who drank from it over the ages had left an imprint of themselves.

'Yes,' Stephen Templeton said. 'I've spent the past four years trying to convince the owner to loan it to a museum for safekeeping and to allow others to view it. Almost won my argument until the war broke out.'

'And your friend? What happened to your friend?' The missus asked.

'I can't find him, nor his wife. I pray they got to safety.' He turned towards Thomas. 'I can't thank you enough for this. I've been wondering if I overstepped by taking on something of this magnitude. You've taken the worry away from an old man. I shall forever be in your debt.'

'I'll keep it safe,' Thomas said. He wrapped it back in the velvet cloth. 'I'll lock it away. Please, everyone, help yourself to tea.' While everyone moved to the dining room, Thomas quickly unlocked the safe and placed the chalice inside. Only when the lock clicked into place did he breathe easily. Hurrying upstairs, Thomas washed his hands and splashed cold water on his face. *I'll be glad when this day is over.* Years of dangerous covert operations had honed Thomas's senses. As such, Thomas had long since learned to trust his intuition, so when his instincts told him to go quietly down the stairs, he did so. Had he not been paying attention, he might not have noticed the glow of light emanating from under the closed door of his study. Careful not to make any noise, Thomas burst into the room, just as Evan Fletcher squatted down in front of the safe, inspecting it.

'You'd better have a damn good reason for being in here,' Thomas said.

As if to show he wasn't intimidated by Thomas, Evan rose and stood nose to nose with Thomas. 'I was checking the safe.'

Evan was twenty years younger than Thomas and very sure of his physical prowess. Unafraid, Thomas stepped closer and met the man's inscrutable gaze. 'Get the hell out of my study,' Thomas said.

Breaking the tension, Evan put his hands in the air and stepped away. 'Sorry. I wanted to see for myself the safe was locked. No disrespect, sir.'

'Apology accepted. The dining room is through there.'

Once Evan had gone, Thomas quickly opened the safe and verified that the chalice was still safely tucked away.

Stephen Templeton and his driver left at nine o'clock. By ten-thirty Beck and the missus had retired for the evening, leaving Thomas alone in his study. He stood before the window with the lights out, waiting for Cat. The shrubs and bushes surrounding the grounds provided a perfect hiding place for someone intent on spying. Thomas shook his head. Standing in the dark office, he scanned the perimeter for suspicious shapes and sudden move-ment, but didn't see anything. The full moon shone bright on Cat as she turned her bicycle into the drive and came riding up. She skidded the bike to a stop and hopped off gracefully. When he opened the door to her, she fell into his arms, laughing all the while. He pulled her inside the house before he closed and locked the door behind them.

'Hello, my love.' He pulled her close to him, intoxicated by the scent of her hair, relieved that she was safely in his care.

'Thomas, stop.' She pushed him away. 'What will Beck and the missus think?'

He grabbed her tighter and whispered in her ear. 'They are retired for the night. We are very much alone.'

She kissed him back before she pulled away and looked into his eyes. 'Did you get it? Can I see it?'

'Yes and yes.' He took her hand and led her into the study. She stood next to him as he opened the safe and took the chalice out. When he pulled the velvet wrapping away, Cat gasped and stepped closer.

'It is absolutely beautiful.' Her voice came out in a hushed, reverent whisper. 'The gold is so rich. May I?'

Thomas nodded.

Cat picked up the chalice, holding it in her hands. She held it up to the light, so dazzled by the shimmer of the gems, she didn't notice Thomas had moved to the window, where he peeked through the curtains.

'Think of all the people who have taken sacrament from this chalice over the centuries. I'll bet kings and queens have touched this before us. I can almost sense their presence.' She set the chalice on the table, never taking her eyes from it. 'What do you know about it? Who did it belong to? Are they still in France? I wonder if they're ...' She paused mid-sentence and cocked her head. 'What's wrong?'

Thomas turned to face Cat, concern etched on his face. 'I have the feeling we're being watched, and I'm worried that some angry husband is going to come after you.'

'You need to stop worrying. Saint Monica's is safe. I'm certain of it. We've been so careful, Tom, really. The doors are locked all the time and Bede has a shotgun loaded and ready. Let me assure you, she's not afraid to use it.'

Thomas sighed. 'I know.'

Cat wrapped the velvet cover around the chalice and handed it to Thomas, who placed it in the safe, closed the door, and turned the lock. 'That's quite a responsibility you've taken on, if you don't mind me saying so.'

'I know,' Thomas said again. His knees cracked as he stood back up and faced her. 'But Stephen Templeton cannot cope with the worry of it. The chalice will be safe enough here, and I'm better equipped to deal with any potential threats to its safety.'

He put his arm around Cat. 'I've been missing you.' He pulled her close. 'I'll feel much better about things once we are married and you're here with me.'

Thomas had known Cat for four years. Despite her ferocious independence and her relentless attempt to keep him at arm's length, they had fallen in love. When Thomas had proposed, Cat hadn't hesitated to accept. All she required was an engagement long enough to allow her to see Saint Monica's up and running. 'I can't be running off to get married while trying to help women who are desperately trying to escape this same fate, can I, Tom?' Although he didn't understand her logic, he went along with her theory, pleased and surprised she had no qualms about coming to his bed. The conditions of their engagement, coupled with their newfound intimacy, only confirmed what Thomas already knew: Cat would always be the sort of woman who required her independence.

She sat next to Thomas on the sofa and ran her hand over his ear and the back of his neck. 'You've got that look on your face, like you want to talk to me about something, but you know I'm not going to like it.'

'Does your intuition tell you that?'

'Bede Turner's been talking to you, hasn't she?'

'Can you blame her? She's afraid Michael Grenville is going to murder you all in your beds.'

'Alice Grenville needs my help more than anyone. Her husband kept her captive in her own home, forced her to cook and clean for him, and beat her if she didn't do his bidding. By god, the woman didn't even have shoes. I couldn't very well send her back to him, could I?' Cat said. 'You should have seen her. She ran away and made it all the way to Cliff's garage before she collapsed. Her husband had beaten her so badly, she could barely walk. He knocked two of her teeth out. Both of her eyes were blackened. How could I turn her away? She was utterly pitiful.'

Thomas bit back the irritation at Cat's stubbornness and tried to make her see reason. 'Michael Grenville is a confirmed criminal. He murders, tortures, steals, forges and extorts. A whole cadre of criminals are ready to do his bidding. Rumour has it he murdered Alice's brother, so Alice could inherit the family fortune. Pushed him down the stairs and left him there for Alice to find the next morning.'

Cat's eyes widened for a moment. Thomas was glad to see the fear there. A healthy dose of terror would go a long way towards keeping Cat and the women she lived with safe.

Shaking her head, as if to convince herself, Cat said, 'He won't find us.'

'You better hope to god he doesn't,' Thomas said. 'I'm wondering if we should get you a guard, just temporarily.'

Cat shook her head.

'Until Alice leaves.'

'No,' Cat said. 'I need to do this my way, Tom. At least right now. If I have any male authority figures at Saint Monica's, it will undermine the feeling of safety.'

'As long as you realise what you're up against.'

'I do. And I'll tell Bede what you said. We'll have to be diligent.'

'As in keeping the windows and doors locked all the time and being aware of people passing by,' Thomas reminded her.

'Of course,' Cat said. 'And checking the house morning and evening to make sure no one has broken in. And by having extra telephones installed, which I've done, by the way, at no small expense.'

'I'm really worried about this.'

'I know. I am too,' she said. She stood and went to him, wrapping her arms around his neck and pressing herself against him. 'Now come and kiss me.'

***

54

Thomas and Cat slept with their limbs entwined, warm and cosy under the eiderdown, until the alarm sounded at six o'clock. They always woke up early enough for Cat to sneak home before the village came to life. The gossip mongers of Rivenby would buzz if word got out that Mrs Carlisle and Mr Thomas were sharing each other's bed out of wedlock.

While Cat rolled over and turned the alarm off, Thomas jumped out of bed. He peeked out the window, studying the shrubs surrounding his house. The sense of foreboding hadn't gone away overnight. After he was certain no one crept around the grounds, he stoked the embers in the fireplace and added kindling. Once the flames flicked to life, he placed another log on the fire, eager for its warmth.

'I'll bring you a cup of tea.' He threw on his clothes.

'Can't,' Cat said. 'I must get back. The girls get up so early, I'm afraid they'll catch me coming in.'

'Soon we will be wedded and we can stay in bed all day if we wish.' Thomas sat down on the chair near the fire and watched Cat as she got dressed. 'You know, once you've got Saint Monica's situated, you could go back to taking pictures. Maybe even write your own book. I'd help you.'

Cat rolled her stocking up her leg, revealing a healthy measure of her thigh as she snapped it into the suspender. She started to give him that sly smile of hers but her face grew serious when she met his eyes. 'Please don't worry.'

'Promise me you'll never let your guard down,' Thomas said.

'Promise,' Cat said.

'I need to tell DCI Kent about Alice Grenville,' Thomas said.

He took it as a good sign when Cat didn't resist his suggestion. 'He'll have to be discreet.'

'I know. I'll explain the situation. But I can't keep it from him because there's the possibility that Michael Grenville will find his wife.'

She came to him and put her arms around him. 'You're really frightened, aren't you?'

'I am. You don't know what Michael Grenville is like. If you did, you might not be so gracious towards his wife.'

'She needs my help,' Cat said.

He stood, moving back over to the window. 'Someone's watching us.' He put his hand on the back of his neck. 'I can feel it.'

Cat stood next to him, leaning in as he wrapped an arm around her. Although she didn't have the sense of being watched, she trusted Thomas's intuition enough to heed his warning. She rose on tiptoes and kissed his cheek.

'I'm off. I'll be careful. I understand how serious this is.'

Thomas stayed at the window until he saw Cat step out the front door. Tying a scarf around her head, she disappeared around the side of the house, only to reappear a moment later, riding away on her bicycle. Just as Thomas started to turn away from the window, he saw the fleeting shape of a man in the hedges near the entrance of his drive. Heart pounding, he focused on the thick shrubs, scrutinising every inch until his eyes lit on a figure crouching there.

Without thinking, he ran down the stairs and sprinted barefoot in the direction of the crouching figure, impervious to the morning frost on his bare feet. At the sound of Thomas's approach, the figure sprang to life, jumped over the hedges and hurried out onto the lane. He heard the sound of a car as it roared away. The car didn't follow Cat. Instead it went in the opposite direction. At least his intuition hadn't led him astray. Someone had indeed been watching him. There was something odd about the way the man had jumped across the hedges and ran away. Thomas ran the scene over and over in his mind like a film, unable to grasp what his mind's eye knew was important.

Chapter 7

The cold morning air stung Cat's cheeks as she pedalled home. Cycling down the lane and onto the village high street, she wished for a warmer coat. *Time to pull out the woollies.* She rather enjoyed the sleeping village in the grey morning light. Smoke wafted out of chimneys as fires were stoked and kettles were boiled. Worries about Alice Grenville's husband niggled at the back of her mind. Even Bede had been concerned enough to speak to Thomas, something she would never do under ordinary circumstances. Bede Turner was outspoken, but she wasn't inclined to meddle.

Cat would have been foolish to ignore the potential danger of their situation. If Alice's husband discovered where his wife had taken refuge, everyone's safety would be in jeopardy. Cat understood men that abused their wives. They liked control and wouldn't think twice about storming the castle and taking their women – whom they viewed as property – away. How would she protect those who relied on her for sanctuary? Should she get a gun? 'They won't find us.' Cat said the words out loud, as if the act of speaking them would give them weight.

A chat with Alice Grenville was the first order of business. If the poor woman was still too afraid to come out of her room, Cat would go to her. They needed to make a plan and discuss

Alice's future, her safety and the safety of the other residents at Saint Monica's. Once Cat was assured Alice had not left any clue as to her whereabouts, she would speak to Lucy Bardwell. There would be no more warnings as far as Miss Bardwell went. One more breach of the rules and out she would go.

With fresh resolve, Cat tucked her bicycle into the shed, slipped in the front door, and crept upstairs to her room. It wouldn't do for her housemates to discover she had taken to spending her nights at Thomas's house. Once she made it unnoticed to her bedroom, she pulled down the covers of her bed and rumpled the pillows. Satisfied the bed looked slept in, Cat stripped off her clothes and soaked in a hot bath until the water ran cold. An hour later, she joined the others downstairs, two packages from Annie Havers tucked under her arm. Cat paused just outside the kitchen, listening to the sounds of laughter and friendly chatter at the breakfast table. When she had doubts about using Saint Monica's as a refuge, she would draw on this memory and remind herself these women had come to her broken and damaged by no action of their own. Saint Monica's provided a safe place for them to recover themselves and start fresh, far away from their abusers. The women were given an education at Emmeline Hinch-Billings's secretarial school, with the promise of job skills to ensure their independence. They did the work. Cat provided the opportunity.

'Good morning, all,' Cat said. She helped herself to tea from the pot and nodded at Bede, who was spooning scrambled eggs onto a serving plate.

'Everything all right?' she said to Bede, speaking just low enough so none of the others would hear.

'Oh, everything is fine. But you might want to mess your covers *before* you go to Mr Charles's house next time.' Bede gave her a sardonic look. 'One of the girls might just wind up in your room.'

'Thank you,' she snapped, taking the serving plate of eggs from the work top and carrying it to the table.

'Jennie, Elaina, these are for you. From Annie.' Cat handed Jennie LaGrange and Elaina Masterson the packages.

'What is this?' Jennie asked. She held the gift in her hand, examining it, a smile on her face.

Elaina tore her gift open, not caring about shredding the wrapping paper. 'Oh, this is lovely!' She held up a small seascape. 'Annie painted it. Open yours, Jen.'

Jennie held up a miniature still life of a vase full of roses. 'Oh, she used my gran's vase.' When Jennie had left her abusive husband, she had taken the small vase she had inherited from her gran. Annie had depicted the vase in the sun, somehow managing to capture the way the light reflected off the etched crystal. 'I'm glad she has time to paint. I thought training to be a nurse was rather gruelling.'

'Annie wanted me to convey her good wishes,' Cat said. She felt protective towards these girls, as if they were her own children. 'I've a little something for you as well. Not as lovely as Annie's gift, but just a little something to help you get started in your new life. I'm so proud of you both.' She handed each of the girls an envelope with money in it. 'You'll need things when you get your own home, linens and such. I'm hoping this will help.' A thickness formed at the back of Cat's throat. Tears filled her eyes. Surprised, she wiped them away. 'You've both worked so hard. I want you to find success and happiness in Scotland. You'll start your new jobs, and hopefully, will forget the bad times.'

Bede brought a fresh pot of tea to the table and sat down. 'I must admit, when Mrs Carlisle first started this venture, I was sceptical. But you two are shining examples of what can be accomplished with hard work.'

They joined hands for a moment, four women from completely different backgrounds. As if in response to their unspoken solidarity, the sun rose and shone brightly through the kitchen windows.

'Enough of this,' Bede said, breaking their connection. 'Let's eat our breakfast. We've all got a big day ahead of us.'

'Where's Mrs Grenville?' Jennie asked.

'She's still resting,' Bede said. 'We'll let her be for the time being.'

'Where's Lucy?' Cat reached for a piece of toast.

'Don't know,' Elaina said. 'I didn't see her yesterday. She's probably having a tryst with her lover.' Realising what she had said, Elaina paused and looked at Cat, a sheepish expression on her face. 'Sorry, Mrs Carlisle.'

'Lover?' Cat asked.

Elaina blushed. 'I shouldn't have said anything. Lucy says she's got an older lover who wants to marry her. But she talks a big game, so I don't know if she's telling the truth. Everyone at school says she's a liar.'

Jennie remained suspiciously quiet.

'What do you mean when you say Lucy talks a big game?' Cat said. A knot formed in her stomach. *What in god's name was Lucy Bardwell playing at?*

Elaina hesitated. She looked at Jennie, as if for confirmation it was okay to speak. Out of the corner of Cat's eye, she saw Jennie give a subtle nod.

'When she first arrived, she said she had fled her abusive brother, who forced her to work like a slave and who had kept her inheritance. But her clothes were new, even though they weren't a rich person's clothes. And she was always buying silly things for herself and eating at the café. She even wanted to take the bus to Hendleigh to go dancing.' Elaina shook her head and set her fork down on her plate. 'All of us who come here have fear, especially at first.' She looked at Jennie, as if looking for confirmation. 'It's hard to explain, but we've escaped something. Being here helped us overcome those feelings of being scared all the time, but it takes a while.' Elaina shivered. 'Not Lucy. She wasn't afraid of anything, not men, not rules, nothing. She didn't seem beaten down emotionally. I always wondered about that.'

Elaina's words resonated in Cat's mind, as she thought of Lucy's initial appearance at Saint Monica's. The girl had been tearful and pleading, her histrionics convincing. She had raised her skirt and shown Cat a generous bruise on her thigh, claiming her brother had hit her. But the injury could have easily been obtained by falling or bumping into something. As Cat replayed her first interview with Lucy, she realised Elaina was right. The girl wasn't harbouring the same deep-seated fear the other girls had. Lucy's psychology was all wrong. And Cat, in her blind eagerness to help all the young girls in distress, had failed to notice that subtle detail.

Jennie, a shy, sweet-natured girl who didn't gossip or speak ill of others, said, 'She's right, Mrs Carlisle. I'm betting Lucy's brother didn't do anything to harm her. If you want proof, go look in Lucy's room. Her bed hasn't been slept in. Her purse is gone, and her night gown is still under her pillow.'

Thirty minutes later, Cat and Bede stood in the lane, waving goodbye as a taxi whisked Jennie and Elaina to the railway station, on to their new lives. After the cab pulled away, Cat and Bede stood in the lane for a moment, as though in a vacuum.

'Well, at least those two are sorted. Come on, Bede. I'll help with the breakfast things.' Cat and Bede headed back into the house. 'I'll admit to being conned by Lucy Bardwell, but I still stand by my position that Saint Monica's is a safe place. We are in no danger. One lying girl doesn't change that.'

Bede followed Cat indoors, shut and locked the front door, double checking the windows in the foyer were also locked. 'I understand why you want to help these women. Since I've started to work for you, I find myself wanting to help them, too. But everyone who reads the newspaper knows what Michael Grenville is capable of. He's a bad man, if you don't mind me saying so. And he'll come hunting for his wife, you mark my words.'

She followed Cat into the kitchen and started collecting the dirty dishes from the table while Cat filled the sink. 'As for Lucy Bardwell, admit it, Mrs Carlisle, she pulled the wool right over your eyes, didn't she?' Bede set the last of the dishes on the work top. 'You need to admit you've made a mistake and ask yourself if you've made any others. Because a mistake in this situation could get us all killed. I've seen what a wife beater can do, the terror they can inflict, which is why I spoke to Mr Charles. I'm sorry if I overstepped my position, but truth is truth. You're so anxious to help these women, you are putting too much stock in your intuition. We need a man on the premises to guard us!'

Angry all of a sudden, Cat said, 'These women are not going to tell anyone where they are. We've been at this for over a year and nothing's happened. Of course, Lucy Bardwell will have to go. But what about Alice? What do you want me to do? Turn her away?'

'No,' Bede said. 'Can't you just move these women to a different house, so they don't have to live with us?'

Cat thought about Bede's suggestion. 'I'd have to build something, Bede, as there isn't a vacant house within miles of here. And to build a house I would need workers. All the men are out fighting. How do you propose we work around that?'

'Why don't you build the bloody house yourself?' Bede says. 'You could probably do it, if you set your mind to it, Miss I Don't Need a Man, I Can Do Everything Myself.'

In spite of herself, Cat laughed and shook her head. Bede didn't share her humour, and Cat realised her friend and housekeeper was well and truly frightened. She picked up a dish cloth and started to dry the dishes as Bede washed them.

'We just need to continue to be vigilant, Bede.'

Bede nodded. 'You're an unusual woman, Mrs Carlisle. Stubborn, independent, but you've a good heart.'

'Thank you for the compliment. Now, why don't I lay a tray for Mrs Grenville? She and I need to have a little chat.'

'I'll be glad when she moves on, I'm not denying my feelings,' Bede said.

Me too. Cat thought the words as a nascent thread of self-doubt sprouted deep within her.

***

Cat set the tray laden with tea, toast and eggs on the hall table and knocked on Alice Grenville's door. She had an idea concerning Mrs Grenville's situation. Now all she had to do was convince Alice of its merits.

'Come in,' a soft voice said.

Hoisting the tray on her hip, Cat let herself into the darkened room and set the tray on the table under the window. Alice Grenville sat in the corner, a silent shadow, still as a statue.

'Do you mind if I let some light in?' Cat didn't wait for an answer. The window had been shut since Alice arrived, and the room had grown musty. When she swept the curtains open, Mrs Grenville cowered in the corner, flinching at the bright light.

'Sorry, Mrs Grenville, but the light will do you good.' Cat opened the window, taking deep breaths of clean, cold air before she poured a cup of tea. 'How do you take your tea?'

'Milk, two sugars,' the woman said.

Cat gave Mrs Grenville her tea and sat across from her on the bed. The woman's eyes, both of them blackened by her husband, were swollen into slits. The bright red bruises had morphed into a deep purple, a sign – at least according to the nurse Cat had consulted – of healing. A nasty lump had formed on Mrs Grenville's forehead, and a spray of bruises trailed up her right forearm.

'Can you see okay?' Cat asked.

'Yes, ma'am.' Mrs Grenville's voice was raspy and tired.

'I'm happy to ask the nurse back, if you'd like.'

'Thank you, but that won't be necessary. And, please, call me

'Alice.' With a shaking hand, Mrs Grenville set her tea down. When she stood, her legs wobbled. Cat reached out to help her, but Mrs Grenville shrugged her away.

'I'll be all right. Just need to get my bearings.' She moved over to the window, staring out over the green lawns and the woods beyond. 'I'm wondering if I've made a mistake. Maybe it's best if I go home and try to sort things with my husband.'

'It's normal to feel that way,' Cat said quickly. 'Guilt, shame, it's part of the process.'

Mrs Grenville turned around to face Cat. 'Process? I don't know what you mean.'

Cat held up her hand. 'I'm sorry. I didn't mean to offend you. The women I've helped have all felt a bit of guilt leaving their relationship. All I'm saying is there are no judgements here at Saint Monica's. I want to keep you safe and help you start a new life. What do you think your husband would do if you were to return home?' Cat knew the answer to her question, but she also knew Alice Grenville needed to see the reality of her situation before she would consent to let Cat help her. 'Is your husband a forgiving man?'

Mrs Grenville shivered. The colour drained from her face. 'He'd kill me. If he finds me here, he'll kill me. I've put you in danger just by being in your home. I should leave.'

'Please, wait. I've come up with a scheme. You've nothing to lose by listening.' Cat rose and led Mrs Grenville back to the chair. Once the woman was seated, Cat said, 'I know about your husband, what people say he did to your brother.' She waited, gauging Alice Grenville's response to her harsh words. 'The whole purpose of Saint Monica's is to help women like you. We can help you train for a job and help you get situated in a place where your husband can't find you.'

'I don't have any money,' Alice said. 'I inherited a nice bit from my brother, but my husband controls the account. The bank won't let me do anything with my money without my husband's approval. I have tried to leave him before. The bloody fool at the bank wouldn't even give me my bus fare. And let me tell you, my husband wasn't happy when he found out I'd been to the bank without him.'

'You have to trust me,' Cat said. 'I've got a solicitor who has more progressive views about women and money. A letter from him will be sufficient to get your money transferred to a different bank. After we get your finances handled, you could move somewhere and rent a house under a new name. The solicitor can send you the money each month and your husband wouldn't be the wiser. I know what I'm doing, Alice. You've taken the first step. Don't you want to be free of this man?'

'Once I take the money out of his control, he'll find me. You don't know my husband. He has very influential friends. He'll find a way to trace the money. He'll find me. I'm certain. And once he finds me, you won't be able to protect me.'

Cat shook her head. 'I don't think so. I've done this before. We'll get your money and get you out of here.'

'Could you get me to America?'

'If you want to risk the crossing,' Cat said. 'Does your husband have friends or family in Scotland? You could wait there until the war is over, and then go to America. We'll get you some new clothes, and maybe a different hair style.'

'Like a disguise you mean?' Cat couldn't help but notice the colour coming back into Alice Grenville's cheeks.

'That's exactly what I mean. A new look and a new identity.'

'If I go back to my husband now, he'll kill me. If he finds me, he'll kill me. I'm dead one way or another. You're giving me a chance, aren't you? Stupid of me not to take it.'

'Perfect. I'll make a call. We can take the bus to Hendleigh. When can you be ready to leave?'

Alice hesitated.

'What is it?'

'If you don't mind, miss, I'd like to leave for Scotland tonight, if possible. Would you mind very much if I just took the train from Hendleigh to Edinburgh after we meet the solicitor? The faster I get away, the better.'

'Of course,' Cat said. 'Maybe one day you'll be in a position to help someone in trouble.'

Alice gave her a weak smile. 'Maybe.'

Cat hated to admit it would be safer for everyone if Alice were to move on as soon as possible. 'I'll make a call and arrange for a hotel. David Masterson-Smith handles my legal affairs, and he's got quite a bit of influence. In fact, he also has an office in London. He'll take care of everything. I trust him implicitly.'

'Why do you do this?' Alice asked. 'You risk so much for people you don't know. Why?'

'I was once in a similar position. Luckily, things worked out okay for me, but the experience left me wanting to help others.'

'Thank you, Mrs Carlisle.' Alice Grenville said. She wiped her eyes with a shaking hand. 'You've given me a glimmer of hope.'

Chapter 8

By the time Thomas arrived at the constabulary, he had worked himself into a state of worry. The idea of Michael Grenville turning his considerable influence on Cat and Saint Monica's caused him grave concern. If there were men available, he would have hired security for Saint Monica's without Cat's knowledge. Before the war, he could have used his connections to populate the property surrounding Saint Monica's with a stronghold of protection, and Cat would have been none the wiser. But times had changed. All the capable men were either off fighting or dead. With these worries on his mind, Thomas was not in the mood for George Hinks, who took one look at him and snapped, 'You're late.' As if Thomas needed reminding.

DCI Kent had his own struggles with manpower. DS Wallace – whose quiet strength had been a perfect buffer against DCI Kent's no-nonsense and rather aggressive approach to police work – had left a month ago. He'd hedged about where he would serve, and Thomas wondered if he was working on some clandestine project. The entire constabulary was feeling the loss of the competent officer with a promising career. In an act of desperation, DCI Kent had hired half a dozen older men, many of them veterans of the previous war. One of those men was George Hinks, a ne'er-do-well with no previous police experience, a condescending attitude and a knack for going missing when there was work to be done. On more than one occasion, Thomas had heard the constables complaining about Hinks, who would often slip away from the constabulary and go to the pub. For his part, Thomas did his best to treat Hinks with professional courtesy, a difficult task at the best of times.

Ignoring Mr Hinks now, who tapped his watch as though he were chastising a school boy, Thomas walked by him towards his desk, only to find Hinks had eaten his breakfast there and had left the dirty plate and teacup for Thomas to clean up.

'Excuse me, Mr Charles?' A police constable – one of the newly hired men, whom Thomas had yet to meet – stood by his desk. 'There's a woman to see you. I put her in the office back there.' He pointed at one of the empty offices in the back of the room.

'And you couldn't bother to tell me this, Hinks?'

'How was I to know?' Hinks said. 'I just got here myself.'

Thomas picked up Hinks's teacup and plate and carried them to the desk where Hinks now sat, a newspaper spread before him. He set the dirty dishes on top of the newspaper. 'Deal with this.'

'I'm not your cleaner—'

'Now,' Thomas said. 'And see that you don't leave the premises when you're finished.'

George Hinks gave him a surly look before he stood, tucking the dirty plate under his arm, scattering crumbs everywhere, and headed for the canteen. *That's the last I'll see of him for a while.* The lazy bugger would spend a good hour on this simple errand, anything to avoid work.

Thomas took a deep breath, thanked the constable, and went to the office with the closed door. He knocked before he entered, surprised to find Bede Turner waiting for him.

'Bede? Is Cat all right?' He closed the door behind him.

'Oh, she's fine. One of our girls has gone missing, and I think I should report it.'

'Not—'

Bede waved her hand. 'Oh, no. Mrs Grenville is doing fine. And you'll be pleased to know that Mrs Carlisle has become more careful about keeping the place secure. You've put the worry in her, and I thank you for that. The girl that's gone missing is Lucy Bardwell. She didn't come home last night. Her bed hasn't been slept in. Her handbag has gone, and her nightgown is still under her pillow. I am worried something's happened to her.'

'Are you wanting to file an official report?' Thomas knew Bede Turner to be a level-headed, practical woman. If she thought this young woman had come to harm, Thomas believed her.

'Yes, sir. It seems the logical thing to do.' She sat upright in the chair, her hat securely pinned into place, her gloved hands clutching the handbag on her lap.

Thomas sat down opposite her, put a fresh piece of paper on the blotter and uncapped his fountain pen. 'Whenever you're ready, Bede. Tell me from the beginning. Give me as much detail as possible.'

'When those girls come to us at Saint Monica's, they have a frightened, haunted way about them. They've been treated miserably and it shows in their faces. They have horrible nightmares, more often than not they wake up screaming, at least for a week or two. A door slams and they jump. Frightened of their own shadows, they are.'

'And Lucy?' Thomas understood where Bede was going.

Bede snorted. Thomas hid his smile. 'Saucy, impertinent, not afraid of a thing. Just the other day Mrs Carlisle caught Lucy in her bedroom trying on her clothes. Can you believe it? I thought she would have been asked to leave right then, but Mrs Carlisle has a soft heart and a blind spot where these girls are concerned, if you'll pardon me for saying so. It is my belief Lucy Bardwell wasn't in difficult circumstances when she came to Saint Monica's.' Bede's eyes flashed as she leaned close to Thomas. 'I think she just wanted to stay in our beautiful house and not have to pay her way. She told us her brother abused her. Lost his leg at Dunkirk and stays home drinking all the time. Two days later, she tells the girls her brother is a priest and wants her to get married and start having children. Her story changes, if you get my meaning. She always seems to have enough pocket money for the cinema. Always bragging about her older lover and sneaking out to go dancing in Hendleigh. Not that Mrs Carlisle would notice. She's rarely home of an evening anymore.' Bede flashed Thomas a look that made it very clear she knew Cat spent her nights in his bed.

'I thought maybe she had run away, but she would have never left her clothes. Not Lucy Bardwell.' Bede paused, collecting her thoughts. 'And she was pregnant.' She met Thomas's eyes, looking for his reaction.

'Pregnant? Are you sure?'

'My sister works as a midwife, sir. I've been around my share of women in the pudding club, if you'll excuse the expression. Lucy Bardwell was in the family way. I'm sure of it.'

'You didn't happen to hear any of the other girls talk about who the father is?'

'Didn't hear talk, but I saw her in the woods with a gentleman. They was carrying on, kissing. It was right embarrassing, I'll tell you. And I'd recognise him if I was to see him again. Older man, much older than Lucy.' Bede shook her head. 'I reckon the poor lass thought the man would marry her.'

Thomas took down a few more details and assured Bede he would look into Lucy Bardwell's disappearance. Anxious to get away from prying ears, he walked her outside. Once they were away from the building, he spoke.

'I'm going to marry Cat.'

Bede patted his arm. 'You two are good for each other. If I may say so, Mrs Carlisle should be married. She needs a husband to keep her out of trouble. I'm not judging you, Mr Charles. It's not like Cat hasn't been married before. And a man like you

– well, I'm sure you're no stranger to love. But Rivenby is a small village. You'd best be careful. Both of you. People do like to talk.'

'Thank you, Bede. We'll heed your advice.'

'Good day. Thank you for helping with Lucy Bardwell.'

Back inside, George Hinks was on the telephone, busily writing a message. Not trusting Hinks, Thomas read over his shoulder. A Colin Whittaker had reported his car stolen. Hinks wrote down the man's address.

'Got it, sir. I'll be right over to take your report.' Hinks hung up the phone and stood. 'Right. I'm off.'

'No,' Thomas said. 'When a call such as this comes in, you wait for DCI Kent to decide how to proceed.'

'Where do you get off telling me what to do?' Hinks stood, eyes blazing.

'I'm pulling rank on you, Hinks. You'll wait for DCI Kent.'

'And if I don't?'

Two constables who had just arrived on shift noticed the tension between the two older men. Not wanting to set a bad example, Thomas stepped close to Hinks and spoke in a soft voice. 'You don't want to fight with me, Hinks. You won't win. Now stand down and wait for DCI Kent.'

George Hinks stepped away from Thomas just as DCI Kent arrived.

'Good morning,' DCI Kent said. With narrowed eyes, he looked at Hinks and Thomas. 'What's happened?'

Hinks spoke first. 'Colin Whittaker called, sir. Said his car had been stolen. Mr Charles was going to go and speak with him, but I thought it would be best to wait until you arrived.'

Thomas closed his eyes, took a deep breath. 'Morning, sir,' he said to DCI Kent before he turned on his heel and walked back to his desk. He picked up the report he had taken about Lucy Bardwell and had just tucked it into the top drawer of his desk, when DCI Kent called out to him.

'Thomas, you're with me. We'll go to Colin Whittaker's. Hinks, I'd like you to go the file room and start getting things in order.'

Ignoring Hinks's glare, Thomas followed DCI Kent out of the building. 'I'll pay for that, you know,' he muttered as they made their way outside.

***

DCI Kent slowed down the car, waiting for two boys as they chased a ball into the roadway. He rolled down his window and called to them, 'Good thing I was able to slow down. Look before you run into the road, lads.' The boys saluted him, and ran off, tossing the ball between them.

'Am I correct in assuming Hinks didn't quite relay the facts correctly this morning?' he asked Thomas. 'And I know you're reluctant to speak ill of a colleague, loyalty and honour and all that. But if you think he's doing more harm than good, I'd prefer to know. I can't watch all my officers every minute.'

Thomas had learned early on in life the best course of action was to keep out of trouble and keep your mouth shut. But DCI Kent deserved to know Hinks wasn't quite up to the job.

As if to encourage Thomas to speak, DCI Kent said, 'I don't trust him, either, Tom. He seems to be lazy. Probably won't last another month, between the two of us. Wouldn't have hired him at all, if I weren't so desperate.'

'He doesn't respect the job. And he certainly doesn't understand the chain of command,' Thomas said. 'If I were you, I would be reluctant to put him out in the field. He's the type who acts without thinking things through. Makes me nervous.'

'Agreed.' DCI Kent downshifted around a tight corner, only to speed up as they hit the open roadway. 'What's on your mind, Tom? You've been distracted all week. Is it something to do with the job?'

Thomas and DCI Kent were cut from the same cloth, both

were stoic and both had seen their fair share of human suffering. They had worked together over the past year and even though DCI Kent was Thomas's superior, Thomas trusted Kent and knew that he could be discreet.

'Cat Carlisle and I are going to marry.'

'Congratulations!' DCI Kent looked at Thomas out of the corner of his eye. 'And that has you worried?'

'No, sir,' Thomas said. 'She's opened a refuge – for a lack of a better word – for women who have been battered by their husbands. These women she's helping live at Saint Monica's while they train for a job at Emmeline Hinch-Billings's school. When they graduate, Cat helps them get situated in a new city.'

'A noble endeavour, but a bit risky.'

'I know. I've offered to find men to work as security guards, but she won't hear of it.'

'But that's not what's troubling you,' DCI Kent said. 'Come on, old boy. Let's have it.'

'Alice Grenville is currently in residence.'

'What? Good god, man, does Cat know who she's dealing with? That's just what we need while we are so short of men. Bloody Michael Grenville in Rivenby. I swear, Tom, that woman is going to drive me to an asylum. She is like a match and a can of petrol, all wrapped up in one tidy package.'

'You need to be discreet, sir,' Thomas said. 'The security of Saint Monica's is in the secrecy.'

'How did Alice Grenville manage to find Cat?'

'She wound up in Cliff's garage, barefoot and beaten. Cat and Cliff are childhood friends, in case you're wondering. A lorry driver found Mrs Grenville on the side of the road on the outskirts of London and drove her here. Of course, Cliff called Cat, who took her in. To make matters worse, for the past couple of days, I feel as though I'm being watched.' Thomas wanted to tell DCI Kent about the figure in the shrubs but decided against it.

'Okay. Thank you for telling me. I'll trust you to monitor the situation, and I'll expect complete candour from Mrs Carlisle. If there is so much of a hint of Michael Grenville's presence, I'll expect to be told.'

'Understood,' Thomas said.

'You've heard of Colin Whittaker, I take it?' DCI Kent asked.

'The novelist? I wondered if that was the same bloke. I read all of his books as a young lad,' Thomas said. He knew that the famous author lived around Rivenby, but rumour had it the old man was a recluse and didn't much like visitors, so Thomas had never met him in person. DCI Kent turned down a narrow lane, obscured by an overgrowth of shrubs and wild climbing vines that wove around the thick tree trunks like so many serpents. They bumped along the rutted road for half a mile, before Colin Whittaker's house came into view. Named after Colin's first novel, Raven's Glass was an old stone house, with chipped paint and even a boarded-up window on the second floor. Someone had attempted a vegetable garden, but only half of it had been cleared and some sorry-looking cabbages were all that managed to grow.

As they rolled to a stop, Colin Whittaker – trailed by three Labrador Retrievers – came from around the back of the house, moving rather quickly in spite of his cane. One of the dogs saw a squirrel and took off after it. In a frenzy of gleeful barking, the other two dogs followed.

'DCI Kent.' He waited while the men got out of the car. 'Thank you for coming so quickly. And you are?'

Thomas extended his hand. 'Thomas Charles, sir.'

The old man squinted at him. 'Are you the same Thomas Charles who writes about the religious houses?'

'Yes,' Thomas said.

'I enjoy your writing style. I'm afraid your trip was wasted, however.'

'Was your car stolen, sir?' DCI Kent asked.

'Yes, it was. Follow me.'

They followed him around the back of the house to a separate building, which served as the garage, to see a blue Vauxhall parked out front, a young boy polishing it.

'This young man is Blue. Arrived from London three weeks ago. He's been staying with me, helping me out around the house. We're starting a garden, but Blue here prefers to take care of the car.'

The young boy stopped polishing long enough to grin at Thomas and DCI Kent. 'He's going to let me drive it someday.'

DCI Kent laughed in spite of himself.

'The car was gone this morning, wasn't it, Blue?' Colin asked.

'Yes, sir. We was going into Hendleigh today, but the car was gone.' The boy tucked his polishing rag into his back pocket and leaned against the car. Thomas guessed him to be about 12 years old. He had a thick thatch of blond hair and bright inquiring eyes. 'And then after breakfast, I came out and here it was.'

'Was anything taken or damaged?' Thomas walked around the car.

'Not a thing,' Colin said.

'It smelled though,' the boy said.

'What do you mean?' DCI Kent said. 'What did it smell like, Blue?'

He squinted in disgust. 'Smelled like a girl.'

'Interesting, isn't it, lads? Seems a woman stole my car.' He laughed. 'I'd like to meet her. Wonder what she did with it? I would bet there's intrigue afoot.' He rubbed his hands together. 'I feel a new novel coming on. Always wanted to write about a female spy.'

'Girls can't be spies,' Blue said. 'They're stupid.'

Thomas opened the door of the car and sat down in the driver's seat. The boy was right. The car smelled of perfume, a heady combination of roses, vanilla and something else – orange?

'Could the car have been stolen last night?' Thomas asked.

Colin shrugged. 'Could have. Haven't driven it for a couple of days.'

'It was there yesterday,' Blue said.

'We can take a report, Mr Whittaker, if you'd like,' DCI Kent said. 'But I advise you to keep the car in the garage, with the door locked for the time being.'

'You think the thief will come back?' he asked.

'We'll be ready for her next time. Won't we?' Blue turned and looked up at the old man.

'We will indeed,' Colin said. He extended his hand first to DCI Kent and then to Thomas. 'Sorry to bring you out here on a fool's errand.'

'Not a fool's errand, Mr Whittaker,' DCI Kent said. 'Call us any time.'

Neither one of them spoke until DCI Kent turned onto the main road. 'Well, what do you think?'

Thomas let out his breath. 'This morning I noticed a figure crouched in the shrubs near my house. I gave chase, but they drove off in what looked like a blue Vauxhall.'

'Colin Whittaker's blue Vauxhall?' DCI Kent asked.

Thomas shook his head. 'Not sure. Could be. But now that I think about it, it wasn't a man who jumped in the car.'

'A woman?'

'Yep,' Thomas said.

'That's curious. The bad news is that we may have a car thief in Rivenby. The good news is that in all likelihood she doesn't have anything to do with Michael Grenville. Wonder what she was doing at your house. Trying to steal your car? Your Hornet Coupe would be quite a treasure to a car thief.'

'During the course of my travels, I met an historian who has made it his life's work to help his friends in the occupied territories keep their historic and religious art safe. My attic has been hosting an assorted collection of interesting but not too valuable pieces. I've recently acquired a solid gold medieval chalice. I've been wondering if someone is out to steal it. God knows, Beck – my valet – is sure we are going to be robbed. Up until yesterday,

I had dismissed his fears, thinking he was just enjoying the excitement of guarding something valuable. But something doesn't feel right.' Thomas sighed and rubbed his eyes. 'And there you have it. I can't be certain that Colin Whittaker's car was the same blue car in front of my house. And why not leave the car somewhere for the police to find? I don't understand why the thief would return it back to Whittaker. It makes no sense,' Thomas said.

'Doesn't make sense yet, but I imagine it will at some point. And I trust your instincts, old boy. You're not the sort who's given to superstitions. If someone's watching your house, Tom, someone's watching you. Let's keep our wits about us. In due time we will know who.'

Chapter 9

The frigid morning air brought Hugh out of his drunken sleep. When he opened his eyes, blinding shards of white searing pain shot through his body. He sat up, took in the empty bottle of Scotch on the floor and remembered drinking the last of it straight from the bottle. He had never made it up to bed. His neck hurt, and he knew his lower back would chime in with pain at some point within the next few hours. The curtain fluttered from the window he had foolishly left open. The news clipping about Martin's suicide had wedged itself under one of the cushions. Hugh picked it up and with fumbling fingers tried to smooth it out, the agony of his friend's death heavy on his heart.

And then he remembered Margaret and her role in Martin's suicide. The rage that he had tried so hard to obliterate by getting drunk returned, worse this time, like a bad rash. It thrummed in his belly. Damn his mother. Damn his wife. He had to do something to avenge Martin. On standing, his knees wobbled, and he sat down before he collapsed. This wasn't the first time he had drunk himself stupid. Clenching his fists until his fingernails dug into the soft flesh of his palm, he waited for the pain to sober him. Today he would pay for last night's self-pity, but he would take the hangover as a form of penance. He stood again, waited until the floor stopped moving, and by sheer willpower closed the window. It took him an hour to rouse himself long enough to splash cold water on his face and dress for a day of outdoor activity.

Desperate for any information about Martin, Hugh searched Margaret's room once more. Determined to be more thorough, Hugh opened the wardrobe and was taken aback for a moment at the two shimmering evening dresses she had left behind, gowns that would have no place whatsoever in Rivenby society. He ran his fingers along the top shelf, but didn't find anything. Turning, he faced the room, his eyes lighting on the writing desk. Rifling through the drawers, he found nothing. A tablet of expensive linen paper lay on the top, words pressed into the blank page. Margaret always had a heavy hand with a pen. Thinking of his childhood etchings from long ago, Hugh tore the page off and took it down to the kitchen. Ignoring his desperation for tea, he took a pencil and rubbed over the remnants of Margaret's scrawling penmanship. *Saint Monica's. Rivenby.*

Hugh had never heard of Saint Monica's. He imagined it was an old church and wondered why his wife had written it down. He kept the paper on the table as he prepared his eggs and toast, glancing at it every once in a while, as if waiting for some revelation. Once he had eaten and cleared up the breakfast things, he grabbed the paper and his coat and headed to Vera's.

Vera. He'd ask her for help. If nothing else, he'd tell her about his situation. Even if she couldn't help him, at least he would get a wee bit of sympathy from her. Hugh's life had been very short on sympathy of late.

The frosty grass crunched under his feet as he walked across the lawn to her house. This morning smoke curled from her chimney, a promise of warmth and good smells in the kitchen. Yesterday she had cleared a space in her greenhouse and together they had started cabbages, shallots, broad peas and a myriad of other vegetables that would stay tucked away over the cold winter months.

'This patch can be yours to care for and use. I'll show you how to tend to it.' At the end of the day, Hugh's muscles ached from all the bending. The simple life suited him, and he had every intention of settling into it. After he avenged Martin's death.

Vera opened the door and greeted him with a smile before he had a chance to knock. 'Good morning. Come in. Have you had breakfast? Are you quite all right?' She put a cold hand on his forehead. 'You look a bit rough.'

He inhaled the scent of apples and spice and Vera herself. *Best be honest and get right to it.* 'No, I am not.'

'Would you like breakfast?'

'No, thanks. I've already eaten. I'm hoping for some advice, actually.'

'Have a seat. I'll be happy to listen as long as you don't mind if I peel apples while we talk.'

She sat across from him, took an apple from the pile and started to peel it. When she was finished, she set the peeled apple in a bowl and reached for another.

'My wife blackmailed my best friend. He committed suicide.' Hugh let the words hang in the air. Vera stopped peeling for a moment. She watched him, a spiral of apple skin hanging from the blade.

Disgusted with himself, he regretted every minute of his marriage to Margaret. 'I'm in a mess, Vera. I feel like I should go to the police.'

Vera set the apple peeler down and reached across the table, covering Hugh's hand with her own. 'Start from the beginning. You'll feel better for the telling of it, promise.'

For the first time in twenty-seven years, Hugh Bettencourt spilled his troubles. He spoke of Margaret's underhanded financial dealings, the blackmail of Martin Shoreham and Martin's suicide. 'We've basically led separate lives for the past few years. I've let her have her freedom. That was easier than taking her in hand. We would go months without seeing each other. I thought – hoped, if I'm honest – maybe she had died or had ran off to America with someone. She's always talking about going to America. I found this.' He pushed the paper from Margaret's blotter across the table. 'I smudged it with a pencil. Do you know anything about Saint Monica's? I've no idea what she's up to. Apparently, she's after an inheritance of some sort. She manipulated me into coming here.' Hugh looked at Vera, meeting her eyes. 'I'm glad she did, be sure of that. We're divorcing. It can't happen soon enough, as far as I am concerned, but I have to avenge my friend's death. I'll never forgive myself for what Margaret's done.'

Vera set the apple peeler down. 'Are you wanting me to say what you want to hear, or are you wanting me to be honest?'

'Honest, please.'

'If your wife is engaged in illegal activity, you need to find out what it is and try to stop her. If you are unable to do that, you must go to the police.'

'But my family—'

'Hugh, you know I'm right. What if someone else gets hurt? And as for seeking vengeance, that's ridiculous. You are not responsible for the actions of your wife. Your friend's death is a tragedy, but you can't fix that. Your wife needs to be taken in hand, Hugh. You're her husband. It's your responsibility.'

She stood and poured them each a glass of elderberry wine. 'It's a bit early in the day, but this situation calls for something a bit stronger than tea. I've a tendency to be blunt at times. I'm going to be honest now and tell you what I would do in your position. First of all, find out what your wife is up to. If she's committed a crime, report her to the police. Let her deal with the ramifications. As for seeking vengeance for your friend, you know as well as I do, vengeance is an elusive thing. You'll never get over Martin's suicide. Nothing you do will take the pain away. You need to take this pain in, pray for Martin's soul and allow your heart to experience the grief. That's how you heal. Vengeance is not for us, Hugh. You know that.'

'I need to get Martin's money back and return it to his wife.'

'Then try to get the money back, or tell the police what

Margaret has done and let them try to get the money back. Just be careful when you speak of vengeance.'

Hugh finished his wine. 'Why are you so kind to me, Vera? What have I done to deserve your charity?'

A wave of desire passed between them, weaving an unspoken bond, bewitching them. They both stood at the same time. Hugh opened his arms. Vera stepped into them without a moment's hesitation. She leaned against him, wrapping her arms around his waist. Intoxicated by the womanly feel of her, the wide hips, the large breasts, the comfortable fullness, he nestled his face in her hair. She smelled of roses and warmth and redemption.

'What a mistake I've made,' Hugh said. 'I'll spend the rest of my life regretting it.' He tilted her chin up to him and kissed her.

When their lips met, she softened and seemed to take him in. But when he groaned, Vera tensed and pushed, her eyes shimmering with unshed tears. 'I can't. I'm sorry. My marriage vows—'

'Vera—'

She shook her head. 'Please. I might become weak and give in. And then I'd never forgive myself.'

Defeated, they sat down at the table, careful to keep a healthy distance between them. Surprised at the surge of physical longing, Hugh ached for the touch of her. He wondered what Vera would do if he swept her up and took her to bed. Pushing his untenable fantasy away, he spoke. 'What should I do?'

Vera picked up the piece of paper that held Margaret's etched note. 'Rivenby is a small village, but now with all the evacuees from London, it would be easy for you to go there and mill around a bit. You could go under the guise of taking a walking tour. A footpath leads from the village through the moors. It's a pretty walk. Blend in. See what you can find out. I know Saint Monica's is one of the nicer houses. I've never been to it, but it should be easy to find. I've a map you can study on the bus.'

'What if I can't find anything?'

'Then we'll see about tracking down your wife's family. You said she is there for an inheritance, correct?'

'Yes, but I don't know anything about her family. She changed her name when she ran away from home.'

'Don't worry about that yet. Let's take things one at a time. Actually, George works at the Rivenby Constabulary. If he wasn't such a fool, I'd ask him to help you, but never fear. We'll figure out the next step when the time comes.' She started peeling the apples again, the skin swirling off the fruit in perfect red spirals.

'You've given me a place to start,' Hugh said.

***

By the time Hugh got off the bus in Rivenby, he was questioning his plan. He was so angry at Margaret, he wondered if he could resist throttling her. As the bus pulled away, Hugh was tempted to chase after it and go home to Vera and the cottage. Home to the fantasy of an idyllic country life. Hugh, with his life of privilege and servants, had never done anything of great importance on his own. The sun warmed his shoulders as he surveyed the quaint high street and the village green, where three young mothers huddled together while their children played a loud game of chase, seemingly impervious to the cold. A stationer's shop was closest, so Hugh set off in that direction, determined to find out what sort of trouble Margaret had stirred up now.

A middle-aged woman with bleached hair and too much make-up was busy dusting a myriad of inkwells on a shelf behind the counter. She dropped her feather duster and brushed off her apron before she turned around, running her eyes over Hugh like a hungry predator searching for its next meal. He found her raw sexuality disturbing. When she spoke, his expression must have reflected surprise at her accent. She smiled at him.

'I'm from London. East End.' She gave him a tired smile. 'I'm having a difficult time adjusting to country life, if you get my meaning. There's no cinema here, and I've got to take a bus to Hendleigh to go dancing. Too quiet for my taste.' She touched Hugh's arm as though they were old friends. 'Have you got a car, love?'

'I do,' Hugh lied, 'but my wife uses it most of the time.'

At the mention of a wife, the woman stepped away. Curt and professional now, she asked, 'How can I help you?'

'I'm new in the area too,' he said. 'I heard there was a walking path here, near a place called Saint Monica's. Can you direct me?'

'There's a house called Saint Monica's. I think there's a turnstile on the path to the moors just past it.' The woman reached under the counter and pulled out a fold-up map, which she opened and spread out on the counter. 'I imagine you're on a bit of a walking tour then? You look like you'd be a good walker. It's your long legs. Anyway, the footpath is about eight miles round trip. Here's the route. Just don't go out there after dark. People get lost.' Using her thumb as a pointer, she gave detailed directions.

'So tell me about the house.' When the woman gave Hugh a curious look, he said, 'I have a fondness for old houses. It's historic, correct?'

'I'm not sure about all that. I like newer houses, myself. Easier to keep warm and no spiders. But the woman who lives in Saint Monica's, Cat Carlisle her name is, came from London to escape the bombs. She's quite famous around here. Her husband was murdered a few years ago. She solved the murder for the police.'

'Is she some sort of detective now?' Hugh asked.

'No,' the girl said. 'She's just a nice lady with a lot of money. Never met her myself, but I heard she likes to help out people in need. Did you want to buy the map? I can take your money over here.'

Hugh paid for the map, thanked the shop assistant and set out to explore Rivenby. He meandered past an old church and graveyard and wove through masses of evacuee children playing in the street. When he reached the lane, he walked slowly past Saint Monica's, towards the turnstile, studying the picturesque village for clues as to why his city-loving wife would want to spend time here. Saint Monica's was indeed a beautiful old house, its brick façade covered in vines whose leaves were turning to autumn's shades of reds and golds. As he passed the house, he caught a glimpse of an elderly lady hanging washing from a line out the back. Hugh paused and thought about approaching the woman. He could pretend to be a lost walker ... The woman saw him. Tossing a piece of wet clothing back into the basket at her feet, she crossed her arms over her chest and watched Hugh with a scowl on her face. *Damn.*

Making a show of being busy, Hugh pulled the map out of his pocket, pretending to plot his route, even though he knew exactly where he was going. He could go through the turnstile and take a side path back to the high street. The two-and-a-half-mile jaunt would stimulate his appetite. He'd take his walk, have lunch in the café on the high street and then return to Much Killham. If he didn't learn anything about Margaret, he would at least have had a pleasant day out.

***

Two hours later, Hugh was sitting in the café, having finished a generous plate of fresh cooked vegetables, accompanied by three biscuits and hot strong tea. He had purchased a newspaper and had taken his time with it over lunch. Having paid for his food, he wandered out into the high street where he saw Margaret. At least, he thought the woman was Margaret, for she had Margaret's build, Margaret's distinguishable hair, Margaret's way of walking. But this woman wore a grey tweed skirt, a frumpy hand-knit jumper, and the uninspired brown lace-up shoes available for purchase with ration cards.

Resisting the urge to call out to her, Hugh stayed back a discreet distance and followed along. Adrenalin coursed through him as he tracked his wife through the village, careful to stay out of sight. When she reached the end of the high street, she continued on a narrow lane, winding up a gentle hill for about two miles towards the woods. Coming to rest at an old dilapidated folly, overgrown with wild vines, Margaret ducked along a narrow trail. Out of breath now, Hugh continued along, mindful of his step. The trail curved, coming to an abrupt stop at a large green lawn, which surrounded an architecturally interesting house situated well off the main road. Woods abutted one side, while the moors loomed in the distance. The house was well maintained, no small feat in this time of supply shortages and lack of manpower. Hiding behind a thatch of overgrown bushes at the edge of the grass, Hugh ducked out of sight, watching as Margaret ran across the lawn to the side of the house. From this vantage point, he saw a woman in one of the upstairs windows flitting around with a dust rag, but Margaret had cleverly positioned herself so she wasn't visible to anyone who might look out the front of the house.

What the devil is she up to? Margaret crept up to one of the windows and stood on her tiptoes, peering in the large window, her hands shading her eyes. She moved onto the next window and was just about to peek in, when the front door opened and an elderly man stepped outside. He had a shotgun over his shoulder. Thinking he should grab his wife and pull her to safety, Hugh watched, unable to move as Margaret darted with the agility of a teenager into the woods. The man took the three stairs down to the path before he yelled in a loud baritone, 'Stay away. Next time I'll shoot.' As if to make his point, the man pointed the shotgun into the air. Hugh had the sense to cover his ears before the old man fired it.

Hugh remained standing as he surveyed the house and its distance to the village. By his calculations, he wasn't too far from the main road. Not wanting Margaret to discover she had been followed, he decided to take the footpath near the road, so he could easily duck out of sight if need be.

Backtracking to the village, he saw Margaret just as she stepped onto the high street. Careful to keep a safe distance behind her, he followed his wife to a row of small brick cottages on the far side of the village green. He watched as she took a key out of her purse and let herself into the cottage on the end, unable to look away when she stepped into the arms of another man. After Margaret's lover shut the door, Hugh stood for a moment, checking his emotions, surprised to find he had none. He wasn't the least bit angry or hurt at Margaret's betrayal. And if he wanted to be brutally honest, he felt a bit sorry for Margaret's latest conquest.

***

'So the old man actually fired his shot gun?' Vera took Hugh's bowl and refilled it with vegetable stew.

'And he yelled at Margaret. The question is, what was she doing there? What is she after?'

'Do you know who lives in the house or what the name of the house is? It seems we should be able to figure out who lives there. Once we know who lives in the house, we are one step closer to finding out what your wife is after.' Vera set another bowl of stew in front of Hugh and sat down across from him. 'Do you think Margaret is going to break in and steal something?'

Hugh played this scenario out in his head before he answered. 'I hope she does. I hope she winds up in prison.' He felt the warmth of Vera as she moved her chair close to his. She didn't wrap her arms around him and press her body next to his, rather she put one arm around his waist in a very platonic way and laid her head down on his shoulder. 'I'll help you, Hugh. We'll get you through this.'

'I know,' he whispered. They ate in silence, sopping up the stew with thick slices of crusty bread, fresh out of the oven. Hugh hadn't eaten this well since boyhood, when Cook had spoiled him with extra portions. When the meal was finished, Hugh watched Vera stack the dishes in the sink. Without thinking, he got up and went to her. Slipping behind her, he wrapped his arms around her waist. 'I'm sorry I kissed you. I won't do it again.'

Without turning to face him, she stilled and leaned against him.

He wanted her. More than that, the feel of her body filled him with comfort and a sense of security he'd never experienced before. *Is this what love should feel like? Dear god, I've been missing out.*

'It's not that I don't want to be close to you. This feels so good, but I can't break my vows.' She turned to face him. Eyes shining, she handed him a towel. 'Help me dry?' They worked together, making quick work of the washing and drying.

'I'm going back to Rivenby tomorrow,' Hugh said. 'Go with me?'

'Can't,' Vera said. 'It wouldn't do for George to see us together. Not that he would care, but people talk. But you should go back. I wonder what would happen if you approached the people that live in the house directly.'

'What?'

Vera shook her head. 'I know it sounds a little absurd, but there's no shame in the truth. Go knock on the door and tell that old man your wife is the one who was looking in the window. Tell him you think she's up to no good. Who knows, he may appreciate the warning.'

Hugh let the idea sink in. In some convoluted way, Vera's idea made sense. 'I'll think about it.' Hugh stood, tired all of a sudden from the events of the day.

'It does my heart good to see you take back your life, Hugh. I wish our situation could be different. I'm so sorry for what we lost, for the chance we didn't take.'

Hugh found he couldn't speak, couldn't respond to those words that tugged at his heart in the most painful way. He couldn't bear thinking of all that he and Vera had missed – a loving home, children, and the prospect of a comfortable old age. He pushed the emotions away. After giving Vera a chaste kiss on the cheek, he said his goodnights and made his way home.

As he lay in bed later, the events of the day replayed in his mind's eye. One thing was certain. Hugh Bettencourt would return to Rivenby. There was something in that house Margaret wanted. Hugh intended to find out what it was.

Chapter 10

Shivering against the afternoon chill, Cat stepped off the bus, glad she had opted for her warm coat when she and Alice left in such a hurry yesterday. For a moment she thought about going to the constabulary and getting Thomas to drive her home, but changed her mind and hurried off to Saint Monica's on foot. She was pleased with herself. David Masterson-Smith had started the process of transferring Alice's money without difficulty. Skilled at explaining things to inexperienced clients, Masterson-Smith had fielded Alice's questions with patience. Arrangements had been made for the Masterson-Smith firm to hold the money in trust for Alice, transferring funds to her each month as required. Cat had overseen what she liked to think of as the metamorphosis, helping Alice choose a hair style and a wardrobe, appropriate for the new life she would create for herself. As Cat had watched Alice model her new clothes, she'd wondered what hell her life must have been under the thumb of her mean-spirited and miserly husband.

Of course, Thomas was right. He often was. Running Saint Monica's wasn't an easy venture, but Cat had overcome the odds – at least as far as Alice Grenville was involved – and had seen the woman to safety. Now Cat would have to turn her attention to Lucy Bardwell with an eye towards determining Lucy's true circumstances. If it turned out Lucy had lied about her abuse, Cat would have no choice but to ask her to leave. If Lucy hadn't yet returned to Saint Monica's, Cat would ask Thomas what she should do. Those decisions could wait until tomorrow. Now all she wanted was a strong cup of tea and a hot bath.

Cat was so engrossed in her thoughts, she didn't notice the two police cars and what seemed to be the entire Rivenby Constabulary traipsing around the exterior of Saint Monica's until she turned up the drive. As she drew near, she saw a constable standing guard, along with another seven men lingering on the edge of the woods. Unexplained shivers ran up the back of her neck. Something compelled her to run, and she approached the edge of the woods just as Thomas and DCI Kent stepped out of the line of trees and spoke to one of the young men who hurried over to meet them. Even from this distance, Cat could see Thomas was pale, his expressions stricken. DCI Kent's face was a blank mask, devoid of emotion as he barked out orders, causing the young men to run off one by one as they received their instructions. Cat heard the end of his words as she approached. 'With a tooth comb, gents. Search the grounds and the woods. We're looking for a handbag, or anything that might belong to the girl. And when you're finished—'

'Thomas.' Cat approached the men. 'What's happened?'

There was no denying the look of relief on Thomas's face when he turned and saw Cat. He wrapped his arms around her, not caring who witnessed this public display of affection. 'Thank god. I've been so worried,' he whispered in her ear.

'I've seen Alice Grenville sorted. She's gone, Tom. We don't need to worry anymore.' Cat tightened her grip on Thomas, feeling a sudden need to lean on him. 'Tell me what's happened.'

Out of the corner of her eye Cat saw DCI Kent watching their embrace, a bemused expression on his face. Thomas held Cat at arm's length and looked into her eyes. 'There's a body.'

'Whose?' Cat asked.

'We're not sure. Might be Lucy Bardwell.'

Cold seeped up through the ground and coursed through Cat's veins. Thomas held her fast as she took a deep breath, deliberately steadying herself by sheer willpower.

'How?' Cat asked, surprised she could bring herself to speak.

'Bludgeoned.' Thomas led her away from the policemen, away from the talk of dead bodies, and searches in the woods. 'Bede's in the house. She's rather shaken. You can go to her in a minute.' DCI Kent had followed them. He and Thomas exchanged a glance. 'Would you mind identifying her? If you're not up to it, I understand.'

'It would help us, Mrs Carlisle,' DCI Kent said.

'You don't have to do this,' Thomas said.

Knowing she could face anything as long as Thomas was with her, she said, 'I'll do it.'

'Come with me.' Thomas held out his hand. Cat took it and allowed herself to be led into the woods. The sun was going down quickly now, taking the warmth of the day with it. Cat's gloves were tucked away in her purse. She craved their protection, wanted them to shield her skin from death and cold. But she didn't have the energy to put them on. The leaves crunched underfoot. Somewhere an owl hooted. As they approached the body, everything seemed to still.

Lucy Bardwell lay on her back. Cat recognised the blue suit. She almost laughed, not surprised Lucy had stolen it. Letting go of Thomas's hand, she moved closer to the body, taking in the beautiful bone structure. Lucy's face, white in death, had frozen into a lopsided grimace. When a fly landed on the blue of Lucy's eye, Cat looked away.

'It's her,' she said.

'Thank you,' DCI Kent said. He stepped away from Cat and Thomas and spoke in a soft, almost reverential tone to a man who wasn't dressed in a uniform.

'Come on,' Thomas said. 'Let's get you back to the house.'

Thomas didn't let go of Cat's hand. Once they were on the smooth mowed grass, he put an arm around her, propping her up as they walked to the house. Cat was grateful for him, as her legs had turned to rubber.

'What have I done? Is this my fault?' Cat moved away from him, claustrophobic all of a sudden. She sucked in deep gasps of air.

'Of course it's not,' Thomas said. 'Cat. Stop.'

The front door opened. Bede stood in the doorway, framed in the warm glow of the house, a linen handkerchief in her hands, a worried look in her eyes.

'Bede, there you are. Let's get her some tea. She's had a shock.'

'Is it Lucy?' Bede asked.

Cat nodded. She had so many questions, but she couldn't make her lips move.

'Have the police found anything?' Bede asked.

'Best not to discuss anything right now. DCI Kent will be up in a few minutes. He'll take Cat's statement and I'll take yours, Bede.'

'Of course,' Bede said.

'Sit down. This is a horrible shock for both of you.' He pulled out a chair for Bede. 'How about a brandy and a cup of strong tea? I'll get it, Bede. You sit.'

Thomas put the kettle on, moving as comfortably in Cat's kitchen as if it were his own. Soon Bede and Cat had tea and a plate of yesterday's biscuits before them. DCI Kent let himself into the kitchen.

'Everyone all right?'

'They're both shaken,' Thomas said.

'Of course they are. Mrs Carlisle, do you mind if my men search Lucy's room?'

'Not today,' Thomas said before Cat had a chance to answer. 'The women have had a shock and don't need policemen trampling under foot tonight.'

'May I remind you I'm your senior officer,' DCI Kent said.

'Sorry, sir. No disrespect. What difference does it make? No one else is in the house tonight. Can't we take their statements now and postpone the search until morning?'

'You understand, both of you, you are not to go into Lucy's room until we've had a chance to search it? There could be information among her possessions that could lead us to her killer. I cannot impress upon you the importance of staying out of her room and not touching her things.'

Cat and Bede nodded.

'Very well. We'll wait until tomorrow to do the search. But I do think it would be best – if you ladies are amenable – to take statements tonight, while events of the day are fresh in your minds. I'll take Mrs Carlisle's statement. Thomas, can you please speak to Mrs Turner?'

After Thomas and Bede relocated to the drawing room, Cat reached for the teacup full of brandy and sipped it. The acrid burn cut through the numbness and shock but did little to dispel the image of Lucy's lifeless face.

'Would you like some tea or something?' Cat stood. 'Brandy?'

'I'm on duty, so tea, please. Would you like me to do it?'

Cat gave DCI Kent a wan smile. 'No, thank you. I'm not as helpless as Thomas likes to think.'

'Thomas tells me you are running some sort of refuge for women?'

'I suppose you could call it that,' Cat said. She filled the pot with fresh leaves and put the kettle on. 'It all happened by chance. There was a need, what with the women coming from London. Some of them were fleeing horrible situations. Emmeline Hinch-Billings refers them to me.'

'Them?' DCI Kent asked.

'Women who live with batterers have certain …' Cat paused, looking for the correct words. 'Certain symptoms. Often the evidence of abuse can be hidden by clothing, but the psychological aspects can't be so readily ignored. Emmeline Hinch-Billings

93

and I can tell if a woman is living in an unsafe situation. They are often shy, apologetic and they have a frightened look.'

'Did you?' DCI Kent stared at Cat inscrutably as she set the teacup down before him.

'Beg your pardon?'

'Did you have a frightened look in your eye when you were married to your abusive husband? Don't look so surprised, Mrs Carlisle. I know about your life in London, in more detail than you can imagine.'

Cat sipped her tea. 'No, DCI Kent. I didn't have a frightened look in my eye. When my husband was abusive, I gave it right back. My parents taught me from an early age not to kowtow to bullies. Luckily for me, my husband grew tired of me and took a mistress. As such, we were rarely under the same roof.' Her voice took on a hard, challenging tone. 'Do you have any other questions about my abusive husband, or do you want to ask me about Lucy Bardwell?'

'You're not a victim, are you, Mrs Carlisle?'

'God no,' Cat said, without thinking. 'At least I try not to be. I admit to having a soft spot – Bede and Thomas will tell you it's a blind spot – for these poor girls with no way out. I got lucky with the money, at least.'

'So you try to help these women?'

Cat nodded. 'My husband would be furious to know what I'm doing with his money. I take pleasure in that, DCI Kent. I'm muddling through. Mistakes have been made. But I'm learning. I help them, with money if they need it. Mostly they need a safe place to stay while they train at Emmeline's school. When they graduate, they get jobs on their own, away from their husbands.'

'Aren't you afraid one of those husbands is going to find out where his wife is and come looking for her? Like Michael Grenville.'

'I see Thomas confided in you.'

'I haven't told anyone, and I will continue to keep your secret.

Thomas was duty bound to tell me. Michael Grenville is a notorious criminal. By harbouring his wife, you put yourself and everyone else in your household in danger.'

Cat sighed, exhausted all of a sudden. 'Honestly, sometimes I think I've taken on too much.'

'Where is Alice Grenville now?'

'She's gone, far away. I'll tell you she's safe. He won't find her.' She paused for a moment. 'Do you think Michael Grenville could have killed Lucy?'

'I suppose it's possible. Although I'm sure if Michael Grenville set foot in this village, I would know about it.'

'I've just thought of something,' Cat said. 'It might not be important, but ...'

'Best to tell me everything and let me decide what's important.'

Cat nodded. 'Alice Grenville and Lucy Bardwell resemble each other. Granted, Alice is a good fifteen years older than Lucy, but they both have dark hair, and are built the same. And for an older woman, Alice carried herself very well. From a distance, it would be easy to confuse the two women.'

'I'll keep that in mind.' DCI Kent looked around the kitchen. 'You're taking a huge risk, Mrs Carlisle.'

'Not now I'm not,' Cat said. 'I don't have anyone left in residence.'

'Tell me about Lucy Bardwell,' DCI Kent said.

Cat thought about the vivacious girl who had no respect for rules. 'Lucy wasn't afraid. In fact, she wasn't the least bit timid. She was reckless and irreverent, almost fearless. She was a liar, changed her story regularly. The girls would sit at this table for breakfast every morning and Lucy would regale them with stories of adventure and travel, all of them lies.'

'How do you know she was lying?' DCI Kent asked.

'Because I actually have travelled a bit, and I can assure you Lucy had never visited the places she claimed. She didn't know what she was talking about. But she could tell a story, DCI Kent.

The girls would be enraptured with her tales of love and adventure.' Cat shook her head. 'She was also a thief. The suit she was wearing belonged to me. I actually caught her in my bedroom trying on my clothes. Can you imagine having the temerity to sneak into my room and try on my clothes? When I caught her in the act, she pretended to be ashamed of her behaviour. She obviously wasn't. She came back and stole the suit and heaven knows what else.'

'But you liked her,' DCI Kent said.

Cat let his statement sink in. 'I did. Her joie de vivre was contagious. People liked her right away.'

'Did you know she was pregnant?'

'Bede certainly thought she was. Honestly, I was in the process of making other arrangements for her. She clearly didn't need my help.'

'Do you know anything of her home life or where she came from?'

'Not sure if this is true, given Lucy's penchant for making up stories, but she said her brother kept her under his thumb. Apparently, he lost a leg at Dunkirk and came home with a chip on his shoulder and an ever increasing love of drink. When he drank, he hit her. I wouldn't be surprised to find she made up the whole thing.'

'One more question. Do you know who her lover was?'

'I don't, but Bede's seen him. Do you think he may have—'

'Anything's possible, Mrs Carlisle.' DCI Kent stood, taking his cup over to the sink. 'As far as I'm concerned, everyone is a suspect. We will eliminate people one by one. I would like to know who she was involved with.'

'How do we go about that? A sketch artist?'

'My sketch artist enlisted three months ago. And there is no *we*, Mrs Carlisle. You're to stay out of this investigation. Do I make myself clear?'

'You do,' Cat said.

'Very well. I'll have a constable outside your door until we determine whether or not Michael Grenville is involved in this nonsense. If he is, you could be in danger. Be careful when you're out and about and keep your doors locked, please.'

***

Later that evening, Cat soaked in a hot tub until the tips of her fingers wrinkled like prunes. She put on a dressing gown and went down to the kitchen where she found Bede chopping piles of vegetables.

'What are you going to do with all of those?' Cat asked.

'Making vegetable soup. We'll just have to eat it for a week. Once I started chopping, I just couldn't stop.' Bede put her knife down, wiped her hands on the front of her apron, and turned to face Cat. 'I just can't believe Lucy is dead. Honestly. I simply cannot believe it.'

'If Michael Grenville is somehow behind Lucy's death, I'll never forgive myself,' Cat said.

'You're to stop thinking this is your fault. Lucy brought about trouble. That's no secret. Sneaking out to go dancing – what? You didn't know she sneaked out at night?' Bede shook her head. 'I knew Lucy Bardwell was trouble the minute I laid eyes on her. So don't you go blaming yourself for whatever she got up to. You do a lot for the women who stay here. Heaven knows you can't watch over them every minute of every day.'

'She didn't deserve to die, Bede,' Cat said.

'I know. And we have to find a way to live with that, don't we? Now, what you need is some nourishment. Tea will be ready in half an hour.'

'I'll go and change.' Cat headed back up the stairs, a dark yoke of guilt sitting heavily on her shoulders. Could she have done more to protect Lucy? If the girl had been sneaking out, shouldn't Cat have known? Was Thomas right? Had she simply taken on a

97

project – albeit with the best intentions – for which she wasn't qualified? She came to a stop as she passed Lucy's bedroom door, testing the knob and discovering it wasn't locked. Surely there would be no harm in a quick search. She wouldn't disturb anything. The young woman had been murdered while staying at Saint Monica's under Cat's care. Besides, no one would know …

Grateful Bede kept the door hinges oiled – one of her many housekeeping pet peeves – Cat slipped into Lucy's room and shut the door behind her. She crept over to the window and peered out from behind the heavy curtains to the front door, where a constable sat smoking a cigarette, oblivious to Cat's presence. She rifled through Lucy's wardrobe, surprised to find one of her old winter coats hanging in a back corner. Three pairs of Cat's leather gloves were tucked away under a stack of expensive chemises. *Thank goodness we don't wear the same shoe size.* Cat spoke too soon. On the top shelf, she found a pair of flat silk evening shoes, along with a matching beaded evening bag. The shoes and the bag had been a long-ago gift from Cat's husband, Benton. Moving over to Lucy's vanity, Cat opened the drawer, surprised by the array of cosmetics it contained, along with a fine brush and mirror. Did Lucy steal those, too? Lucy's nightstand contained a stack of letters wrapped in a green ribbon and tied with a bow. Cat undid the bow and looked through them. All the envelopes were written in the same masculine handwriting. She took the most recent letter and held it under the light.

Dear Sister,

I hope this letter finds you well and your studies at the secretarial college are keeping you busy. I often try to visualise you taking down shorthand and typing letters, but somehow can't quite manage it. For some reason, I see you as a movie star or aeroplane pilot. In any event, I'm terribly proud of you for setting out on your own. Things have been difficult since I came home. Believe me when I say how sorry I am.

Money is enclosed. Please let me know if you need more. As we discussed, I'm happy to find you a house of your own if you wish. I'll do anything to help you.

Have you made any decisions about Christmas? Please do say you'll come home. I could do with some cheering up, and it's not too far to travel.

Warm Regards,

Ambrose

Cat read the rest of the letters, which all had the same kind and generous tone. Ambrose – at least in his writings – seemed like a loving and concerned sibling, who took responsibility for his shortcomings. Cat searched between the lines for hints of violence. It wasn't there. *I've been duped*, Cat thought.

Taking note of Ambrose Bardwell's address, she tucked the letter back into the envelope, re-tied the bow and set the letters back in the nightstand.

***

Unable to sleep as thoughts of Lucy Bardwell lying dead in the woods ran through her head, Cat tossed and turned, finally giving up on sleep at 5.30 a.m. She wondered if Alice Grenville's husband had killed Lucy. Had Mr Grenville been lurking outside Saint Monica's? Had he mistaken Lucy for Alice? Alice wasn't terribly forthcoming about her husband's occupation or his penchant for violence. Cat had been shocked when Thomas told her the horrid truth about Michael Grenville. How could she have been so utterly stupid? If she kept Saint Monica's open, which was highly unlikely given the current state of affairs, she would need to conduct a more rigorous vetting of potential residents. Bede Turner was an excellent judge of character. Cat would certainly involve her. As much as she hated to admit it, she would probably have to hire a man to serve as guard and protector.

She shook her head, as if to clear the cobwebs, and headed downstairs, desperate for tea. Things could be worse, Cat reasoned.

99

She could have a house full of frightened women in residence now, who would be scared to death by Lucy's murder and the police presence. *Funny how things work out.* Cat didn't have anyone in the house now, and she was well and truly inclined to walk away from this business while she could. Rather than crusade to help women who had suffered at the hands of men who should have cared for them, Cat could step back from the drama, the heartache and – she hated to admit it – the danger. Maybe it was time to turn her attention back to photography and her upcoming wedding. Could she be satisfied without a challenging project to occupy her time and her restless mind? She put the kettle on the hob and pulled her dressing gown tighter against the morning chill.

The kettle boiled. With her mind made up, Cat poured the tea. Bede would be happy. And if the rooms were empty, she may as well offer to take in an evacuee family, maybe with young children. It would be nice to have a child's laughter in the house. As she sipped her tea and contemplated her future, a figure passed by the window, pausing before the kitchen door. Heart pounding, Cat looked for something she could use as a weapon. Grabbing a knife, she crouched on the floor, hoping whoever was outside hadn't seen her.

'Hello?' A woman's voice called out. 'I know someone's in there. I saw you through the window. Please. Help me.'

Unable to stop herself, Cat stood up, set the knife on the counter and opened the door.

The woman wore a coat that had clearly once been a rich green. Now it was covered in a patina of grime and gave off a musty smell. The stitching around the lapels was frayed, the elbows worn thin. Her forehead was scratched, as though she had run through brambles, and her cheeks were ruddy with cold. Her right arm lay bent up next to her chest, held fast in a sling made out of a very fine blue velvet scarf. 'I'm sorry to come to your back door, but there was a policeman at the front and I didn't

100

know—' She stopped speaking, waiting for the inevitable invitation to come into the house. 'Are you Mrs Carlisle? This is Saint Monica's? I heard you might be able to help me.'

Unable to avoid social decorum, Cat stepped aside. The woman entered the kitchen, careful with her injured arm as she passed through the door.

'Have a seat.' Cat pointed to the chair closest to the stove.

The woman shivered. 'I've been waiting for a decent hour to come knocking. Why have you got a policeman here?'

'A body was found in the woods by my house. A young girl who was staying with me was murdered.' Cat set a steaming mug of tea down before the woman. The woman didn't flinch at Cat's blunt statement.

'Thank you.' The woman picked up the teacup and sipped. 'Did the woman's husband kill her?'

'The police don't know. It just happened yesterday. How can I help you?'

The woman closed her eyes. 'My husband held me against my will. Told me if I left, he'd kill me. When he went out for food, I grabbed my coat and ran.'

'Are you saying you've been living rough since you left your husband?'

The woman nodded as she wrapped her hands around the teacup.

'What's your name?' Cat sat at the table.

'Margaret.'

'And your surname?'

The woman's eyes darted to the door. Cat could sense she was gauging how quickly she could run if she needed to. 'Smith. Margaret Smith.'

'That's not your real last name, Margaret,' Cat said. 'We won't worry about that right now. How did you come to be in Rivenby?'

The woman had eyes as grey as the winter sea. The paleness of her skin accentuated the dark circles under them. They shimmered with tears now. But Cat, in light of what she had discovered about Lucy Bardwell, wasn't so easily taken in. Not this time. She bit back the expected desire to help, which had become her rote response to situations like this, and forced herself to wait for the woman to speak.

'I'm so ashamed,' Margaret said. She winced as she reached into her coat pocket for a handkerchief. 'He beats me – he beat me. I'm not going back to him. You've probably heard all this before.'

'I'm assuming he's beaten you or threatened you, somehow frightened you to such an extreme you were willing to run away. But I need to know the details, especially if I'm to help you. I can offer you a safe place to stay, assistance with training for a job and starting over someplace else if need be. But I need to know what I'm dealing with.'

Margaret finished her tea. 'I understand.'

Cat sliced four pieces of bread and put them under the grill just as the sun crept up. She had planned on spending the day outdoors. The beds needed to be mulched and the vegetables that were starting in the greenhouse needed thinning. Once those chores were complete, there were apples to preserve. Gardening wasn't a hobby anymore. The war and its accompanying rationing of food was real. Cat thought of Bede Turner and the way she would react when she came downstairs to discover Cat had taken in yet another wayward soul in need of her assistance.

'Have some toast. After you've eaten you can take a bath and rest. I've got some clothes you can borrow. When you're feeling better, we can discuss your future.'

Margaret breathed a sigh of relief. 'Is that what you do here? Help women who are having difficulty?'

'I've helped a few.' Cat hesitated, not quite sure how to express herself to this woman without frightening her. 'I need to make something clear to you, Margaret. I will help you. But when we discuss your circumstances and how you came to be at my doorstep, I expect you to be honest with me. And I will need your real name. If I discover you're lying, you'll have to leave. Immediately. Do you understand?'

Margaret met her gaze directly before she looked away. 'Of course. Thank you.'

'I'll help you get away, if that's what you want.' Cat didn't mention she would verify Margaret's story before she helped her. If Margaret Smith were lying, Cat would find out.

Half an hour later, Cat found Margaret sound asleep in the room Cat had given her. She put fresh clothes on the chair near the bed and headed back downstairs, Margaret's filthy clothes over her arm. She found Bede waiting for her in the kitchen, an angry look on her face.

'You've got us another one of those women, haven't you? As if yesterday's events weren't bad enough.'

'I couldn't turn her away, Bede. You should see her.'

'You're gullible, Mrs Carlisle. Gullible.' Bede turned her back on Cat, mumbling as she washed the teacups and plates.

'Maybe I am,' Cat said. 'But she's been sleeping rough and it was my duty to offer her a rest. Bede, stop what you're doing and sit down, please. Let's talk this out.'

Bede's attitude became more surly by the second. She sat at the table, a scowl on her face.

'How about this,' Cat said. 'We'll mend her clothes, feed her, let her rest for a day or two and see what happens. She'll tell me – tell us – her circumstances, and we'll make a plan. Meanwhile, I'll get Thomas to help me verify what she says is true.' At the mention of Thomas's name, Bede uncrossed her arms and leaned back in her chair.

'I'm assuming Thomas can check the woman's background without letting her husband know where she is. If he finds anything the least bit untrue, if he discovers this Margaret Smith is lying, I'll give her some money and send her on her way.'

'If word gets out you feed, clothe and give money to anyone who knocks on your door, it will never end. You'll have a stream of women – especially those from London, who are bored of country life – begging for a handout,' Bede warned.

'I'm not going to continue, Bede. My reckless generosity may have caused Lucy Bardwell's murder. It's time to turn my attention back to my photography and look forward to my wedding.'

Bede nodded her head. 'You're making the right decision, miss. You can't save everyone. You can't save the world.'

'When Margaret wakes up, we'll sit down and talk to her together, okay? We'll plan for her future together. She's older and might not want to train for a job. We'll just have to see.'

'And after she leaves, we're finished?'

Cat hesitated for just a moment. 'After she leaves, we're finished.'

'You've got that look in your eye, Mrs Carlisle. You say you're finished, but I don't think you are. A body knows these things.'

Cat ignored Bede's cynicism. 'You wouldn't have any interest in travelling to Hendleigh with me, would you? I'd like to pay a visit to Lucy's brother.'

'Mr Charles won't be happy with our meddling. But I suppose we've got an obligation to that poor girl.'

'I went through Lucy's room and found a letter from her brother. It seems, Bede, darling, you were correct all along. Lucy's brother wasn't abusive. In fact, at least based on the tone of his letters, it seems he couldn't have been kinder.'

Triumph blazed in Bede's eyes.

'Please don't say "I told you so", Bede. I see the error of my ways, honestly.'

'And a good thing you do, miss,' Bede said. 'You're a good woman, who has a soft spot for those who aren't as fortunate. That's understandable, really, given how your husband treated you. But you can't fix everything, miss, not on your own.'

'Come with me to visit Lucy's brother. I need you to keep me out of trouble.'

'When you put it like that, how could I say no? Now, if you'll let me attend to those dirty clothes, I'll get on with my chores.'

'Very well. I'll be out in the garden.'

Taking a hot mug of tea to the greenhouse, Cat settled into the routine of moving down the row of small containers that held seedings and thinning them. Soon they would be transplanted into bigger pots. By springtime they'd be ready to go outside into the world. Enjoying the routine of the mindless physical labour, Cat thought about Margaret Smith, picturing her on the doorstep, her arm wrapped in that beautiful scarf. Something about the woman struck Cat, some characteristic niggled at the back of her mind. What was it? Had she met Margaret Smith before? She didn't even know where the woman had come from and wondered if they had met in London at one of the many parties Cat had attended with Benton. Cat sensed an inauthentic quality in Margaret Smith, as though the woman were acting a part in a play.

Soon she and Bede would speak to Margaret about her husband and the circumstances that had caused her to flee. They wouldn't make any definitive plans until Thomas verified Margaret's story. For her part, Cat vowed to be relentless in her questioning. She vowed to replace the usual empathy and compassion she felt for the unfortunate women who came to her for help with a fair measure of scepticism and ruthlessness.

Cat had learned her lesson with Lucy Bardwell. She wouldn't be fooled again.

Chapter 11

Thomas hurried home, ready for dinner on a tray, a glass of blood-red claret, and a book before the fire. The lads had been working non-stop on Lucy Bardwell's murder. In response to their exhaustion, DCI Kent had reorganised the shifts and sent half the men home for a good night's sleep. George Hinks had gone missing at one point, only to be found at the pub. Thomas let himself into the house and found Beck pacing in the drawing room, his shotgun slung over his shoulder.

He gave Thomas a wild-eyed look. 'A woman came creeping around here. Looking in the window, she was. I chased her away. Fired my gun in the air.'

Thomas felt what promised to be a banging headache threaten. Had the wrong person found out about the chalice? *So what if they have?*

'He's making a fool of himself, if you ask me,' the missus said, as she pushed the door open with her hip. As if reading Thomas's thoughts, she carried a soda siphon, two glasses, and a bottle of whisky. 'Pardon me for speaking truthfully, but you'd both best share a spirit and discuss this. Maybe you can knock some sense into him. He's running around here acting like a teenager. I didn't see no woman. He's just conjuring up excitement where there is none.' The missus placed the tray on Thomas's desk.

'Now don't you go saying that I made that up,' Beck snapped.

The missus stepped near him, hands on her hips and a look in her eye that Thomas knew was the portent to trouble.

'Both of you, stop,' he snapped. 'Please. The chalice is safely tucked away. We've done everything we can to ensure its safety.'

'Tell that to Beck. He won't let me do my weekly shop tomorrow because he's going to be away.'

'You can have them deliver what you need,' Beck insisted.

'I like to pick my own vegetables, thank you very much,' the missus said.

Beck put his shotgun down and poured drinks for both Thomas and himself. 'I was just being careful.'

'Thank you for that, Beck.' Thomas took his drink and sipped, enjoying the warmth as it ran down the back of his throat. 'Listen. Let's just carry on as usual, all right?'

'I tell you there was someone there,' Beck snapped.

'You've been seeing shadows all day,' the missus snapped back.

She walked up to her husband and placed her hand on his arm. 'Been married to you for forty years, Beck. I've never seen you so worked up. Go and see your brother tomorrow. I know you've been missing him.' She turned to Thomas. 'Are you expecting us to treat this house like a museum until the war is over?'

'Of course not,' Thomas said. 'But I do believe there has been someone creeping about the property. So when you are here alone, I expect you keep the doors locked. More importantly, I expect you to be on your guard. If you sense anything suspicious, or if you see anyone approaching the house, no matter how innocent they may seem, I expect you to call for the police. Do not open the door for anyone. Do I make myself clear?'

'I understand,' the missus said.

'Beck, go and see your brother tomorrow. I'll see if I can get a constable to patrol every hour or so.'

Beck grunted his acknowledgement, not bothering to hide his disapproval.

If someone had actually tried to break into the house, the only thing left to do was console himself with the knowledge his safe was well hidden and impenetrable. Even if someone actually entered the house, they wouldn't be able to open the safe. Of that, Thomas was certain.

***

Rivenby was coming to life when Hugh stepped off the bus. Shop owners swept the pavement, while the horse-drawn milk cart made its way through the streets with its deliveries. Hugh meandered through the village, his rucksack on his back, looking like just another day-walker heading out to the moors. Reaching the end of the high street, he turned away from the path the walkers took and headed in the opposite direction back to the woods. Following the trail from yesterday, he wound up once again at the house in the clearing and took his time looking for a quiet place to spread out the small rug on the ground. After he found a vantage point that allowed him to see the house clearly, he arranged himself comfortably on the ground, ready for a long wait. Margaret would show up. The question was when. Pulling out a well-read, tattered copy of *The Sittaford Mystery* by Agatha Christie, Hugh settled down to read, enjoying the susurration of the trees in the breeze and the sound of the birds chirping overhead.

When the front door of the house opened, Hugh set his book down and looked through his binoculars at the old man who had fired a warning shot at Margaret yesterday. He strode out of the house, surprisingly nimble and spry for someone with grey hair and stooped shoulders, coming to a stop in the middle of the lawn. He scanned the woods, as if searching for an intruder. Hugh tensed when the old man studied the shrubs where Hugh was hidden. His gaze lingered, as if he sensed Hugh's presence. Through the binoculars, Hugh had a clear view of the man's shrewd, intelligent face. With the shotgun over his shoulder, the man circled the house twice before he went back inside. Fifteen minutes later, the old man, accompanied by a younger gentleman – tall, athletically built and dressed in a bespoke suit – left the house together, taking great pains to lock the front door. The younger man also surveyed the area surrounding the house. He spoke to the old man, who nodded in response, before they set off at a brisk pace down the drive. Was the house now left unattended? For a brief moment, Hugh thought about going to the front door and knocking. If someone answered he could claim he'd got lost and ask for directions to the moors. Alas, his better judgement prevailed. What if he was knocking on the door and Margaret appeared? Best to wait, patience being a virtue and all that rubbish.

It didn't take long for Hugh to get lost in his book. An hour passed quickly. He ate two slices of his bread and drank almost all the tea he had packed for himself. When his bum became sore and his legs numb from sitting on the ground, he stood and stretched, walking around until the circulation started flowing again. When he sensed movement in the bushes directly across the clearing, he tossed his book down. Grabbing his binoculars, he scanned the shrubs, half expecting to see a squirrel or a stray dog. Instead he saw Margaret, dressed in tight fitting trousers and a sleek, no-frills top. She had a scarf over her hair, but he recognised the slope of her back and the curve of her hips as she bent over an army-style satchel. Hugh didn't have the best vantage point. But when Margaret crouched down in the bushes, he felt a touch of pride that he was able to spy on her without her knowing.

Soon a car pulled into the drive. Hugh watched as it came to a stop before the house, and a man – Hugh recognised Margaret's lover – strode up to the front door and knocked. No answer. He knocked again. No answer. The man looked in Margaret's direction and waved. She ran across the lawn and into the man's arms. A long and passionate kiss answered any questions about the nature of their relationship. Margaret stood by while her lover took a small leather case out of his pocket. He unzipped it and turned his attention to the front door. While the man bent over the lock, Margaret kept watch. Soon the door opened and the man slipped inside. Margaret waited by the car. Unable to stay still, she paced and checked her watch over and over. Minutes ticked by. Soon the man came back, carrying something under his arm, which he handed to Margaret. They kissed. The man jumped in the car and drove away, while Margaret scurried back to the woods, carrying whatever it was he had stolen.

Knowing Margaret was too focused on the task at hand to notice him tracking her, Hugh grabbed his binoculars and moved deeper into the shrubs. He knelt on dead leaves, ignoring the shooting pain from a long-ago war injury on his left knee. *What the devil is she up to?*

A shovel leaned against the thick trunk of an ash. Margaret picked it up and started to dig a hole. As far as Hugh knew, Margaret hadn't done a day's worth of physical labour in her life, yet she worked the shovel with surprising industry. Once finished, she buried the parcel, hid the shovel in the shrubs and hurried out of the woods. Hugh waited a good half an hour before he walked the circumference of the lawn, staying well hidden in the shrubs, just in case Margaret decided to come back.

Retrieving the shovel from its hiding place, Hugh dug the hole back up and removed a black holdall about the size of a hatbox. Not wanting to linger, he tucked it in his rucksack and hurried towards the bus stop. When he was on the bus, the mysterious parcel tucked safely under his seat, Hugh thought things may well be turning in his favour. Margaret had stolen something. If

Hugh played his cards right, he could use this evidence of Margaret's misdeeds to retrieve Martin Shoreham's money and return it to Hermione. As long as he got some vengeance for his friend, he didn't care what happened to Margaret.

***

The Rivenby Constabulary was buzzing with activity when Thomas arrived the next morning. All the desks were occupied, as uniformed constables set about the various tasks assigned by DCI Kent. Thomas had been charged with the sole objective of discovering the identity of Lucy Bardwell's lover. Every single student at Emmeline Hinch-Billings's secretarial school needed to be interviewed, with their stories double checked. Although Thomas had never participated in a murder inquiry before, he was duly impressed with DCI Kent's organised assignment of tasks. He compared the process with the casting of a net over Lucy Bardwell's entire life. Once everything was covered, the police would reel the net in, hopefully with a murderer ensnared in its centre.

DCI Kent wove through the throng of men, his coat over his arm. When he saw Thomas he nodded, pointing at the door. Thomas met him there. 'You're with me.'

'Where are we going?'

'Hendleigh. We are going to speak with Ambrose Bardwell.' DCI Kent tossed Thomas the keys. 'You drive.'

Ambrose Bardwell lived on a quiet street, in a row of detached houses with small swathes of lawn in front. The houses were all neatly kept, the only incongruity the occasional vegetable patch. Other than an old woman carrying a shopping bag, Thomas didn't see a soul and reckoned most of the residents were at work. They approached the cottage and knocked on the front door. Nothing happened. Thomas knocked again, and called, 'Police, Mr Bardwell. We need to speak to you.'

They heard movement inside. Out of the corner of his eye,

Thomas saw a curtain flutter. He knocked again. 'Mr Bardwell? Please. We must speak to you.'

'All right. Give me a minute,' a voice growled behind the door.

They heard shuffling, the sound of something being knocked over, followed by a mumbled curse. A man on crutches opened the door.

'Ambrose Bardwell?' DCI Kent stepped forward. 'DCI Kent. Rivenby Constabulary.'

Ambrose Bardwell gazed at Thomas and DCI Kent through red-rimmed eyes. Thomas was struck by the sense of utter defeat he saw there. Dark stubble covered his face. When he spoke, his voice was surprisingly cultured.

'How can I help you?'

'We're here about your sister, Lucy,' DCI Kent said.

'Lucy? What's she done now? Better come in.' When he moved out of their way, Thomas noticed Ambrose Bardwell's right leg was missing from the knee down. As if reading Thomas's mind, he said, 'Lost it at Dunkirk. Nearly lost my life. Follow me.'

DCI Kent and Thomas fell into step behind the man, who led them down a dark hallway and into a well-lit, spanking clean kitchen.

'Tea?'

'Thank you,' DCI Kent said.

Thomas took out his notebook, knowing DCI Kent would expect him to play amanuensis, despite his utter lack of shorthand skills. They waited while Ambrose made tea. Despite using a crutch with one arm, Mr Bardwell moved around his kitchen with quiet grace. He put out milk, sugar and a plate of what looked like fresh biscuits. Thomas took in the row of copper cooking pans, all polished to a high gleam. A row of tins containing flour and sugar were arranged in an orderly fashion on the shelves. It struck Thomas this was no ordinary kitchen.

'Did you bake these yourself?' DCI Kent bit into a biscuit. 'They are delicious.'

'I did. Had to find something to do with myself. I've been experimenting with biscuit recipes, thinking I might start a company. When the war's over, of course.' Ambrose poured himself a cup of tea. 'Now why are you here? What sort of trouble is my sister involved in now?'

'When was the last time you saw your sister, Mr Bardwell?' DCI Kent asked.

An unnameable emotion flashed in Ambrose Bardwell's eyes. 'Where's Lucy?'

'Please answer my question. I need to know the last time you spoke to her and what she said,' DCI Kent said.

'Why? What's Lucy done? I'm not going to answer any questions until you tell me what's happened. Where's my sister?'

Although it seemed a bit cruel, Thomas understood the logic of questioning Ambrose Bardwell before he knew of his sister's death.

'I'm afraid your sister is dead, Mr Bardwell.'

Thomas observed Mr Bardwell's face as it paled in shock. For a moment he thought the poor chap was going to faint. DCI Kent caught his eye and gave his head a subtle shake. They both waited for Ambrose to collect himself. 'Would someone please get me a glass of water.' Thomas jumped up and fetched it for him. Ambrose Bardwell took it, raising it to his lips with a shaking hand. Pulling a rumpled handkerchief from his pocket, he held it to his face for a few seconds. Still they waited. When he finally tucked the handkerchief away and met their eyes, Thomas had a flash of insight. *He didn't kill her.* Thomas knew this in an instant.

'How did she die?' Ambrose finally asked, his voice tremulous as he fought his tears.

Unsettled by the raw emotion, Thomas couldn't bring himself to look Ambrose Bardwell in the eyes.

DCI Kent cleared his throat. 'I'm afraid she was murdered.'

Ambrose didn't move. He sat in his chair at the table, looking

113

straight ahead. He didn't blink. It seemed as though he barely breathed.

'I say, are you all right?' Thomas ignored DCI Kent and moved over to Ambrose Bardwell, whose skin had turned ashen grey. His breathing became shallow and fast. When he wobbled on his chair, Thomas grabbed him.

'I beg your pardon, gentlemen. I'm going to be sick.'

'He needs medical attention,' Thomas said. 'Mr Bardwell, can you tell us how to reach your doctor?'

'Number is by the telephone. Hallway.'

'Take care of him, Thomas,' DCI Kent said. He hurried into the hallway.

'I'm going to move you to the floor, Mr Bardwell. Can you put your arms around my neck?' Once Thomas had arranged Mr Bardwell on the floor, he moved back into the front room and grabbed an old throw rug along with a pillow off the couch. By the time he returned to the kitchen, Mr Bardwell was shaking so hard his teeth were chattering.

'I'll be all right in a minute,' Ambrose said. 'Not the first time.'

Thomas put a hand on the man's shoulder, a feeble effort to provide comfort.

By the time the doctor arrived, Ambrose Bardwell had stopped shivering. He lay quietly on the floor, eyes closed, his breathing laboured.

The doctor, a stooped elderly man with a lion's mane of white hair, squatted down as he took Ambrose's pulse. 'This isn't the first time this has happened. He's still recovering from his battle scars. Help me get him to bed, would you?' Thomas and DCI Kent, with the doctor's close supervision, moved Ambrose Bardwell to his bed. Once he was situated, they waited in the hallway until the doctor finished.

'I've given him an injection. He'll sleep and wake up fine. I'll send a nurse over to stay with him over night. He'll be right as rain tomorrow.' The old man put the leather case, which held his syringe and his stethoscope, back into his medical bag. He looked at DCI Kent. 'I know you. You're a policeman, correct? I testified at one of your cases. Dr Towers? You probably don't remember me. It was years ago.' His mood sobered. 'Why are you here? Why is Ambrose involved with the police?'

'It's Lucy. She's been murdered,' DCI Kent said.

Thomas saw the sadness wash over the doctor's face. 'Oh, that's terrible. No wonder Ambrose was so shaken. He's been worried sick about his sister since she left.'

'Why was he worried about his sister?' Thomas asked.

The doctor hesitated for a moment.

'Dr Towers, Lucy was murdered. The more we know about her, the quicker we can find out who killed her. Please. If you know of anything, we'd appreciate it if you would tell us,' DCI Kent said.

'I delivered Lucy in that bedroom.' Dr Towers nodded towards the closed door. 'She was a feisty one from the day she was born. Her parents and her brother doted on her, spoiled her. Some children quickly learn how to get what they want, if you take my meaning. Lucy was no exception. Ambrose and Lucy lost their parents when Lucy was just 8 years old. Ambrose was 18 at the time, a young man just starting out in life. But he insisted on keeping Lucy himself and taking care of her. The child should have been sent away to school, but Ambrose wouldn't hear of it. He did his best, but a young girl needs a woman's influence, especially in their developmental years. When Lucy turned 15 she fell in with a bad crowd. Ambrose did his best …' Dr Towers let his words trail off.

Out of the blue, DCI Kent asked, 'Could Ambrose have killed his sister?'

'God no,' Dr Towers blurted. He took a deep breath and shook his head. 'I understand human nature, DCI Kent. Seemingly good people commit murder when pushed to their limit. But Ambrose Bardwell went through hell at Dunkirk. Do you know how he lost his leg? He refused to leave his injured men. He went back into danger four times to retrieve his injured comrades. Slung them over his shoulder and carried them out, surviving the ordeal by divine grace. He got shot in the leg while he was carrying the third man to safety. Despite his injuries, he went back for the fourth man, and nearly died trying to save him.'

'That will change a man,' Thomas said.

'It will indeed,' Dr Towers agreed.

'What about Lucy?' DCI Kent persisted.

'I'm betting that Lucy had a lover,' Dr Tower said. He hesitated for just a moment, as if he wanted to say something more. 'Forgive me if I've shocked you, but she was the type. Spent her money on fancy clothes and garish make-up. Tried to make herself look like a film star. Lucy had a penchant for married men. She liked the chase.'

'Do you happen to know who Lucy's lovers were?'

Dr Towers shook his head. 'I'm sorry. A bit out of touch.'

DCI Kent shook Dr Towers hand. 'Thank you, sir. We may need to speak with you again. Meanwhile, if you can think of anything else, I'd appreciate a telephone call.'

'Very well.' Dr Towers followed them out. They watched as he headed down the hallway and out the front door.

'Now all we need to do is find Lucy's lover,' DCI Kent said.

'Possibly,' Thomas agreed.

***

When Thomas and DCI Kent returned to the constabulary, they discovered three constables working at the desks, transcribing reports from the notes they had taken during the countless interviews and leads they had followed. George Hinks sat off by himself, reading the newspaper.

'Excuse me while I find something to occupy Hinks,' DCI Kent said, his voice laced with sarcasm.

One of the constables noticed them coming in, picked up a piece of paper from his desk and headed over to Thomas.

'Sir, there's a message for you.'

'Thank you.' Thomas read the message. It was from Stephen Templeton.

'He said it was urgent,' the constable said.

Heart pounding, Thomas walked back to his desk and returned Stephen's call.

'Thomas, is that you?' He didn't give Thomas a chance to answer. 'Oh, Thomas. I've made a dreadful mistake. It's Evan Fletcher, the lad who accompanied me when I delivered the chalice. He came today to make the delivery.'

'What?' Thomas cried out, causing everyone to look in his direction. 'What do you mean?'

'The real Evan Fletcher – and I've checked his credentials, of that you can be certain – showed up at my door two hours ago. He said he received a telegram changing the date of the transport. It seems the young man whom I thought was my security detail was a fraud.'

'You sound awfully calm about this,' Thomas said.

'I seriously doubt anyone could get into your safe, Thomas. Just continue to be diligent. I am sure all will be well.'

'And if it isn't?' Thomas snapped. 'Never mind. I'll call you back.' He hung up the phone, grabbed his coat and ran all the way home.

By the time he turned up the drive, sweat dampened his shirt. His lungs felt as though they were about to burst, and his regret at agreeing to guard the chalice grew by the second. He burst through the front door of his house and hurried to his study, knowing what he would find from the minute he received Stephen Templeton's news.

The missus sat at his desk, her head bowed as she wept. 'This is all my fault.'

Thomas hurried over to her and put a comforting hand on her shoulder. He didn't need to look at the safe. Didn't need to see the door hanging open and the empty inside of it taunting him, like some ill-timed jape.

Chapter 12

Dusk fell just as Hugh stepped off the bus, the rucksack slung over his shoulder. Any curiosity he had about the mysterious thing his wife had stolen was overcome by his utter exhaustion. He trudged back to his cottage, mindful of his aching back and sore feet, knowing tomorrow he would pay for the hours he spent sitting on the ground. Eventually the pain would be better. Even though he wasn't sure what Margaret had stolen, or how it would help him get vengeance for Martin's suicide, he felt smug pleasure at besting his wife. He would have paid dearly to see the look on her face once she discovered her treasure had been stolen. Although he may not have any evidence for the police, he was surprised at how much joy he took in thwarting the woman who had made him so miserable for so long.

Now he longed for Vera's kindly ministrations. How lovely it would be to go right to her cottage, put his feet up, and have a drink while she puttered around the kitchen. He had been tempted on the bus ride home to peek at the contents of his rucksack, but it only seemed fair to share the revelation with Vera. After all, she had encouraged him to find out what Margaret was up to and take control of his life.

Hugh trudged up the stairs and soaked in a hot bath until the water turned cold. As he lay in the tub alone with his thoughts, he wondered how long it would take Margaret to discover her parcel was missing. When the keen pleasure at the day's shenanigans crept up, Hugh pushed it away. This was not the time for arrogance or over-confidence. He had poked the proverbial hornet's nest. The situation required caution, lest he get stung. He dressed quickly and had just come downstairs when Vera knocked on the kitchen door. Through the window Hugh could see she carried a basket of food.

He let her in, overwhelmed with the joy he felt at seeing her, and stood watching as she unloaded half a roasted chicken, potatoes, green beans and carrots. His stomach rumbled.

'I've brought dinner. And dessert. Fresh apple pie.' She set the food on the worktop while Hugh got dinner plates and cutlery out of the dresser.

'George is home tonight.' Vera spoke nonchalantly, but something in her voice gave Hugh pause. 'He's trying to be kind to me. It's all very odd.'

'Have you asked him if anything's wrong?'

'No,' Vera said. 'He wouldn't tell me if there were. We don't talk much, and we certainly don't share our day-to-day woes. When I grabbed this basket of food and headed over here he wasn't too pleased. I left him home, eating the lunch leftovers. Would you think me presumptuous if I unpacked this lot and set the table?'

'Not one bit,' Hugh said as he brought the rucksack into the kitchen.

'What have you got there?'

'I spent my day sitting on the ground in the woods, watching the house Margaret went to yesterday. My back will pay for it tomorrow, let me tell you. In any event, Margaret stole this' – Hugh nodded at the rucksack – 'from the house, with the help of her lover. After they buried it in the woods, I dug it up and brought it home.'

119

'What's inside?' Eyes sparkling, Vera set the plates she held on the table and stood next to Hugh.

'I don't know. Let's find out.'

Hugh pushed the cutlery aside and opened the rucksack. He placed the object, wrapped in the blue velvet scarf he had bought Margaret for Christmas the previous year, on the table.

'Go ahead, Vera. You do the unveiling.'

Vera unwound the scarf to reveal a faded velvet sack with a drawstring. Her hands were those of a worker, with short nails and callouses, so unlike those of his wife, which had never done a day of work. Vera untied the drawstring and peeled the velvet wrapping away. 'It's heavy.' As she held up a heavy gold chalice, they both gasped.

'My god,' Hugh said.

'That's the most beautiful thing I've ever seen,' Vera whispered at the same time. She gingerly touched the rim of it, running her hands over the encrusted jewels, a look of reverence on her face. 'Do you think this is real gold? This is a religious chalice, Hugh. I'm sure of it. This came from a church somewhere.'

Hugh pulled the velvet wrap back over the chalice and tied the drawstring. What if the police found him in possession of this precious relic? There wasn't a shred of proof of Margaret's involvement. The police would think he was the thief and send him to prison. Margaret would have the last laugh after all.

Vera put her hand on his arm. 'Hugh? What is it?'

'I can't believe what an idiot I've been. Do you know what will happen to me if the police discover this in my possession? I'll go to prison, that's what. For a crime my wife committed.'

'No. You could return it to its rightful owner and explain what happened.'

Hugh Bettencourt was a man of average intelligence. As a child, he did moderately well at school, but he learned from an early age he was no super intellect, like his older brother and his mother. As an adult, Hugh had always been disgusted by the manipulative games people played as they jockeyed for position in the business world. Whenever Hugh set out to engage in manipulative shenanigans – and he had been forced to try on more than one occasion, thanks to his mother and brother – he always found himself on the losing end of the proposition, the brunt of the joke. Despite this disadvantage, he knew Vera's idea made perfect sense. As far as Hugh could see, only one thing could go wrong.

'What if they think I'm the one who stole it? What if they think I had second thoughts, and returned the chalice out of guilt?'

'Don't tell them.' Vera put the chalice back in the rucksack, which she zipped up and tucked under the table out of sight. After arranging the plates and putting the food on the table, she sat down and started to serve them.

'What?'

'Just take it back to the house and leave it on the doorstep. You can wait in the bushes to make sure no one interferes. No need to explain yourself. Once the chalice is safely back in the house where it belongs, you creep away with no one the wiser.'

'Which still leaves me at Margaret's mercy.'

'Oh, but it doesn't,' Vera said. 'Margaret doesn't need to know you returned the chalice. In fact, best for her to think you've got it hidden somewhere. I know it's not true vengeance for your dead friend, but at least you have the satisfaction of making your wife uncomfortable.'

'You're brilliant,' Hugh said.

'Not brilliant. Just sensible,' Vera said. 'I feel guilty at being so petty. But I've lived with a husband who has betrayed me over and over. Vengeance is against God's will, I know that. But sometimes ...' Hugh understood what she meant. He squeezed her hand, grateful when she didn't pull it away.

They ate in comfortable silence. When they finished and Vera had stacked the plates in the sink, Hugh said, 'Tell me about George.'

121

Vera turned and met his eyes, an expression on her face that he couldn't place. Worry? Guilt? She wouldn't meet Hugh's eyes. Instead she folded her hands on her lap and looked down. The shame she carried broke Hugh's heart. He wanted to reach out and take her hand, but he didn't, opting instead to stay quiet while she told her story.

'I've never told anyone this.' Her voice had a jagged quality to it. She cleared her throat and found her voice. 'The weekend that we married, George had an affair with a 19-year-old shop girl. I caught them in the act. I've never been so humiliated in my life. George confessed, explaining the girl seduced him. I was so young and foolish. George was so handsome back then. I wanted to believe everything he told me. In fact, as I look back, I remember being amazed that a man like him would love me. I forgave him and tried to forget about the incident. He assured me it would never happen again.

'He worked for my father at the furniture store, until one day he came home and said he had taken another job and that we were moving. He demanded I sell this house, but I didn't. I found out later he had been stealing from my parents. They didn't want to tell me.' Vera shook her head. 'We moved to Hendleigh for a while, but soon George lost that job, too. I had my small income from my grandmother, which kept food on the table, but we struggled. And fought. The war did something to George, I think. There were times when he seemed to just lose his reason. We no sooner moved to Hendleigh, than I heard George had gotten a young girl pregnant.

'I hated my husband, hated myself for being such a fool. One night George went to the pub, I packed my bag and came here, fully expecting to never see George again.'

'Obviously he came back to you,' Hugh said.

Vera looked up, meeting Hugh's eyes for the first time. 'I can't take this anymore, Hugh.'

She wept. Without thinking, Hugh pulled Vera to her feet, wrapped his arms around her, and kissed away her tears.

122

'We'll get through it, Vera. I love you. It's like no time has passed. I won't let you get away again.'

She sobbed again, as a fresh wave of grief washed over her. He let her cry, holding her and comforting her all the while.

'Tell me you love me, Vera,' he whispered in her ear.

'Of course I love you. I've never stopped' She wrapped her arms him and buried her face in his chest. Finally, shaking her head, she pushed away from him. 'I'm sorry.' She wiped the tears with the back of her hand. 'I can't.'

Chapter 13

Alex tucked himself between two overgrown hawthorn bushes and waited in the cover of darkness for Margaret Bettencourt. The night was quiet, save for a pair of owls who hooted at each other every few minutes. Alex longed to extricate himself from Michael Grenville's clutches. Under normal circumstances, once he had the chalice safely in hand, he'd slip away and never be heard from again. But Margaret Bettencourt had changed that scenario.

Like a fool, Alex had allowed Margaret to manipulate her way into his world, turning his simple existence entirely upside down. Careful to keep her at arm's length with regard to his business dealings, they had spent an intoxicating weekend together in Edinburgh in an opulent hotel under the name of Mr and Mrs Peter Smith before coming to Rivenby. Alex didn't like small villages, preferring the anonymity of London or Edinburgh. The last thing he wanted was to be noticed. That wouldn't do at all.

Replaying the series of events that had enabled Margaret to finagle her way into his work life, Alex recalled the day he got the telephone call with the information about the chalice. She had been in the bathtub, doing all the things with potions and unguents designed to keep her looking young. He didn't give her a second thought as he wrote down the logistics of the job, the name of the man to whom he would deliver the chalice and the address of Stephen Templeton, the vicar who had the chalice now. He hadn't realised Margaret was stood behind him, eavesdropping. After Alex hung up the phone and tucked the piece of paper into his jacket pocket. Margaret stepped close to him, a sultry smile on her beautiful face.

'Who were you talking to?'

'I wish you wouldn't sneak up on me. No one important. Work. You smell divine.' When she didn't answer him, he met her eyes, surprised by the look of sheer rage he saw there. 'What's the matter?'

'I heard what you said. Who's Thomas Charles?' Margaret's voice became shrill, the portent of yet another emotional storm. Alex – in a metaphorical attempt to batten down the hatches – held up his hands in supplication as he stepped away from Margaret. 'You need to stop eavesdropping on my conversations, Margaret. That was a work phone call. It doesn't concern you.'

She nodded at his coat pocket where the piece of paper lay. 'Thomas Charles? In Rivenby? What is your business with him?'

'You know this man?' Alex realised he had made an egregious error and had underestimated Margaret.

'Let's just say dear Mr Charles has something that belongs to me. You're going to steal from him, aren't you?' She crossed her arms, allowing her dressing gown to fall open, revealing a bare shoulder and just enough of her breast to titillate. 'He's quick, smart and – no offence, darling – much more powerful than you will ever be. Bet your friend on the telephone didn't tell you that.'

Alex had learned early on it was easier to just let Margaret have her way than try to dissuade her. When she had come up with the idea of burying the chalice in the woods, he had been duly impressed. 'What if this Mr Grenville takes the chalice from you and doesn't pay? Best not to turn the chalice over until you're holding the money.' In hindsight, Alex realised he had been so busy focusing on the job at hand, he had failed to notice Margaret's increasingly erratic behaviour.

Their plan had gone off perfectly. The chalice had been removed from Thomas Charles's house in less than five minutes. Now they were going to retrieve it, so Alex could give the chalice to Michael Grenville and get his money. Once Alex had the chalice in hand, he would have to find a way to escape Margaret once and for all.

Where was she? It started to rain, more like a gentle mist, pretty to look at but chilling to the bones.

'Over here, darling.' Margaret stepped into the moonlight, dressed head to toe in black, her hair pulled back from her exquisite face and held in place with a dark scarf. God, she was beautiful. He felt the familiar stirring as she walked up to him and stood on her tiptoes to be kissed. 'I've had the most marvellous day of rest. Saint Monica's is a really lovely home.'

'And the woman who owns it just took you in out of the blue?' Alex hoped she wouldn't detect the incredulity in his voice.

'She did.' Margaret twirled like a schoolgirl in a new skirt. 'I've got the loveliest room, with lots of light and a silk counterpane. And the cook – she's rather surly, but she is masterful in the kitchen.'

Stepping close, he took Margaret into his arms and whispered into her ear, letting his lips linger there. Gently touching Margaret's cheek – she responded to physical affection like a spoiled cat – he said, 'Keep the noise down, love. Let's get what we've come for and get out of here.'

Margaret took his hand and led him through the woods. 'What I wouldn't give to see the look on Thomas Charles's face when he discovers his precious chalice is missing.'

'Why do you hate him so?'

'Never mind that, darling. That's a story for another day. The minute I get the money, we'll get out of here. Where shall we go?'

He lied easily, knowing that he was going to have to slip away from her.

Alex stepped over the trunk of a toppled tree, offering his hand to Margaret. She took it and jumped over, spry as a deer. Margaret tightened her grip on his hand. As if reading his mind, she said, 'You're not going to leave me, Alex. I won't let you.'

Just then the moonlight bathed the fine planes of Margaret's face. Alex met her eyes and saw the steely determination there, along with something wild and unfathomable. *Good god, I'm afraid of her.* Taken aback by this revelation, Alex acknowledged Margaret Bettencourt had some sort of an agenda, and his stupidity had allowed her to use him to carry it out. Maybe Margaret was after Thomas Charles. Maybe she was simply on a reckless thrill-seeking mission. Her motivations didn't matter. Alex had to get away from her before she ruined him.

They trudged along in the moonlight for a good ten minutes before Margaret pushed Alex aside and walked ahead of him on the narrow path. Through the bushes he could see the outline of Thomas Charles's house, Heart's Desire, against the night sky. The windows were dark from the blackout curtains.

'Oh, my god,' Margaret cried out, as she broke into a run. She came to a stop by a pile of dirt. Alex stood beside her, and together they stared into the empty gaping hole.

'I cannot believe this. The bastard. He took it.' She kicked at the mound of dirt before she turned and strode towards the house. She had just stepped onto the large expansive lawn, in plain view of anyone who cared to look out one of the many windows that faced it, when Alex caught up with her. He grabbed her hand and pulled her back into the bushes.

'Let go of me.' Her shrill voice cut through the night, silencing the rustling nocturnal creatures. She broke free from Alex and kept running. He hurried after her, this time wrapping his arms around her from behind and holding her fast. As he picked her up and carried her back to the protection of the woods, she started to scream. As soon as they reached cover, Alex pushed Margaret against a tree and used one hand to cover her mouth. He nearly screamed himself when she sank her teeth into the fleshy skin of his palm.

'Be quiet. Do you want them to hear us?' He waited until she stilled in his arms. 'If I take my hand away will you keep quiet? If you scream, I'm leaving. I mean it, Margaret. I'll throw you to the ground and disappear into the night. You'll never hear from me again. Do not think for one minute you can outsmart me.' He took his hand away but kept her arms pinned, just in case she decided to dart back towards the house.

'I'm sorry. He makes me so mad.'

He turned her to face him. 'Who is Thomas, Margaret? Tell me.'

Her eyes blazed with unabashed hatred. 'He's my brother. And he stole my inheritance.'

Her brother? Oh, god. What had he done? For the first time in his entire adult life and professional career, Alex acknowledged the error of allowing Margaret to get close to him.

'This is what we need to do.' She spoke quickly, her words merging together in one long maniacal rant. 'We'll rob him. Yes. That's it. When he leaves the house in the morning, you will attack him from behind. Not too bad, just enough to knock him out. Then I'll steal his keys …'

Careful to keep his voice low and calm, Alex rubbed her arms in a slow, sensuous movement. 'Listen to me.'

She stopped talking, but her eyes were wild. He kept stroking her, as if trying to calm a frightened animal.

'Of course I'll help you,' Alex lied easily. 'But I won't be part of your plot to seek revenge. Seeking revenge will get us caught.' He kissed Margaret's forehead. 'It will be all right. We both need a good night's rest. Let me see you back to Saint Monica's, and we can decide how to proceed tomorrow.' He interrupted her before she could continue, stepping close and pulling her to him. 'Don't worry. I'll get the chalice back.'

'I don't care about the chalice,' Margaret hissed. 'My brother needs to pay for what he's done.' She grabbed Alex's arm, harder this time, her fingers like claws, relentless hooks that would surely trap him if he didn't extricate himself from this situation.

Alex took a deep calming breath. With a gentle touch, he cupped Margaret's chin, and spoke to her in a gentle, coaxing voice. 'Let me do my job. Then we can discuss your brother. How does that sound?'

With a violent shift her mood changed. The wild recklessness replaced by utter sorrow. Her body weakened. The tears came. She sobbed so hard her shoulders shook. Not knowing what else to do, Alex took her in his arms and cradled her like a child. 'Don't cry, Margaret. Everything will be all right. I promise.'

When she stopped crying, he dried her tears and, taking her hand, led her through the woods back to Saint Monica's, neither of them speaking. When they arrived at the clearing near the house, Alex kissed her forehead, careful not to trigger another emotional tirade.

'Sleep well, my love. Come to me tomorrow.' Alex waited until Margaret slipped into the kitchen door, knowing that he would never see her again. As he walked back to the cottage, he made plans. He would pack quickly and find another place to stay, a safe place where Margaret couldn't find him. Then he would figure out his next move. Margaret's mental state gave him pause. The poor thing needed medical help. Her brother would need to be warned. Alex exhaled. Things had become very complicated indeed.

Chapter 14

'I'm leaving her sliced bread and butter. She needs to eat, but I don't want her cooking in my kitchen,' Bede had said. 'She'll have to make her own tea. Aren't you worried about leaving her here alone?'

'Not really,' Cat said. She wove her arm through Bede's as the two women stepped out of Saint Monica's and hurried down the lane to the bus.

'You are a trusting soul, Mrs Carlisle,' Bede said.

'Bede, you liked Margaret just fine when she was praising your cooking.'

'I couldn't be rude, could I? She's every bit as bad as Lucy Bardwell – forgive me for speaking ill of the dead.' Bede slid into her seat next to Cat, ignoring the woman across the narrow aisle who turned to stare at them.

As the bus pulled away, Cat leaned into Bede and whispered. 'Keep your voice down. Everyone's listening.'

The bus was filled with mostly women office workers, en route to their office jobs in Hendleigh, along with a few women who – as evidenced by the shopping bags they carried – were off to market. As the bus sped away from Rivenby, Cat had second thoughts. What if Margaret robbed her blind? She envisioned

Margaret running off with their linens and clothes. She shook her head. *Stop being ridiculous.* Bede had fallen quiet as the bus left the village and wound through the countryside.

'I'm glad Mr Charles will be involved with this one,' Bede said. 'He's got a good head on his shoulders. If Margaret Smith is up to no good, he'll see right through her.'

'Bede, just because Lucy Bardwell conned us – conned me' – Cat corrected herself when Bede's expression became indignant – 'doesn't mean everyone else is a liar. Margaret couldn't have faked her injuries.'

'Oh, really? And did you examine her? Did you see the bruises on her skin? See the swelling on her allegedly injured knee? I didn't think so. Don't you find it strange she spends so much time in her room? How much sleep does a body need?'

'I do not think it's strange. She's exhausted.' Cat wondered if she had given Bede too much authority by asking her to be involved in vetting Margaret. 'I don't want to speak of this again. You'll have your say when we sit down with her. Meanwhile, we will treat her with respect until we are given a reason to do otherwise.'

'Very well, but I'll say one more thing, if you don't mind. How did she come to show up on your doorstep? At least ask her that,' Bede said, turning her back on Cat and staring out the window, leaving Cat alone with her worries about Lucy Bardwell's murder and the mysterious woman who she had left alone in her home.

***

Dark ominous clouds greeted them when they got off the bus in Hendleigh. Rather than get stuck in the rain, Cat and Bede opted for a taxi ride to Ambrose Bardwell's house.

'Will you look at this garden,' Bede said, as the taxi pulled up in front of Ambrose Bardwell's detached cottage. Fat cabbages sat in rows, ready to be picked in the small area in front of the

131

house. 'There's not a weed among them.' Bede stooped and picked up a handful of the black soil, running it through her fingers. 'This dirt looks so rich. He must be using some special fertiliser. Do you think he'll tell us what it is?'

'It's manure mixed with water.'

Bede and Cat turned to face a man dressed in work clothes, who had come around the side of the house. His right leg was missing from the knee down. His right hand clenched a single crutch. His left hand held a trowel. 'You have to be careful not to make it too strong or you'll burn the plants and you can't use it until they are well underway. I let it sit for a couple of weeks, and then use one cup of that mixture in ten gallons of water.' He dropped the trowel and walked over to them, surprisingly graceful, despite his missing leg. 'I'm Ambrose Bardwell. You must be here about Lucy.'

'How do you do, Mr Bardwell. I'm Cat Carlisle and this is Bede Turner. Lucy lived at my home until she was—' Cat stopped, embarrassed at her insensitive remark.

'It's a terrible business. The police were here yesterday. I had a bit of an episode. Haven't been able to handle things since I left the service. Shell shock, that's what the doctor says. Why don't you come in. I could use a cup of tea about now.'

They followed him around to the back of the house, where the smell of fresh biscuits emanated from the kitchen. There were stacks of them, arranged in racks on a professional looking baker's shelf tucked into a corner.

'What's this?' Bede exclaimed, not bothering to keep the surprise from her voice. 'Did you bake these?'

'Yes, ma'am,' Ambrose Bardwell said. He put the kettle on. 'We'll sit in here. Have a seat.' He pointed to a table in a windowed alcove which looked over a fenced-in garden area that boasted another well-tended rose garden, complete with an obelisk upon which three different varieties of clematis grew.

Soon the three of them were drinking tea, eating biscuits and discussing the pros and cons of mulching roses, as though they were old friends.

When the tea was drunk and the biscuits consumed, Ambrose turned to Cat. 'What happened to my sister? Is it true they found her in the woods behind your house?'

'I'm so sorry, Mr Bardwell.'

'Call me Ambrose.' He stared out the back window, not meeting Cat's eyes, as he struggled with his grief. When he spoke, his voice was wistful. 'I just can't take it in. Can't believe she's gone.'

'She was under my care and I feel responsible for her somehow,' Cat said.

Ambrose Bardwell looked at Cat with sympathy. 'Don't try to take responsibility for Lucy's actions. That's a fool's errand. Spoiled she was, by my parents – god rest their souls – and by me after they died. Lucy was a pretty thing, but she had a wild streak. As much as I hate to admit it, I knew she was headed for trouble. She was boy crazy, for one thing. Didn't listen, either.'

As if reading her thoughts, Ambrose Bardwell said, 'It's not your fault, miss. I'm surprised it didn't happen sooner. The truth of the matter is Lucy is what they call a *fast* girl. I know she's had boyfriends, some of them married. She had a reputation, but there was nothing I could do about it. Once some of the ladies came to my door and offered to help me with Lucy, get her involved in church activities and the like. But she refused, laughed in their faces. Told them what they could do with their church ways.'

Cat sighed. 'I feel as though I should be honest with you, Mr Bardwell – Ambrose.'

'Honesty's always best. I've never been one for false words or pretence. Tell me about my sister. What sort of trouble did she stir up in Rivenby?'

'You don't sound surprised,' Bede said.

'Nothing shocks me anymore,' Ambrose Bardwell said with a hint of sadness in his voice. 'And Lucy had a way of influencing other young girls around her, those that were easily led astray.'

133

'She told lies,' Cat said, gauging Ambrose Bardwell's response.

'Oh, no doubt. Lucy could spin a yarn. She were a right good liar,' he said.

'I run a home for women who have been battered by their husbands and families. Lucy came to me, claiming you abused her and withheld money from her. She was desperate to train to be a secretary, so she could get away from you. Horrible accusations, I know, but that's what she said.'

'Mrs Carlisle is a bit gullible,' Bede said.

Ambrose Bardwell tipped his head back and laughed. Cat and Bede looked at each other as his laugh became louder and louder. Finally he slapped the table before he stood and picked up the dirty tea things. 'I've never laid a hand on my sister. My parents were non-violent. They never even spanked us as children.' He gave Cat and Bede a serious look. 'My sister was a liar, ladies. That's the sad and sorry truth.'

Cat thought about the things Lucy had done, stealing Cat's clothes, lying about her situation. She believed Ambrose. 'Ambrose, would it be an imposition for us to see Lucy's room?'

'Of course not, miss. If you'll follow me.' He led them down the hall, into a spacious bedroom situated in the back corner of the house.

'This was our parents' room,' he explained. 'But I let Lucy have it when she turned 13. I thought if I gave her this room, she'd stop being so wild.'

'It didn't work?' Cat asked.

Ambrose shook his head. 'She started leaving school, sneaking out at night, stealing alcohol. It was a difficult situation. In hindsight, she might have done better with a mother figure.'

'This is beautiful,' Bede said. She stood in the centre of the room and turned a slow circle, surprised at the canopy bed, the large wardrobe, and the chaise tucked under the window. She shook her head. 'Looks like one of them pictures you see in magazines. Fit for a princess, this is.'

'I don't understand why she'd want to leave,' Cat said.

'I was good to my sister,' Ambrose said. 'She received a generous allowance. Our parents left us both pretty well situated, but I'm the trustee of Lucy's money. Given her reckless nature, I had to be diligent. Before she left, she started seeing someone. Wouldn't be surprised if he were married.'

'Why do you say that?' Cat asked.

Ambrose Bardwell looked sheepish. 'I eavesdropped on her phone conversations and heard her talking about it. He didn't come right out and say he was married, but he never took her to the cinema or out on the weekends.' Ambrose shrugged his shoulders. 'I just had a feeling. When I suggested this man wasn't available to court her properly because he was married, she became angry with me. Told me to mind my own business, insisted I give her control of her money. When I refused she told me she hated me and didn't care if she never saw me again. The next morning, she packed her things and left. Didn't even say goodbye.

'About a month ago, she came home to visit. Dressed in fancy new clothes. Said she was training to be a secretary, and she was getting married. When I asked questions about her beau – as her brother and guardian, I felt I should meet him – she became angry. But she needed money. I wrote her a generous cheque and agreed to start her allowance again. She seemed satisfied, and we left on good terms. That was the last time I saw her.'

'And you've no idea who her boyfriend was?'

'No. Lucy's had many boyfriends, but she grew bored easily,' Ambrose said. 'Some will say she deserved what she got.'

'She didn't, Mr Bardwell. No one deserves to have their life taken,' Cat said. 'And we should be going. Thank you for the biscuits and for taking the time to talk to us. I'm at Saint Monica's in Rivenby. If you think of anything, or if I can do anything to help you, please contact me.'

***

135

The bus ride home was a quiet one. The meeting with Lucy's brother had proved enlightening, and Cat – thank goodness – was realising Lucy Bardwell had indeed created a dangerous situation for herself. *Could I have done more to keep her safe?*

'It's not your fault, Miss Catherine,' Bede said, as if reading her mind. 'Women like Lucy Bardwell often wind up in trouble. Now don't get me wrong, I'm sorry she was murdered, but the police will find out who killed her. You did a kindness to Lucy and your heart was in the right place. And if anyone ever says otherwise, they'll have me to contend with.'

'Bede, I don't think we should tell Mr Charles we've visited Ambrose. He may take our visit the wrong way and think we're meddling.'

'I don't like keeping secrets, but I do see your point.' With that, Bede crossed her arms over her ample bosom and drifted off to sleep.

Cat dozed too and didn't awaken until the bus pulled into Rivenby, Bede snoring softly next to her.

'Bede, wake up,' Cat said, shaking her gently.

Bede startled awake. 'I wasn't asleep. Never have been able to sleep in a moving vehicle.' As the women stepped off the bus, Bede clutched her purse to her chest. 'I'll just run to Mrs Henson's and pick up the eggs. No need for you to come with me. You go on home and put your feet up. There'll be omelettes and green beans for dinner.'

Cat buttoned her coat against the afternoon chill, longing to see Thomas and wishing for a cup of tea before a toasty fire. As she turned onto the lane to Saint Monica's, she saw Thomas and a surly-looking man dressed in ill-kempt clothes and in need of a shave loitering in front of Beth Hargreaves's house. Beth – who now lived in Scotland and worked as a professional baker for a fancy Edinburgh hotel – had decided to leave her house empty until she was certain of her new position. When Thomas saw Cat, he pointed to his colleague and walked in her direction with a purposeful stride, an intense look on his face. Cat's heart quickened. Something was wrong.

When he drew close, she was dismayed by the dark circles under his bloodshot eyes and the deep lines etched into the sides of his mouth. Why hadn't she noticed his exhaustion? She longed to run to him and wrap her arms around him, but something in his manner gave her pause.

'Thomas,' she said, when he got close. She almost kissed him, but stopped herself again. 'What's wrong?'

'Blasted newspaper reporters. They're camped in front of Saint Monica's. I'm here to convey you through the woods to your back door to make sure they don't bother you.'

'Thank you,' Cat said.

The other man came striding up behind Thomas, not bothering to hide his displeasure. Cat wondered why he was so angry.

'How do you do?' she said, thinking if she were polite to him, he would reciprocate in kind.

'Very well.' The man nodded and looked at Thomas. 'What do you need me for? I need to get back to the station.'

'Where's Bede?' Thomas asked Cat.

'Mrs Henson's. She went to get our eggs.'

'Hinks, wait here until Bede Turner arrives. Then bring her through the woods to Mrs Carlisle's back door. I'll be there waiting for you. Understand?'

'I'm not daft,' Hinks said. 'And I don't know why you think you can order me around.'

'Just do it, Hinks. For god's sake, man, just do as you're told.' Thomas took Cat's hand and led her towards the woods.

Exhausted all of a sudden, Cat didn't give voice to the questions running through her head. She walked next to Thomas, enjoying the feel of his warm hand in hers. When they stepped up to the back door of Saint Monica's, Cat turned to him. 'What's the matter? Something's wrong. And don't tell me it's Lucy

137

Bardwell's murder and the reporters camped in front of my house. I know you too well.'

For a brief moment, the anger and exhaustion lifted. Thomas reached out and touched her cheek. 'Let me get you inside. I'll tell you while you put on the kettle.'

Thomas kept watch while Cat unlocked the back door and let them in.

'Thank goodness you don't have any women living here now,' he said.

'But I do,' Cat said. The bread and butter Bede had left out for Margaret stood untouched on the counter. 'A new woman arrived yesterday.'

'Okay. Well, find out where she is. Make sure she's safe,' Thomas said. 'I'll shut the curtains in the front of the house.'

Cat left Thomas to his own devices and hurried up the stairs. Margaret's bed was unmade, a damp towel thrown across it. But Margaret was nowhere to be seen. Cat grabbed the damp towel and headed back downstairs, where she found Thomas in the kitchen pouring hot water into the teapot.

'Do you want some brandy?' Cat asked. 'No offence, Tom, but you look like you could use it.'

Thomas turned to face Cat, the look on his face one of defeat and despair. Her heart broke looking at him. 'Tell me.'

'The chalice has been stolen.' He walked over to the table and sunk down into one of the chairs. 'The guard who came with Stephen Templeton was an imposter. I found him checking the safe. When I confronted him, he said he was making sure the chalice was securely locked away. I took him at his word.' Thomas rubbed his eyes. 'I'm getting soft in my old age.'

'Stop it,' Cat said. She sat down across from him at the table. 'That's not true and you know it. Tell me what happened. Don't leave anything out.'

He told her about Stephen Templeton's phone call, the guard who turned out to be an imposter and the empty safe.

'That's unbelievable,' Cat said.

'It was planned. The entire fiasco was an orchestrated scheme.' Thomas sighed. His shoulders slumped. 'And I didn't bloody see it.'

Cat stepped behind Thomas, rubbing his neck and shoulders until she felt the tension start to lessen.

He reached back and took her hand. 'How the devil am I going to fix this?'

'Are you asking a real question or a hypothetical?'

'Neither. I don't see how I can remedy this situation. Stephen Templeton trusted me. I let him down.'

'Don't be ridiculous. Stephen Templeton allowed an imposter into this scenario, not you. He's not going to blame you, Thomas.'

'I know. But I still feel responsible.'

'Of course you feel responsible. If I were in your shoes, I'd feel responsible, too. Are you not even going to try to find the chalice? Thomas, you've dealt with men far worse than this common thief. Find him. Find the chalice. You've seen him, you know what he looks like. Does he have a car? Where is he staying? Is he still in Rivenby? Surrounding villages? Has he tried to sell the chalice? Surely you can use your connections and investigation skills to get some answers.'

They reached for each other, impervious to George Hinks and Bede Turner approaching the back of the house. When George Hinks banged on the back door, a devious grin on his face, Cat and Thomas both jumped. Thomas yelped. Bede stepped inside, white-faced and wild-eyed, while Thomas went outside to speak to George Hinks, shutting the door behind him.

'Bede, whatever's wrong?'

'That's him,' Bede whispered. 'As I live and breathe, that's him.'

'Who? Mr Hinks? Bede, what are you talking about?'

'Mr Hinks is the man I seen Lucy Bardwell kissing in the woods.'

Cat had been living in the same house with Bede Turner for

well over a year. Never had she seen any incident shake Bede's stubborn sense of calm. The terror on Bede's face now prompted Cat to lock the back door. 'You're safe, Bede. Thomas won't let anything happen to you.'

At the mention of Thomas's protection, Bede nodded. 'You're right. We must tell the police. I expect they'll want a statement?'

'Probably. Why don't you go and take off your coat and hat. I'll get Thomas away from George Hinks and tell him myself.'

Bede scurried out of the room, unpinning her hat as she went.

Cat watched as Thomas and George Hinks continued their rather spirited discussion, Thomas speaking non-stop, George Hinks pretending to listen, an exasperated look on his face. Finally, George Hinks turned on his heels and left. Thomas headed back to Cat, a grimace on his face.

'I have tried my best to show Mr Hinks every professional courtesy, but he continues to argue with me. One of these days he's is going to irritate the wrong person—'

'I need to talk to you.'

'What is it?' Thomas said, concern etched on his face.

'Bede just told me George Hinks is – was – Lucy's lover.'

Thomas cocked his head, a bewildered look on his face. 'George Hinks?'

'Yes. She's rather shaken, Tom.'

'I had better call DCI Kent.'

Cat left Thomas alone in her study to telephone DCI Kent. Meanwhile, Bede came back into the kitchen, still pale, but determined to carry on. After DCI Kent arrived, Cat polished the silver in an attempt to keep herself occupied, while Bede gave her statement in the drawing room. After the men had left, Bede and Cat ate dinner and retired to their rooms early. Margaret never returned. Cat wondered if they had seen the last of her.

Chapter 15

During the sixteen months Thomas had known DCI Kent, he had always admired his superior officer's keen intellect and open mind. Now, as Thomas watched DCI Kent's face redden and the small vein on his forehead throb, he made a mental note not to wind up on his DCI's bad side.

'The bloody idiot didn't think he should tell us about his relationship with this girl? He bloody well knew we were searching high and low for the identity of Lucy's mysterious lover.' They were in DCI Kent's office with the door closed. Although the constabulary was lightly staffed in the evening, Thomas knew everyone outside the office had stopped working in hopes they would hear something to indicate the source of Kent's agitation.

'That may not be true, sir. You did assign him to the file room. And he hasn't been involved in the investigation.' Thomas had Lucy Bardwell's file on his lap and was thumbing through the scant information they had so far. He pulled two photographs of the dead girl out, glanced at them briefly and placed them on top of the myriad of papers and reports that waited for review and processing.

'What if he's killed her, Tom? What if I hired a murderer to work with my men?' DCI Kent stood up, knocking his chair over in the process.

'You're overreacting,' Thomas blurted without thinking. He regretted his impetuous outburst the minute he said it. 'No disrespect intended.'

'What the devil are you saying then? Explain yourself.' DCI Kent sat back down at his desk.

'You couldn't have known what he was up to, could you? Everyone knows your police force is frighteningly short staffed. Your qualified and trained officers are off defending queen and country. There are scant resources to vet the men you hire and virtually no time to train them. You're doing the best you can.'

DCI Kent placed his hands on his desk, palms down, closed his eyes, and took a deep breath. 'Thanks, Tom.'

'I didn't tell you anything you don't already know, sir.' Thomas stood, clutching the Bardwell murder file. 'Are you coming with me?'

DCI Kent nodded. 'I'll just observe. Don't trust myself to speak to that idiot.'

It was 8 p.m. by the time George Hinks had been fetched from his local pub in Much Killham and returned to the Rivenby Constabulary. When the constables arrived at his pub to retrieve him for questioning in connection with Lucy Bardwell's murder, Hinks thought he was being sought after for his expertise. When he was placed in an interrogation room, he became indignant. When DCI Kent and Thomas entered the room, he started to speak, but quickly closed his mouth, his eyes darting back and forth between the two men.

'What's going on here? Why have you brought me to an interrogation room? I demand to know what's happening.'

When Thomas sat down across from him, George Hinks turned in his chair and spoke to DCI Kent. 'What's this about? I am not talking to him.'

'You will speak to him, Mr Hinks. And you will answer questions truthfully. Because if you lie – and believe me, I'll find out if you do – I will personally throttle you. Do I make myself clear?'

George Hinks realised the gravity of his situation. He swallowed, his Adam's apple bobbing, as he slunk down in his chair. 'All right, then. Let's have it.' He nodded at the folder on the table in front of Thomas. 'What've you got there?'

'Never mind that for the moment,' Thomas said. 'Where were you on the morning of October 7th?'

'I was here,' George Hinks said. 'And you bloody well know it.'

'Not sure, Hinks,' DCI Kent said. 'I looked for you in the file room, but you had left the job. I'd like to know where you went.'

At least George Hinks had the grace to look embarrassed. 'I might have taken a quick walk to the pub to find out what they were to serve for lunch. But there's no harm in that, is there?'

'Yes, there is,' Thomas said. 'You don't just arbitrarily walk away from the job without telling anyone.'

'You can just—'

'Tell me about your relationship with Lucy Bardwell,' Thomas interrupted.

'The murdered girl?' Confident now, George Hinks gave Thomas a smirk. 'Is this why you had me removed from my pub and forcefully brought here? If I knew anything about her, don't you think I'd have said when she turned up dead?' He turned around to face DCI Kent. 'You believe me, don't you?'

'I do not,' DCI Kent said.

When George Hinks turned around to face Thomas, his expression became unsure.

'You were seen, Hinks,' Thomas said. 'We have an extremely reliable witness who saw you in the woods behind Saint Monica's kissing Lucy Bardwell. Did you kill her?'

'Kill her?' George jumped up, angry red splotches on his cheeks.

'Sit down,' Thomas said.

For a moment, Thomas thought George was going to argue with him, but the man thought better of it and sat back down. A sheen of sweat broke out on his forehead. He wiped it with his forearm and gave Thomas a pleading looking.

'Look here, we was seeing each other a bit. Nothing serious,

143

mind you. But Lucy was a good-time girl. She knew where things stood between us. But I didn't kill her. I swear.'

'When was the last time you saw her?'

'The day before she was killed. She said she needed to talk to me about something. We set up a meeting at the folly near the church. Lucy never showed. I didn't wait around because I didn't want to be late for work.'

'Maybe she wanted to tell you she was pregnant,' Thomas said.

The colour drained from George Hinks's face. 'Pregnant? Lucy? Are you sure?' Any bravado left in George Hinks seeped out, as he slumped in his chair.

'Very sure.' Thomas opened the folder and took out the two photos. Slowly he set them on the table and watched as George Hinks took one look at his lover's corpse and fell to the floor, unconscious.

***

Following DCI Kent's orders, they left George Hinks in jail overnight. Although Thomas felt certain that Hinks didn't have the type of anger needed to bludgeon Lucy, DCI Kent wasn't comfortable letting Hinks go until he discussed matters with his superior. They had left him snivelling in his cell, protesting his innocence all the while. Hinks may not have murdered Lucy Bardwell but withholding evidence in a police inquiry was another matter. Thomas didn't concern himself with that. They had a killer to catch. DCI Kent and Thomas both knew that Michael Grenville was their likely suspect. He had seen Lucy sneaking around Saint Monica's, mistaken her for his wife, and beaten her to death. All they had to do was find him.

Pleased to see the newspaper reporters had retired to the pub for the night, Thomas walked through the dark to Cat's doorstep. Without speaking, she took his hand and led him upstairs, where she quietly removed his clothes and took him to bed. Their lovemaking was intense and deeply satisfying. They lay tangled in the sheets, the flickering flames of the bedroom fire making shadows dance along the wall. Safely tucked away in the cocoon of Cat's bedroom, Thomas felt as though he could sleep for weeks.

'You're finally relaxed,' Cat said. She kissed his shoulder and got out of bed. Thomas watched, admiring her naked body and her lack of inhibition as she wrapped her wool dressing gown around her waist. *My wife.* The sentiment, surprising as it was, came to him unbidden. They hadn't had the ceremony yet, but as he watched Cat in her nakedness, he thought of her thirty years from now, with stooped shoulders, greying hair and arthritic knees. There was no question their love would withstand the test of time. His challenge – and he must never forget it – was to allow Cat her freedom. He would always feel protective of her. His drive to keep her safe from harm would always be there. It was up to him to make sure Cat never felt smothered with it. Smiling over her shoulder at him, she reached into the back of her wardrobe and pulled out a navy-blue paisley dressing gown, which she tossed to him.

'Why do you have a man's dressing gown in your wardrobe?' Thomas wrapped himself in its warmth, enjoying the feel of the soft fabric against his naked skin. He wished he could stay here, away from the stress of Lucy Bardwell's murder investigation, away from the anguish of his utter failure as guardian of the chalice. 'If you're sharing your bed with another lover, I'd rather not know about it.'

'Don't be an idiot. I bought it for you. Forgive me for being forward, but I knew at some point you would wind up in my bed, darling.' Sitting next to him, she furrowed her brow in the expression Thomas had come to recognise. She gave him a worried look. 'Have you found out anything about Michael Grenville?'

'Only that he's looking for his wife and he may well have murdered Lucy Bardwell.'

'What a horrible coincidence, but there's no denying the resemblance. Lucy and Alice really do resemble each other, especially from a distance. Never fear. Alice is well hidden,' Cat said. 'He won't find her.'

My worry, love, is that he'll find you. Thomas didn't say these words out loud.

'I have a favour to ask,' Cat said.

Thomas took Cat's hand and kissed her palm. Laughing, she pulled it away.

'Don't try to distract me. I want you to help me vet this woman who arrived on my doorstep. If she's going to stay at Saint Monica's, I feel as though she should be thoroughly investigated.'

Serious now, Thomas sat up. 'Why?'

Cat pursed her lips and met his eyes. 'As you well know, Bede's been harping on at me for being reckless since I started this venture. I hate to admit it, but she has a point. This woman is going to be a test for me. With proper vetting and a cohesive plan, I should be able to help her in a more …' She paused, searching for the proper word. 'A more professional way. So will you teach me how to investigate someone's past? Look into their background? If she's got a criminal husband, for instance, she'll have to go.'

Thomas sighed with relief as he pulled Cat into his arms. 'Of course. We'll start on it as soon as possible. Let me know a good time to meet her. I'll start with asking her some questions and we'll go from there.' He nuzzled Cat's neck. 'Marry me.'

'I already said I would, darling,' Cat said.

'No. Marry me now. Why don't we get married and then have a second, more proper ceremony when Lydia and Annie arrive.'

'I can't, Thomas. Lydia would be disappointed and Annie would never forgive me.' She gave him a sheepish smile. 'After all the things happening lately, I'm craving a quiet life.'

'Would you sign something to that effect?'

Cat picked up a pillow and hit Thomas with it.

'In all seriousness,' Thomas continued, 'next year will be a quiet one for us. I'm going to cut back on my work for DCI Kent and we will take a proper honeymoon.' He sat up and walked over to the fire. 'How do you feel about going to America? After the war, of course. I wouldn't risk taking a boat now. We could go for a visit and see if we like it. I was thinking I'd like to see Los Angeles or San Francisco.'

'America?' Cat's voice sounded dreamy and full of promise.

Thomas smiled. 'We'll just think about it, shall we?'

***

Thomas awakened slowly, moving his body into one of the dappled sunbeams that warmed the bed. The prior evening had been the perfect finish to an otherwise horrid couple of days. Cat. He yawned and realised, as he slowly came awake, she was next to him, her legs pressed against his. Noises in the kitchen and the smell of bacon – he couldn't help but wonder how in god's name Bede Turner managed to get bacon – caused his eyes to spring wide open.

'Cat,' he whispered.

She woke up and smiled at him, until she realised their predicament. 'Oh no.' She jumped up, crept to her bedroom door and peeked out into the hallway. 'You're going to have to sneak out, Thomas. The reporters may come back.'

DCI Kent had given a detailed interview to the press yesterday, so Thomas felt certain they would be occupied this morning. But one could never be sure, so Thomas jumped out of bed and dressed in a flash. Pulling Cat into his arms, he kissed her. 'I'll see you tonight?'

'Yes. I'll come late.'

'No. I'll walk you over. I don't want you out by yourself. Not now.' *Not with Michael Grenville on the loose.*

Cat kissed him. 'Very well.'

Surprised Cat had acquiesced so readily, Thomas slipped out the front door. Once he was certain the reporters hadn't returned early, he took off at a run across Saint Monica's sweeping lawn. When he reached the lane, he turned right and cast a glance back at the house, just in time to see a curtain flutter on the second floor.

'Damn,' he cursed out loud. Someone had seen him, in all likelihood the new boarder.

147

Thomas hurried down the lane and up the high street. The shopkeepers hadn't opened yet, but soon they would be putting their vegetables out, sweeping their pavements and getting ready for the day. Luckily he didn't pass anyone. If anyone had seen him scarpering home, eyebrows would raise and within minutes the entire village would know that Thomas and Cat spent their nights together. He didn't mind what others thought of him, but Cat's reputation had to be protected at all costs. He smiled at the thought of their lovemaking the previous night and spent the rest of his walk in the chill autumn morning pleasantly distracted by the memories of it. When he got close to home, he saw a lone walker carrying a rucksack and a walking stick pass the lane that led to his drive. Suspicious, his senses fired. Why was this man near his home? He looked like an ordinary walker, one of the hundreds of people who sought the trails to the moors and through the forest. But the only trailhead here was directly from Thomas's property.

The man walked towards him, at a leisurely pace. Alert to the potential of danger, Thomas exhaled and slowed, his muscles taut. He had known his fair share of danger, and although he had taken a few punches, had somehow always managed to come out the victor. When they reached each other, the man met Thomas's eyes, smiled, bade him good morning and carried on walking. After they had passed each other on the lane, Thomas waited a few seconds before turning around. The man continued his insouciant pace. Something wasn't right. Breaking into a run, he turned down the long drive that led to his home. When he reached the steps to the front door, he bent over, clutching at the hellish cramp in his side, trying to catch his breath. He almost missed the blue velvet bundle tucked behind a large ceramic pot filled with ferns.

When he reached down and picked it up, the fabric fell away, revealing the chalice, the stones encrusted around the lip glittering in the morning light.

Chapter 16

Cat threw on a pair of old trousers accompanied by a thick fisherman's sweater. Before she headed down for breakfast, she peeked through her window, glad to see the reporters had yet to arrive. Her stomach rumbled when she smelled the bacon on the cooker, knowing full well how dear those slices were. Bede would serve them their share and save the fat to season the vegetables she would cook later. *What a perfect start to a chilly autumn morning.* She thought of Alice Grenville and hoped she was settling into her new life of freedom. Hoping the reporters would stay near the front of house, so she could be outside without their prying eyes, Cat looked forward to a day of physical labour. So wrapped up was she in these thoughts, she didn't notice the sly smile on Margaret's face when she walked into the kitchen.

'Good morning,' Cat said.

'Morning, Miss,' Bede said, placing a plate of bacon, eggs and toast at Cat's place at the table. She turned to Margaret. 'Are you finished then?'

Margaret, who wore a midnight-blue skirt, a crisp white blouse and a very fine jumper, leaned back in her chair. She crossed her silk stockinged legs and stared at Cat. 'Yes, thank you.'

Bede took Margaret's plate away and set in the sink. 'I've the

149

linens to deal with. I'll be upstairs if you need me.' She hung her apron on its hook and left Margaret and Cat alone in the kitchen.

'You had a guest last night,' Margaret said, her voice sultry and knowing. 'I saw him slinking out of here at the crack of dawn.'

Cat ignored Margaret as she poured out her tea, adding a generous dollop of milk and sugar.

'You're lucky you can eat like that and remain so slim,' Margaret said.

'I'm blessed with good genes,' Cat said. She sipped her tea and met Margaret's eyes. 'This is my house, Margaret. I'll thank you not to question me and meddle in my business. Do I make myself clear?'

'Forgive me, Mrs Carlisle. I've always been a little outspoken. My husband certainly never liked this unfortunate characteristic.'

'Where were you yesterday evening?' Cat gauged Margaret's response, looking for the tell-tale signs of a lie. 'There were reporters everywhere when we got home. I came to your room to check on you. You weren't there. Where did you go?'

'I met a friend, who managed to get into my house and retrieve some of my clothes.' Margaret smoothed the sleeve of her jumper. 'Thank goodness.'

'That's good news at least,' Cat said. She picked up the teapot. 'Were you able to avoid the reporters when you got back?'

Margaret had the grace to blush. 'As it turns out, I didn't return home until very late. I'm sorry. I should have left a note, or at least told you where I was going.'

'In the future you'll have to be more forthright, Margaret. I'll need to know where you are for your own safety.'

'You said we needed to speak. Are you going to allow me to stay here?'

'We'll need to ask you some questions about your circumstances, your husband, any potential danger we may be exposed to, things of that nature. I can't make that decision alone. We need to assess the risk of danger,' Cat said.

'Who is *we*, if you don't mind my asking? I don't want to put anyone in jeopardy. Perhaps I should go—' Margaret started to stand up.

'No. Wait. Let me clarify.' Once Margaret was again seated, Cat continued. 'I'm not saying I won't help you. We just need to sit down and discuss how best to proceed.'

Cat noticed a very fine calfskin handbag hanging on the back of Margaret's chair. Margaret reached into it and withdrew a silver cigarette case. 'I quit smoking five years ago when my husband threw this cigarette case at me and cut my eye rather badly. Luckily, the scar is under my eyebrow, so you can't really see it. I thought he was going to kill me. I never smoked again, but I kept the cigarette case to remind me of what he was capable of.' With a forlorn look, Margaret gazed out the window, her focus far away. She shook her head. 'The state of women is a sad one, isn't it? Society doesn't seem to trust us to do anything on our own. Seems rather ridiculous, doesn't it?'

'It makes me angry,' Cat said. 'That's why I started Saint Monica's.'

'How come I'm the only one here? Forgive me for being forward, but this house is so big, it seems there should be other people here. Surely I'm not the only woman in need of protection in Rivenby.'

'There were others, but they've moved on to start a new life. But we were discussing you. How did you come to find me?'

'Find you? What do you mean?'

'I don't exactly advertise my services, Mrs Smith. How did you come to be knocking on my back door?'

Margaret furrowed her brows and cocked her head. 'I must have heard about you from somewhere. That secretarial school, maybe? Or at the church? I went to the church for a while and spoke to the vicar.' Margaret put the cigarette case back in her purse. 'Is it important? I can't remember at the moment.'

'Probably not,' Cat said. 'What exactly do you need from me?'

'It's a bit complicated. I am waiting on an inheritance. Once I get it, I can move far enough away to set up house on my own. I simply require a safe place to stay for another week, maybe two. After I receive the money I'm due, I'm happy to pay you for my room and board.'

'I can agree to that, but there's a condition attached. I'll need to check your story to make sure it's true. If you could write down your full name and address, I can get started.'

Margaret's eyes grew big, her lips paled. 'My husband will know if you start asking questions about me.'

'Be assured your husband will be none the wiser. I'll be discreet.'

Margaret hesitated.

'You're going to have to trust me, Margaret. I'm trusting you. This has to work two ways.'

Margaret sighed. 'I really don't have much of a choice. I cannot go back to sleeping outside.'

'More tea?' Cat picked up the teapot. As she stood to refill Margaret's cup, her engagement ring came untucked, swinging across the table like a pendulum. Margaret reached out and grabbed the heavy gold band.

'Are you engaged?' She held the ring fast, surveying the fine gold with Thomas's promise of eternal love engraved on the inside.

'I am.' Cat pried the ring out of Margaret's fingers, hiding it away again under her jumper.

'Why ever would you hide such a beautiful ring? Doesn't it fit?'

Cat took the chain from around her neck. She undid the clasp and slipped the ring on her finger.

'It looks like an heirloom. Is it old?'

'It is,' Cat said. She stood and collected the dishes from the table. 'It belonged to my fiancé's mother.'

'How come you keep it tucked out of sight?' Margaret gave Cat a sheepish smile. 'No prying. I understand. I'll just get busy

152

on these dishes.' She took Bede's apron off the hook and tied it around her waist. 'Thank you, Mrs Carlisle. I am afraid I will owe you a debt of gratitude.'

***

Cat had spent the majority of her adult life in London, with access to shops, cafés, and a house full of servants to deal with stocking the larder, preparing food, and tending to the day-to-day household chores. The outbreak of war and the move to the country had opened Cat's eyes to the endless tasks needed to keep a household running smoothly. She had lived in Rivenby for over a year now and since that time had come to appreciate the way chores were aligned with the seasons. Spring was for cleaning and planting, summer for growing, autumn for harvesting and planting the next round of vegetables, while winter was a time of rest and hibernation. A perfect circle.

Leaving Margaret to do the dishes, Cat headed out into the morning chill towards the garden shed, her mind worrying over the veracity of Margaret's story. Donning her gloves, she raked the vegetable bed, mixing in the mulch they had ordered specially. By springtime, the bed would be rich and fertile and ready for the vegetables they started in the greenhouse. As she worked, she thought of her upcoming marriage. Thoughts of Thomas distracted her so thoroughly, she didn't see the man sneaking out from behind the greenhouse, a shovel slung over one shoulder. Like a perfect predator, he paused for a moment, staying just outside Cat's line of vision, until she squatted down with her back to him, vulnerable and unable to defend herself.

Cat didn't sense his presence. Out of the blue, she felt a strong hand on her back, followed by a hard push, which sent her sprawling onto her stomach into the dirt.

Adrenalin coursed through Cat's body as she landed. She turned on her back and met the eyes of a short, wiry man, with a lined face and angry eyes. He towered above her, brandishing the shovel. By the look on his face, Cat could tell he enjoyed his dominant position. Forcing herself to stay calm, she took a deep breath. 'Mr Grenville, I presume.'

'We're going to have a little talk about my wife,' Mr Grenville said. 'Get up.' He offered Cat his hand.

She ignored it and stood up on her own, grabbing the hand trowel as she did so.

The manoeuvre wasn't lost on Mr Grenville. He gave Cat a smirk and slung the shovel over his shoulder again.

'Get off my property,' Cat said. She was a good three inches taller than Mr Grenville. She bit back her fear, keeping her voice strong. 'The police are looking for you in connection with a murder. Someone inside the house will see you and call them.'

'Not true, Mrs Carlisle. You've got your housekeeper in there, but she's weak and old. I'd say that I'm safe from her. Surely you didn't think I'd approach you without evaluating the situation.' He stepped closer, once again brandishing the shovel like a weapon in an effort to intimidate. 'And I didn't kill that girl.'

Cat took a step closer to him. 'Get away from me.'

'You've got spunk, I'll give you that. You just tell me what you've done with my wife, and I'll be on my way.'

'No. My singular purpose in life is to keep women like your wife away from men like you.' Cat regretted the taunt immediately as Mr Grenville's placid, semi-amused look became one of anger. He circled Cat, like a boxer in the ring. Having no choice but to reciprocate, Cat countered his every move. They mimicked each other, like two dancers in a violent tango. Over Mr Grenville's shoulder, she saw Bede Turner's startled face in the window.

Please, Bede, get help.

Mr Grenville attempted to step closer to Cat. In perfect panto-mime, Cat stepped away. She eyed the house. Could she make a dash for safety?

'You can't outrun me, Mrs Carlisle. And I don't know what my wife told you, but we were happy together. I was good to her.'

Cat laughed. 'Hardly. She hated you. Couldn't wait to get away.' Cat should have noticed the twitch in Michael Grenville's left eye, the portent of his rage. 'She's rather a fine lady. Not surprising considering her wealth. Her wealth, Mr Grenville. Not yours. No, you won't be finding her. She's safely tucked away, safe from your influence, enjoying all her lovely money.'

'She loved me,' Michael Grenville insisted.

'You beat her,' Cat said. 'I saw the bruises.'

'Only when she needed it. A man needs to take his woman in hand. Maybe I should give you a beating right now. Teach you a lesson.' He leered at her. 'It'd serve you right and ain't nothing you can do about it.'

Cat knew women often cowered around their aggressive husbands. But she hadn't flinched when her husband – now long dead, thank the heavens – threatened. Benton had been tall and strong, and every bit as angry as Michael Grenville, but Cat had never backed down. Familiar hot rage ran through her. She stepped close to Michael Grenville and pushed him hard on the shoulders. He didn't have enough time to react. His eyes opened wide as he stumbled and landed on his backside.

'Get away from her,' Bede Turner shouted, as she strode towards them.

Michael Grenville scrambled into a standing position and held up his hands. 'You've won this round, Mrs Carlisle, but I'll be back. You can be sure of that.'

Cat moved nearer to Bede, who pointed a shotgun at Mr Grenville. 'I won't mind shooting you.' To make her point, Bede pointed the gun in the air. Cat covered her eyes just as Bede fired. Michael Grenville turned and walked in the direction of the woods.

Keeping her gun pointed at Michael Grenville's disappearing form, Bede shouted, 'Get to the house. I'll shoot him if he follows.'

Once they were in the kitchen, Bede slammed the door and locked it.

'We need to check all the doors and windows,' Bede said. 'I'll take upstairs. You do down here.' Bede propped the shotgun over her shoulder and headed upstairs, spry as a teenager. Cat hurried through the bottom floor of the house, heart pounding as she fumbled with the windows and doors, doubling checking they were properly locked. Not wanting to be alone, she followed Bede upstairs. Once both women were in Cat's bedroom, she shut the door and locked it, her breath coming in short, hard gasps.

Bede stood at the window. 'I can see him on the road.'

Cat hurried to the window. Standing next to Bede, she watched Michael Grenville hurry down the lane towards the high street.

'We should call the police,' Bede said.

'He'll be back,' Cat said. 'He told me so.'

The tears came unbidden. Cat wiped them with the back of her hand as she looked at Bede, her eyes imploring. 'I can't do this anymore. I can't protect these women and us by myself.'

Bede put a comforting arm around Cat's shoulders. 'It's all right, love. You don't have to. Mr Charles will help you. He'll keep us safe. I'll just go and call him.'

Something deep inside Cat shifted, tempering her reckless courage with a healthy measure of fear.

***

Thomas manoeuvred around a lorry overladen with bales of hay, while DCI Kent distracted himself with the scant file they had on Lucy Bardwell. The mysterious return of the chalice and the feeling that things were in play around him over which he had no knowledge or control caused Thomas concern. At the back of his mind, he wondered if Michael Grenville was orchestrating some scheme to get the chalice back. Beck, eager to see that no one took the chalice again, had taken to sleeping near the safe, his shotgun and his Webley service pistol at the ready. The next person who broke into Heart's Desire would have a surprise waiting for them. Thomas decided to trust Beck's security measures, for there was nothing else to be done about it.

Back at the constabulary, a select group of constables focused on pinning down Lucy's time of death and tracing her activities before she was murdered. A trusted few had been told that Michael Grenville may be involved in Lucy Bardwell's murder. Specifically instructing these men to search for evidence of Michael Grenville, or anyone affiliated with him, DCI Kent had managed to investigate Grenville without jeopardizing Saint Monica's. Thomas took a deep breath as he manoeuvred around another lorry, this one towing a horse box. In another mile, they would be on the main road to Much Killham, where they would interview George Hinks's wife.

'I know you think Hinks is innocent, Thomas. Let's assume you're correct for a moment. If Hinks didn't kill Lucy, who did?'

'Michael Grenville,' Thomas said. 'He's the logical suspect. The resemblance between Lucy Bardwell and his wife is remarkable.'

DCI Kent shook his head. 'I don't think Grenville would kill the wrong woman.'

'So if it's not Grenville and it's not Hinks, who? The brother?'

DCI Kent shook his head. 'Not likely. He telephoned to apologise for his behaviour towards us. Not that he needed to. I just don't see him killing anyone, not after his experiences in the war. In any event, he claims to have been participating in an injured veteran's support group at a hospital in Hendleigh. Says he was there for three days under constant supervision. I have a constable verifying his alibi.'

Thomas thought for a moment. 'Lucy Bardwell was a pretty girl. Her friends say she was a bit wild. I am interested to know who else she spent time with when she wasn't with George Hinks. She may well have had another lover. Maybe she jilted him, and he didn't like being tossed aside. I admit that I'm surprised that such an attractive young girl would be interested in the likes of George Hinks, but I've learned not to question the motives of young women.'

'Hinks may not have been totally honest with her,' DCI Kent said. 'Maybe he led her to believe he was well-to-do, had money from an inheritance or something of that nature.'

'Lucy Bardwell would like that,' Thomas said. 'She seems the type who would appreciate a man with a nice bank account.'

'Agreed.' DCI Kent unfolded a map and read it quickly. 'Take the next left. We're looking for the last cottage on the right.'

The car slowed as they drove past a row of detached cottages, most of them with sections of lawn converted to vegetable gardens. Rosebud Cottage, with its bright red door and window-sills, stood out among the others. Thomas was surprised to find George Hinks's house – a lazy man if there ever was one – was so well tended. The garden was three times as big as the others along the lane. A large pile of freshly raked leaves was nestled against the stone barrier wall. Six apple trees had been recently plucked of fruit, their leaves turning a pleasant shade of red and yellow. Furls of smoke wafted out of the chimney, completing the storybook scene. Curious now, Thomas wondered about George Hinks's wife, for he was certain this image of bucolic bliss had little to do with George Hinks, a philandering ne'er-do-well, if ever there was one.

'This should be interesting,' DCI Kent said to Thomas before he got out of the car and headed up to the front door.

Thomas followed him up a cobbled pathway. A woman with a strong jawline and vivid blue eyes opened the door before they had a chance to knock. She was dressed in country tweeds, and a gold cross hung from a chain around her neck.

She cocked her head, giving them a curious look, as though she were waiting for someone else. 'Can I help you?'

'DCI Kent. Rivenby Constabulary.' DCI Kent showed his iden-tification. 'This is Thomas Charles. May we come in?'

'Is it George? What's he done? Is he dead?' Vera Hinks's hand went to the cross.

'He's very much alive. We just need to speak with you.'

Vera stepped aside. 'Come in. I'm preserving today. Do you mind if we speak in the kitchen?'

'Of course not,' DCI Kent said.

Vera Hinks was an attractive woman. Her ruddy cheeks spoke of physical strength and time spent outdoors. Her kitchen, as Thomas expected, was immaculately turned out. Rows of gleaming jars sat ready to be filled, with piles of peeled and sliced apples ready to go into the boiling pot. The whole scenario reminded Thomas of his own childhood, and the apple butter his mother used to make every autumn. But his mother's kitchen was nothing like Vera Hinks's. Thomas remembered his childhood kitchen as one of charming clutter, unlike this orderly kitchen, with everything lined up like so many rows of soldiers. Unfortunately for Vera Hinks, Thomas and DCI Kent were about to introduce chaos into her organised life.

'Have a seat.' She pointed to an old-fashioned pine table, the scars and scratches on its top a testimony to the kitchen as heart of the household. 'Tea?'

Thomas would have killed for a cup, but DCI Kent gave his head a small, nearly undetectable shake.

'No, thank you. Mrs Hinks, would you mind sitting down.'

Vera set the kettle down and turned to face them, a worried expression in her eyes. 'What's happened?'

'Did you notice your husband didn't come home last night?' DCI Kent said.

She sat down across from Thomas. 'No. I didn't. He stays at a friend's house in Hendleigh most of the time. When he's here, we have separate rooms ...' Her voice trailed off. She removed her glasses, revealing dark crescents under intelligent eyes. Her right hand, calloused and roughened from time spent gardening, reached once again for the cross hanging around her neck. She fondled it, a worried expression on her face. 'Why are you here? What's happened?'

DCI Kent hesitated before he pulled a snapshot of Lucy Bardwell out of his jacket pocket. The picture flattered Lucy, accentuating her thick dark hair and her bright smile. He placed it on the table and pushed it towards Vera. 'Have you ever seen this girl before?'

Vera put her glasses back on and stared at the picture. Seconds ticked by. Vera rubbed the picture with one of her fingers and mumbled what sounded like a prayer.

'Have you seen this woman before?' DCI Kent repeated.

'No. Wait. Is this the girl whose picture was in the newspaper? The girl that was murdered in Rivenby?'

'I'm afraid she is.' DCI Kent took the picture and put it back in his pocket. 'Mrs Hinks, I am afraid your husband was involved with this young woman.'

Vera Hinks, who had been staring at her lap, gave DCI Kent a stricken look. 'Involved?' Her voice broke when she uttered the word. 'She was one of his – one of his – oh my god.' Vera Hinks pushed away from the table and with a choking sob, ran from the room. Neither Thomas nor DCI Kent spoke after she left. They listened to Vera's quiet sobs, which were eventually replaced by the sound of running water. After a few minutes, Vera joined them, her eyes red from crying.

'I'm sorry. George is not – has never been – a faithful husband.' She pulled the picture of Lucy Bardwell closer to her. 'But I had no idea he was involved with this girl.' DCI Kent didn't speak. Vera stared at him. 'What aren't you telling me?'

DCI Kent cleared his throat. Thomas did not envy him this task. 'She was pregnant.'

Vera Hinks's face blanched as the blood drained away. Thinking she was about to faint, Thomas leaned forward in his chair, ready to rush to her should the need arise. She turned the picture over, so it was face down on the table. 'That poor girl. You don't think George killed her, do you?'

'That's what we're trying to find out, Mrs Hinks. Was George here on the morning of October 7th?'

Vera sighed and shook her head. 'I can't say for sure. I don't think so. Like I said, when he's here, we're in separate rooms.' For the first time, Vera turned her attention to Thomas. 'My husband is a coward. He can't stand the sight of blood, can't even bear it when I clean a chicken. I don't know if that helps, but it's the truth. There's no love lost between my husband and me, but he's no killer.' Vera Hinks stood. 'And now I'd like to lie down.'

DCI Kent and Thomas both stood.

'We may need to speak to you again,' Thomas said.

'I understand.'

Vera Hinks ushered them out the front door, slamming it shut and locking it behind them. They didn't speak until they were well away from Rosebud Cottage.

'Interesting,' DCI Kent said. 'The first thing she asks is if her husband is dead.'

'Wishful thinking perhaps? She's hiding something,' Thomas said.

'Like what, Tom? She's a simple countrywoman, religious, devoted to her husband. Along we come with questions about a girl who was not only murdered, but who was involved with her husband, and who was in all likelihood carrying her husband's child. That's enough to make anyone react strangely. I'll have to talk to her again, probably at the constabulary. If she's hiding something, I'll find out what it is,' DCI Kent said.

Thomas didn't doubt it.

Chapter 17

Thomas and DCI Kent returned to the constabulary to find a group of men gathered around Sergeant Jeffers's desk, which was now covered with a large piece of butcher paper, nearly filled with handwritten notes.

'What's this?' DCI Kent asked.

'We've got our timeline pinned down, sir,' Sergeant Jeffers said. Using a pen as a pointer, he went down a list of dates and times. 'On October 6th, Lucy Bardwell was seen by a number of people at the Dance Palace in Hendleigh. She left at 11.30 a.m. by herself. Apparently she stayed in a hotel across the street. I've got a constable checking on that right now. Then she was seen on the morning of October 7th at the bus stop on the Rivenby high street. I'm assuming she took the bus from Hendleigh, but still need to verify that.'

'Dancing?' Thomas said.

'Yes, sir,' Jeffers coughed. 'Apparently she sneaks out of Saint Monica's on a regular basis. Two witnesses saw her at the bus stop, sir. She wasn't seen again until approximately 3 p.m., or thereabouts, when Emmeline Hinch-Billings saw her get out of a car in front of the school.'

'What kind of a car?' DCI Kent asked.

'Don't know, sir.'

'Go on,' DCI Kent said.

'The two lads who were playing in the woods discovered her body at four-thirty, sir. Which means she was in all likelihood walking back to Saint Monica's when she was ambushed in the woods.' Sergeant Jeffers picked up the photographs of the woods, some of them depicting Lucy's body in situ. 'It looks like someone waited for her to walk by, hit her hard enough to stun her, and then hit her a second time, which finished her. And then they turned her onto her back.'

'To make sure she was dead?' DCI Kent asked.

'Don't know, sir.'

'To hide the wound on the back of her head, maybe,' Thomas said. 'Maybe he saw the bloody mess and felt disgusted by it.' He took the timeline from Sergeant Jeffers and studied it.

'Good work, Jeffers,' DCI Kent said. 'We have an hour and a half of unaccounted time. Go back to the person who saw her in the car, find out exactly where they saw Lucy. Interview shop-keepers, anyone who may have seen her after she got out of that car.'

'Yes, sir,' Jeffers said. He hurried away, nodding at two consta-bles as he went. They jumped up and followed him.

'You do realise the implication here, sir?' Thomas said. 'Lucy wasn't murdered in the morning. This clears George Hinks. He was in the office on the afternoon of Lucy's murder. We are his alibi. We are back to the beginning.'

'I know.' DCI Kent rubbed his hand over his face. 'Go home, Thomas. Get some rest. I need to call the Superintendent and tell him we no longer have a suspect.'

Thomas grabbed his hat and was heading out the door, when a constable hurried over to them, waving a telephone message in his hand. 'Bede Turner just called. There's been an incident, sir. Michael Grenville tried to attack Mrs Carlisle at Saint Monica's. No one's been hurt, but they're a bit shaken.'

163

The sound of pounding blood thrummed in Thomas's ears as DCI Kent barked out orders. Around him, men jumped into action. Thomas burst out of the building and sprinted to the car.

DCI Kent grabbed his arm. 'Thomas, stop.'

Without thinking, Thomas pushed Kent's hand away. In a surprising show of strength, DCI Kent grabbed him once again, pulling him to a stop.

'Look at me, damn you.'

Thomas met DCI Kent's level gaze.

'If you're going to act irrationally, I'll leave you here. The constable said the women are not injured, just shaken.' He reached out for the keys. 'I'll drive. We can discuss how to proceed on the way.'

Behind them, two cars screeched out of the parking area, leaving clouds of dust in their wake. Thomas eyed the car.

'Tom, give me the keys.'

Thomas knew DCI Kent represented the voice of reason. Where Cat was concerned, he tended to take on the role of warrior knight with his sword unsheathed. Rational thought told him this behaviour wouldn't do. Not now. 'Sorry, sir.' He handed DCI Kent the keys.

By the time they reached Saint Monica's, Thomas's jaw was sore from grinding his teeth. At this rate, he'd wear them down to nubs by dinnertime. Ignoring DCI Kent's protestations, Thomas jumped out of the car and hurried in the front door. He found Cat in the kitchen, sitting with a blanket around her shoulders, with Bede Turner clucking over her like a mother hen. When she saw Thomas, relief washed over her face.

'Thank god you're here,' she said.

'Cat,' Thomas said.

She stood up and faced him, the blanket falling to the floor. Her eyes looked haunted in her pale face. 'Oh, Tom. He scared me.'

He pulled her into his arms. 'You're safe now.' Over Cat's head, Thomas looked at Bede. 'What happened?'

'I was upstairs, stripping the beds when I happened to look out the window and saw him come at her. When I saw him, I grabbed my husband's rifle – I always keep it under my bed, in case the Germans come – and ran downstairs. I was afraid for Mrs Carlisle. I wouldn't let no harm come to her. Would have shot him first. But she handled herself. Pushed him down on his bum.' Her look became serious. 'He said he'd be back.'

Cat wriggled out of Thomas's grasp. 'I believe him. He wants to find Alice. Bede, where's Margaret? I just realised she's missing. Been so preoccupied with Michael Grenville ...'

'She's gone,' Bede said. 'Nowhere in this house. I searched after I called the police. Her handbag is gone, so is her coat and her holdall. I think she was planning on leaving anyway.'

'Margaret?' DCI Kent asked.

'A new boarder. Allegedly she fled a rather abusive situation. I'm betting she ran when the police showed up,' Cat said.

Bede snorted. 'Good riddance.'

'Should we try to find her?' DCI Kent asked.

'I'm not worried about her. I have a feeling Margaret Smith is capable of taking care of herself,' Cat said.

'Very well. We need to decide what to do here,' DCI Kent said. 'I don't like the idea of you two here by yourselves. I'll have constables outside, but I'd feel much better—'

'I'm taking Cat to my house,' Thomas said. 'You too, Bede. I've got plenty of room. You're both welcome.'

'Wait,' Cat said. 'I have an idea.' She walked to the window and stood with her back to them, overlooking the sloping lawn behind Saint Monica's, and the pastures beyond, now filled with bales of hay that would sustain the livestock over the winter. 'I think I know how we can catch Michael Grenville.'

Bede coughed. 'I'd rather go to my sister's. I could do with a break, if you don't mind me saying so.'

'Very well. And I'll go to Thomas's.' She turned her eyes to DCI Kent. 'What do you think about not having a constable outside the house. Let's make it look as though Saint Monica's is empty, as though we fled out of fear. But it won't be. You can have men inside. Keep the curtains closed and the lights out. When Michael Grenville comes back to search for information about his wife – I'm betting he'll go straight to my office to see if I keep records – you can nab him.'

DCI Kent leaned against the kitchen worktop, his eyes closed. Thomas knew he was dissecting Cat's plan, looking for flaws, playing out the worst-case scenario.

'It makes sense, sir,' Thomas said. 'If there's going to be a confrontation with Michael Grenville and his men, best have it here, away from the village.'

'Agreed. In fact, knowing Grenville the way I do, I wouldn't be surprised if he had men watching the house now.' DCI Kent turned to Cat and Bede. 'Why don't you ladies pack what you need to take with you.'

Once Cat and Bede were upstairs, DCI Kent explained the plan to the three constables who had followed them into the house. Half an hour later, the half-dozen constables who were charged with searching the premises, along with DCI Kent, Thomas, Bede Turner, and Cat, made a very deliberate show of leaving Saint Monica's. Although the house now looked empty, the three constables remained. As they pulled out of the drive, Thomas turned and stared out the back window of the car, searching the woods and surrounding premises for any signs of Michael Grenville or his men.

***

Although she claimed to be fine, Thomas couldn't help but notice the way Cat's hand shook as she took a sip of water. When the missus accidentally slammed a door in the kitchen, Cat yelped and looked at Thomas with frightened eyes. It didn't take much to cajole her into a hot bath, scented with the bath salts he knew

166

she preferred. He left her alone, while Beck patrolled the house with his gun and the missus fussed in the kitchen, preparing a meal guaranteed to 'put some meat on that woman's bones.' DCI Kent had personally agreed to drive Bede Turner directly to her sister's. Since Thomas hadn't heard anything to the contrary, he assumed all went well and Bede was safely tucked away at her sister's farm. There was no reason for Michael Grenville to go after Bede. Motivated by a desire to find the wife who had taken her money and abandoned him, any attempts at retribution, Thomas felt certain, would be directed at Cat.

'Sir, why don't you go out for a walk. The cold air and sunshine will do you a world of good. I'll see to Mrs Carlisle. Not that she isn't capable of taking care of herself,' Beck said.

Thomas didn't have to be asked twice. He dashed up the stairs to tell Cat he was going out. The missus had put Cat in the room next to his. He found her lying on the bed, wrapped in his dressing gown, snoring gently. After covering her with the heavy counterpane, he kissed her forehead and whispered, 'Back soon, my love.'

Thomas filled his lungs with the country air and immediately felt better. The leaves crunched under his feet as he took the familiar walking path towards the woods. He walked with a sure stride up the footpath, stopping to enjoy the sweeping view of the pastures where the sheep grazed in the summer. His mind wandered, as it often did when he was alone, to his upcoming marriage and how country life agreed with him, when something hit the back of his knees, sweeping his feet out from under him. Landing flat on his back, the sudden fall knocked the wind out of him. As he struggled for breath, he saw Stephen Templeton's fraudulent driver standing over him.

The imposter guard who had arrived with the chalice, hovered over Thomas, looking down on him. Today he wore a soldier's uniform and carried a cane, playing the injured hero.

'Sorry for the ambush,' the man said. 'I need to talk to you.

No disrespect intended, sir, but I'm younger and faster, so don't think of trying anything.'

After a few seconds, Thomas found he could breathe again. Alex held out his hand. 'Here. Let me help you up. I'm not here to harm you. In fact, I'm here to give you a warning.'

Thomas took the man's hand, resisting the urge to overpower the little git and teach him a lesson.

'You stole the chalice,' Thomas said, brushing debris from the seat of his trousers. 'Why did you return it?'

Alex shook his head. 'I didn't.'

'I don't believe you. Why are you here? What do you want? Tell me quickly before I grab you and give you a beating.'

If the man was afraid of Thomas, he didn't let on. 'You're not a stupid man, Mr Charles. Surely you've sensed there are things in play, about the chalice and about you.'

Something in this man's demeanour gave Thomas pause. 'About me?'

'Your sister. Margaret.'

'Margaret?' The word came out as an incredulous question. Margaret. Blood thrummed in his ears, as images of the sister he had adored and loathed in equal measure ran through his mind. He had spent years of his adult life searching for Margaret after his parents died. They had sent her to an asylum which had burned to the ground, along with all of its patient records. Over the years, he had hired numerous private investigators to take over the search. In 1924 one of them had traced his sister to a winery in the south of France. By the time Thomas had arrived at the small village she called home, Margaret had vanished, along with a very fine painting, which she stole from her lover. After years of fruitless efforts, Thomas had given up the search for his sister.

'Is she all right? Can you take me to her?'

'I don't recommend that,' Alex said.

'That's not for you to decide. She's my sister—'

168

'Whom you haven't seen in decades. Do you know anything about her? I didn't think so. She's not healthy.'

'Is she in hospital?'

Alex held up his hand. 'Please. Let me explain. I met your sister at a dinner party in Scotland. She wasn't terribly forth-coming about her situation. She seduced me, inveigled herself into my life. I've since discovered she blackmailed someone into financial ruin. The man ended up killing himself. I'm sorry about the chalice. Margaret should not have been involved in that. My problem, and I'm dealing with it. But she's after you. Says she's got an inheritance coming.'

'If you'll tell me where she is ...' Enervated now, feeling the burden of his years, especially when compared to this younger and stronger man, Thomas pushed away the overwhelming sense of loss and shame. Would he have been able to change Margaret's life if he had found her sooner?

'Mr Charles, you don't know me. God knows, you've no reason to trust me. But your sister means you harm. She is unstable. I personally believe she would benefit from commitment to a psychiatric hospital. Medical intervention would help her. Although she claims she wants money from you, I believe that's not true. I found a bag with a knife, a rope and belladonna tablets. She's going to come for you. You'll offer her a drink of some sort, and she'll slip you something. Do not think for one minute she won't hurt you. She will.'

'She sounds irrational.'

'She is. And her behaviour is escalating.'

'Why are you telling me this?'

'Michael Grenville hired me to steal the chalice from you. Actually, he blackmailed me, forced me to steal from you against my will. I don't like being controlled. These circumstances made me sloppy. In any event, I lost the chalice. My sense is that Mr Grenville's loyalty lies with money. My belief is that he is in bed with the Germans. This is an intuition, mind you. I could be wrong. I don't know who stole the chalice and I have no idea why it was returned to you. But you need to know that Michael Grenville wants it. You also need to know your sister means you harm.'

'I'll ask again. Why are you telling me this?' Thomas asked.

'Honour among thieves? I've a passion for justice and felt it only fair you should know. Michael Grenville is focused on his wife right now, but he may or may not turn his attention to the chalice and to you. But your sister will come for you. And she'll claim her visit is about money. Do not be swayed by her. She needs to be committed. She needs medical help.'

'I can't do that without seeing Margaret for myself. What if she just needs a good rest?'

Alex shook his head. 'I am going to get Margaret the medical care she needs, with or without you.'

'You can't have my sister committed,' Thomas said, more confident now. 'You're not related to her. You're not married to her. Frankly, you've no authority in this matter.'

'I have my ways, Mr Charles.' He held out his hand. 'I'll see your sister gets the care she needs. I've said my piece. Good day, Mr Charles. Apologies for ambushing you. I realise it wasn't the behaviour of a gentleman.'

'Wait,' Thomas called after him.

The man stopped walking. He paused for a moment before he turned to face Thomas.

'Where does my sister live?'

'She finagled herself into some women's boarding house. Saint Monica's, I think it's called.' With that, the man turned to walk away.

***

Timmer Ashcourt was born and raised in the slums of Bermondsey. His father earned his living shovelling coal, while his mother took

170

in laundry. Both of Timmer's parents worked themselves to the bone, but despite their efforts, there was never enough. Of anything. Timmer grew up hungry, dressed in rags and angry at the conditions his family and neighbours were forced to live in. He learned at an early age the only way out of poverty was through criminal enterprise, so after his mother died of influenza and his father drank himself to death, Timmer took to thieving. Like all tasks born of desperation, he was good at it. With his clever mind and a cadre of like-minded young men, he soon developed a sophisticated method for successfully passing on the things he stole. Soon Timmer discovered he had a knack for forgery. His passports and identification papers garnered him even more respect among the criminal elite. As time went on, Timmer learned to keep his identity and whereabouts secret to all but just a few choice friends. Alex was one of those friends. Now, he waited for Alex in a café in Hendleigh, dressed in a Savile Row suit, harmlessly flirting with the buxom waitress who brought tea.

'Are you meeting your wife?' The waitress set the teapot on the table and set about arranging the cups and cakes.

Timmer wondered when women had become so forward. He liked a woman with the reserved sophistication that came with good breeding. His smile didn't quite reach his eyes. 'No, ma'am. Just an old friend. And here he is.' The girl hurried away as Alex came limping into the café, dressed in a soldier's uniform. He poured the tea as Alex sat down.

'Thank you for service to queen and country.' He smiled as he handed Alex a cup of tea. 'I'll let you add your own milk and sugar.' Timmer surveyed Alex, taking in the gaunt cheeks and the loose clothing. Despite his friend's obvious hunger, his smooth veneer remained intact.

'Did you do as I asked?' Alex loaded his plate with two slices of cake and a sandwich.

'Of course. You're hot right now, Alex. You need to be careful.

171

Grenville has a price on your head. He's got men looking for you.'
He ran his eyes over his old friend, impressed with his disguise.

'I no longer have the stomach for this work. I'm getting out,'
Alex said. He set his fork down and leaned back in his chair.
Timmer noticed the exhaustion in his friend's eyes.

'I don't think people like us get to walk away from this life,
friend,' Timmer said. 'Grenville will never stop searching for you.
It's a matter of pride for him. Your walking away will undermine
his authority.'

'You let me worry about Grenville,' Alex said. 'What about the
safe house?'

'Arranged. Of course, you can't go there right away.' Timmer
removed an envelope from his pocket and slid it across the table
to Alex. 'You'll stay two to three nights at each of the addresses
listed in there. Once you memorise the list, burn it. Each house
will take you closer to London. Once it's determined you're not
being followed, you'll be moved to the next safe house. I've
arranged someone to come and bring you food every other day.
You'll have to take care of domestic duties yourself. If you are
careful, you'll be out of Grenville's reach. The bombs are another
thing.'

'I'll take my chances against Hitler's bombs, as long as Michael
Grenville can't find me.'

'I'm sorry you fell in with him, mate,' Timmer said.

Alex shrugged. 'Maybe it's a blessing. If I survive, I'll be able
to live a quiet, law-abiding life.' Alex opened the envelope and
fanned through the notes. After removing the list of addresses,
he tucked the envelope away in his pocket before he turned his
attention to the addresses of the safe houses. Once those were
memorised, he tore the page up into tiny pieces. 'What of Lady
Trevelyan's diamonds?'

'Everything broken up and sold, except this brooch.' Timmer
handed Alex a small velvet box. Alex swept it away and put it in
the pocket of his coat. 'And the sisters have been relocated to a

very fine boarding school in Scotland.' Timmer laughed. 'You should have seen Lady Trevelyan's face when she discovered the girls had inherited money. Demanded to be made their guardian.'

'And the other matter?'

Timmer raised his eyebrow. 'I've never seen you so concerned for a woman before, Alex. Have you fallen in love?'

'I just need to see her sorted. Her family will step in when they realise her situation.'

'Whatever you say. Sir Kettering almost didn't speak to me. His clerk reiterated how careful he is about which clients he takes. Of course, they capitulated when I named your price. Are you sure you want to do this?'

'Honestly, I don't *want* to deal with this woman, but I feel obligated. She needs help before she hurts herself or someone else.'

'Your charitable deeds will be your undoing, mate,' Timmer said.

Alex chuckled. 'Thank you, Timmer. You've been a good friend to me. I won't forget you.'

'Just do me a favour and stay alive, will you? I won't see you for a while. You realise you can't contact me?'

Alex nodded. He finished the last of his tea and reached for his wallet.

'This one's on me. Now get out of here.'

Timmer watched as his old friend put on his hat and hobbled out of his life.

173

Chapter 18

Thomas sprinted back to the house, his thoughts on his sister and her violent past. His anguish was fuelled by the idea of Margaret at Saint Monica's and the danger she could have posed to Cat. By the time he reached the converted stable, his lungs were burning. He jumped into his beloved Hornet Coupe and went flying down the drive, gravel spraying behind him. The old girl sputtered a bit. Not her fault. Thomas hadn't been driving much since he moved to Rivenby. He eased off the accelerator and gave her a chance to collect herself before he barrelled down the lane, past the high street, and onto the dirt road towards Saint Monica's. Hands gripping the steering wheel, he skidded to a stop in front of the house. The front door was locked. He pounded on it. Weren't there constables there? Why the devil didn't they answer the door? He continued banging away until a voice came to him through the thick slab of wood.

'Go around the back, sir. Get the key from underneath the flower pot. We need to assume we're being watched. And you know the house is to look empty.' Thomas didn't miss the irritation in the young man's voice. Feeling like an idiot for jeopardising the scheme to catch Michael Grenville, Thomas pretended to jiggle the handle for the benefit of anyone watching before he hurried around to the back of the house, found the key, and let himself in. Two constables were drinking tea at the kitchen table. The man who had spoken to Thomas through the front door stepped into the kitchen wearing an exasperated look. 'Does DCI Kent know you're here, sir?'

'Not now, lad. Carry on. I'll be out of your way in a moment.' Thomas took the stairs two at a time. He opened the doors to the bedrooms, searching for the one most recently occupied. He recognised his sister's perfume immediately, a strange combination of orange and vanilla she used to steal from their mother. This scent from his childhood invoked memories of a family long forgotten, emotions so rich and full, Thomas nearly fell to his knees.

Margaret, five years his senior, had been advanced for her age. Her friends – what few she had, given the rural village in which they lived – were often much older than she. The few times Thomas had tried to tag along on their shenanigans, he had been sent home. He understood siblings didn't often like each other. He knew from an early age that his birth had forced Margaret to give up her position as the singular apple of their parents' eyes. He had wanted to love his sister. In fact, he remembered trying over and over to prove he was worthy of her time and affection, but she always pushed him away. As Thomas grew older, Margaret became cruel, destroying Thomas's toys and blaming him for her troublesome acts. Thomas didn't dare tell on his sister. He feared her wrath more than he feared his mother's switch.

Always a pretty child, Margaret's tall lanky body developed curves during the summer of her fifteenth birthday. Suddenly the boys Margaret and Thomas played with changed towards his sister. They backed away from friendship, they pulled closer and tried to steal kisses. One by one, Margaret rebuffed them. One boy, whose name he couldn't remember, had tried to pin Margaret's arms so another boy could kiss her. The boy who had tried to kiss her got sent home with a black eye. After that,

Margaret turned her attention to the boy who had held her arms and tried to subdue her. She beat him with a rock, leaving him so damaged the boy's parents had demanded Margaret be held accountable for her actions. Despite his youth, Thomas knew the situation with his sister was not going to end well.

Shortly after that incident, Thomas was awakened one night by voices coming from the kitchen. Getting out of bed, he crept by Margaret's room. She lay on her side with her back to the door, but Thomas was certain she was awake. Careful not to step on floorboards that he knew creaked, Thomas hid in the shadows, eavesdropping on his mother and father as they sat before the fire. His mother's despair broke his heart, for he was helpless to do anything except stand quietly by while his father did his best to comfort her.

'We'll have to send her away,' his mother had said. 'I don't know what else to do.'

'She needs treatment, love. Something's not right with her.' Thomas's father, usually so stern and commanding, held his wife while she sobbed. He recalled the tracks of tears on his mother's cheeks as clearly as if it were yesterday. They never noticed the little boy on the stairs, a silent witness to their anguish. After what seemed an eternity, Thomas had crept up to bed, but he hadn't been able to fall asleep. The next morning, two men had come for Margaret. She had refused to go, and had kicked and screamed and had even bitten one of the men so hard she drew blood. Finally one of them subdued her, while the other gave her an injection of something that caused her to slip into lethargy. Thomas's last view of his sister was as she was being carried out of the family home, in the arms of an orderly, while his broken-hearted mother sobbed uncontrollably.

The time after Margaret left blurred in Thomas's mind. Without Margaret's disquieting presence, family life slipped back to normal. Every now and again, he would catch his mother eyeing Margaret's place at the family table. His parents spoke of their daughter in hushed whispers after they thought Thomas was in bed. Although he had vague memories of his mother crying over his sister's picture, he didn't remember much else. Memories of Margaret grew dimmer with the passage of time. Thomas had gone to university and had nearly been killed in the war. After his parents passed away, he had sold the family land, tucking Margaret's share away in the bank, where it had earned interest all these years. As an adult, he had tried to find her. Obligated by an outdated sense of family, Thomas had hoped he and Margaret could mend their fences, perhaps be friends. She was his only living relative, and at times he wished for a connection to his childhood and his roots. His attempts had been in vain, however. Now she was back. And – if this Alex was to be believed – she was dangerous.

He moved over to the wardrobe and ran his fingers over the battered coat Margaret must have left behind. What game was she playing? How did she find her way into Cat's house? More importantly, just how psychologically damaged was she? As he turned his attention to her dresser and did a quick search with no results, Thomas acknowledged he was trying to cope with a situation that he didn't understand. He surveyed the room one last time. With a sigh, he closed the door behind him and headed home to Cat.

***

By the time Thomas tucked the coupe away, he had worked himself into a state of worry. Would he even recognise Margaret if he saw her? These thoughts whirled through his head, as he stepped into his house, where Beck hurried to meet him. After Thomas handed over his coat and hat, Beck said, 'Mrs Carlisle is in your room, sir. She asked for dinner on a tray for the both of you, if that suits?'

Thomas exhaled, soothed by the idea of dinner with Cat before a warm fire. In his bedroom, no less. His hand went to the Webley he wore holstered under his jacket. There would be no sleep for him. Not until Margaret and Michael Grenville were dealt with. Keeping Cat safe was his priority. His stomach rumbled. 'Thank you, Beck.' He hurried up the stairs to the woman who had his heart.

He found Cat in his bedroom, still wearing his dressing gown, her red hair glimmering like burnished copper in the firelight, as she arranged the plates on the small table.

'Tom!' She gave him a bright-eyed smile as she walked over to him. The dark half-moons under her eyes had diminished. To his relief, the look of fear had faded as well. 'I must have been exhausted. Look how long I slept.' Taking his hand, she led him to the table. 'You'll be pleased to know I've come to a decision about Saint Monica's.' Cat sat down across from Thomas and tucked her legs underneath her. 'You were right. I should never have taken on a project of that magnitude by myself. It was a dangerous undertaking. After my encounter with Mr Grenville, I've learned my lesson.'

'Thank god,' Thomas said.

'I realise the worry I've put you through, darling. And I'm sorry for it. Apparently I'm one of those women who learns by failure.'

'You didn't fail. You've accomplished what you set out to do, helped those women by providing training for jobs and a fresh start,' Thomas said. He ladled vegetable soup from the tureen into the bowls.

'Thank you for not saying I told you so.' Cat untucked her legs, pulled her chair up to the table, and tasted the soup. 'I thought to close up the house and be finished with it. But I have a better idea.'

Oh, no. Here it comes. Thomas forced a smile.

'Surely you can understand how difficult it is for me to walk away from people who need help.' She paused, watching him, as if gauging his response. 'What about hiring a board of directors to manage Saint Monica's, along with a proper security detail to ensure all those who are involved stay safe? I can provide the financing, thereby using Benton's money in a beneficial way. But I will step away from the day-to-day running, maybe limit my involvement to a behind the scenes, titular level. What do you think?' She watched him, waiting for his response.

Thomas resisted the urge to leap out of his chair and jump for joy. 'I think that's a brilliant idea.' He understood Cat's need to help the wretched women who had been beaten down by domineering families, be it husband, father, brother, or even – as on one occasion – an overbearing mother. He imagined during the course of their life together, Cat would stumble across other people who needed help, and it would be incumbent upon him to let her navigate her way through these scenarios as well. Cat wouldn't have her wings clipped. Any attempt to do so would likely result in disaster, or – even worse – chip away at the love they held for each other. Thomas closed his eyes and exhaled. He had to tell Cat about his sister. There was no getting around it.

'What's wrong?' She put her spoon down and looked at him with that all-knowing penetrating gaze.

'I – something's happened.'

'What is it? Tell me.' The panic in her voice broke his heart. 'It's not Michael Grenville, is it? Surely DCI Kent will have—'

'No,' he said. 'I need to talk to you.'

'Oh, god. You're not going to tell me you have a long-lost wife, are you?'

Thomas chuckled in spite of himself. 'No. But I do have a sister. The woman that was living in your house.'

'What? Margaret?' Cat looked at Thomas, her brow furrowed as it always did when she was deep in thought. 'You know, now that you mention it, she looks like you. I wondered how she found me.' Cat dabbed her mouth with her napkin. 'I knew she wasn't being honest. Why didn't she tell me who she was?'

179

Thomas launched into his story, starting with his encounter with the mysterious Alex and backtracking to the day Margaret was taken from their childhood home, against her will. He replayed those events of long ago in his mind one more time, filling in details he missed earlier. He told Cat about the fear that his sister, so reckless and wild as a young girl, had become damaged and dangerous in her adulthood.

Cat didn't speak until he finished. 'She's rather beautiful. And just so you don't think I am foolishly gullible, Bede Turner and I were suspicious of her from the beginning. That's why we wanted you to help us vet her.'

'I've not seen her in over thirty-five years. You've spent time with her. Do you think she's dangerous?'

Cat studied him for a moment before she gave the slightest nod. 'Maybe. If she was pushed. The man in the woods – this Alex – said she'll act like she wants money? If she comes here, can't you just give her what she wants and send her on her way? Now that we know she's coming, we can be ready for her.'

'That seems a logical way to proceed. In my experience, logical plans often fail when dealing with someone who is not quite sane.' Thomas finished his soup and pushed the bowl away. 'There's something fishy about this whole situation, and I don't know what it is. When we were little a boy held my sister down while another boy tried to kiss her. She beat the boy who held her down with a rock. His parents were furious. My parents sent my sister to an asylum. I've hired investigators to find her, but they couldn't. There's much I do not know about her.'

'Understood. So what will we do? Can we inform the police?'

'And tell them what? I have a sister I haven't seen in thirty-five years, and the man who broke into my house and stole a valuable relic ambushed me on the moors to warn me she's dangerous?'

'You don't think she had anything to do with Lucy Bardwell's murder, do you?'

Thomas thought of that battered child from so long ago. 'I don't know.'

'So we wait for her to show up demanding money. We'll tell the missus and Beck.' Cat served them each a spoonful of potato souffle and green beans. 'At least she won't have the element of surprise.'

Thomas agreed. There was really nothing else to do but wait. After dinner, they passed the evening reading before the fire. While Cat prepared for bed, Thomas checked his service revolver and placed it in the drawer of his nightstand, within easy reach. Later, when they lay together, entwined in each other's arms, Thomas bit back a frisson of fear and enjoyed what to him felt like the quiet before the storm.

***

Frustrated that he hadn't found any actionable evidence against Margaret, Hugh decided to get satisfaction from knowing that he had returned the chalice to its rightful owner. After penning an inquiry to his solicitor in Scotland about divorce proceedings, he decided to go to the cottage where Margaret lived and search for her ill-gotten gains. If he found the money she blackmailed from Martin, he would take it to the police, explain how Margaret had come to have it, and instruct them to return it to Hermione. And then he would step away and figure out what sort of life he could have with Vera.

Hugh stepped off the bus, glad for his warm coat. There were no more buses this evening, but Hugh didn't care. He'd dressed for the weather and would sleep rough if he had to. With fresh resolve, he walked around the village green on the lookout for Margaret and her lover. It wouldn't do for them to catch him out before he had a chance to actually find the money. But once he did, and once it was safely stowed away in his pocket, he would welcome a long overdue confrontation. It was time Margaret realised she hadn't gotten the best of Hugh Bettencourt. Win or lose, Hugh needed this fight.

When he reached the row of redbrick cottages, he sat on one of the benches and pretended to read the paper in the dimming daylight. Before darkness fell, Hugh hurried around to the back of the cottages, careful to walk like he knew where he was going, just in case anyone saw him loitering and became suspicious. As luck would have it, there was a tall wooden fence between the back of Margaret's cottage and her next-door neighbour's, which provided him a bit of privacy from inquisitive neighbours. Hugh stood on his toes and peered in the windows at the tiny kitchenette and open living area. A rumpled bed sat in the middle of the bedroom. Surprised at the dingy conditions, Hugh circled the cottage once, just to make sure no one was home. The back door was a glass-panelled affair. It didn't take long for Hugh to find a rock and use it to break the panel of glass nearest the doorknob. Within seconds he let himself in.

There's no going back now. For the briefest moment, Hugh thought about turning around and heading back to Much Killham, but thoughts of Vera and their lost chance of happiness sparked a flare of anger. He used that spark to fuel his courage, easily blaming Margaret for his lifetime of misery. Walking through the living room, Hugh took in the chairs and the small writing desk. He rifled through it quickly. Nothing. The heels of his boots clicked on the wooden floor as he walked to the bedroom. Heart pounding, he began to search, noticing right away there was no evidence of Margaret's lover, no shaving kit, no men's slippers. Interesting that Margaret had driven him away so quickly.

Margaret had always been lazy about picking up her things. Her cruel nature made it difficult for her to keep a maid, and after a number of years, Margaret had given up and learned to live with her own squalor. Hugh surveyed the familiar disarray of the room, clothing everywhere, cosmetics strewn across the dressing table, piles of clothes stacked on the only chair, the chaos a metaphor for their relationship. Opening the door to the wardrobe, Hugh went through it inch by inch. He searched each individual shoe, looked in all the hat boxes, and checked the pockets of the clothes that remained on hangers. Nothing. After rummaging through the clothes scattered about the room and stacked on the chair, he still hadn't found Martin's money. Surely Margaret hadn't spent it already? Put it in a bank? No. Margaret wouldn't do that. Not only did she not like banks, she liked the actual feel and smell of the bank notes. Slowly turning around, his eyes settled on the top of the wardrobe. Standing on the vanity stool, he ran his hand over the dusty top, giving a quiet cry of glee when he felt a thick envelope.

Stepping down, he opened it, surprised once again at how much money there was. Feeling smug at his success, Hugh pushed the wad of notes deep in his pocket but stopped in his tracks when the front door opened and then slammed shut.

Panicked, he hurried to the window only to discover that it was painted shut.

'Damn,' he said.

'What the hell are you doing here?' Margaret stood in the doorway, hands on her hips, red-cheeked with fury.

'I've come to tell you I've got the chalice,' Hugh said.

When her eyes widened in surprise, Hugh felt a moment of triumph.

She thrust out her hip and gave him that sultry smile that up until now never failed to arouse him. 'Clever you. How did you do it?'

'I've been following you. I watched in the woods while you and your lover broke into that man's house. After you buried what you stole – stupid idea by the way – I simply dug it up. I'm finished, Margaret. Finished with you, with your schemes. I'm taking the chalice to the police, so they can return it to the rightful owner. After they prosecute you, of course.'

Margaret jeered at him. 'It will be your word against mine.'

'And who do you think they'll believe? My family has standing and respect. You—'

'Oh, stop. I am so tired of your family. Face it, Hugh. You can't prove anything.'

'Maybe not. But I can certainly return the money you black-mailed from Martin, along with the letter from him that you were stupid enough to leave behind.'

At the mention of the money, Margaret's eyes darted from the top of the wardrobe, to the vanity stool.

'You're bluffing,' she said.

'No. I'm not.' Hugh moved to the door. 'Goodbye, Margaret.'

The hairs on the back of Hugh's neck stood up when Margaret screamed, a primordial wail that breached the stillness of the cottage and – in all likelihood – the entire village. Certain one of the neighbours would now fetch the police, Hugh became anxious. Time to get out of here. Before he had a chance to rush out, Margaret pounced, biting, kicking and clawing at him. He felt the sting of her fingernails along the side of his cheek, followed by the wet damp of his blood as it dripped down his face. With tight fists, she tried to box his ears, but Hugh was tall and she couldn't quite reach. She kicked his shins. He covered his groin and stepped sideways just in time. When the toe of her shoe connected with the long muscle in his thigh he cried out in pain. There was nothing to be done but wait. Although this was the most violent tantrum Hugh had ever seen, it was not the first. Finally – as had happened so many times before – Margaret stopped, her temper spent. She stood before Hugh, teeth bared, breathing heavily. Dark mascara ran in tracks down her pale cheeks. Her hair had come loose from its pins giving her the crazed look of a madwoman.

'Don't. Look. At. Me.'

Hugh took an involuntary step back. During the course of their marriage, Hugh had seen his wife angry, defiant and reck-less. But this woman, this version of Margaret, was something altogether new. For the first time in his life, Hugh was frightened of his wife.

'You bastard,' she hissed.

Hugh ran for the door. Margaret launched herself at him once more. This time she jumped on his back, wrapping her legs around his waist and her arms around his neck in a choke hold. He felt a jolt of pain as her teeth bit into his earlobe. When he backed into the wall, throwing all his weight into it, Margaret yelped and loosened her hold enough for him to push her onto the bed. She lay there on her back, her eyes full of fury. Hugh felt the blood gush from his torn earlobe.

'Martin Shoreham was a fool. He's been trying to get me to be his lover for years. You and Hermione were too stupid to realise it,' she called after him.

'We're finished.' As he turned to walk out of the room, he picked up a white silk blouse from the pile of clothes on the chair and used it to staunch the blood from his dripping earlobe. When he stepped out into the cold autumn air, he took a deep, cleansing breath and realised he no longer cared about his wife, nor about the social constraints forced upon him by his family. His future was in Much Killham, in the humble cottage next door to Vera Hinks. For the first time in his life, Hugh Bettencourt was free.

***

Hugh hurried home from the bus stop in the dark, his hands and feet getting colder by the minute. His ear throbbed where Margaret had bitten it. The passengers on the bus had given him strange looks as he stumbled to his seat, one hand holding the silk blouse to his still bleeding ear, the other resting on the envelope of cash in his coat pocket. By the time he disembarked, the blouse was soaked through. Who knew ears could bleed so much? He tossed the blouse in the first rubbish bin he came across and trudged home, not caring that his only coat was becoming sodden with the blood that still dripped from his ear. He hurried past his own house, choosing instead to go right to Vera. Her cottage was dark, with the exception of one light in the kitchen. Passing the front door, he went around to the side. Knocking twice to announce himself before he opened the door and stepped into the warmth and good smells of Vera's kitchen.

Vera sat at the kitchen table, a dismantled handgun in front of her, tears running down her face. Without thinking, he hurried over to her.

'What's wrong? Why've you got a gun?'

She wiped her tears. 'Don't mind me. There's a fox around the hen house. I've had a rotten day.' She looked up at him, her eyes immediately travelling to his bloody ear and stained coat. 'What have you done to your ear? Sit down before you bleed all over the place. Here, take my chair. I'll get supplies.' Cabinet doors opened and closed. Soon she returned with a first-aid kit full of bandages and potions. The unguent she dabbed on his ear stung, but Hugh bit back his cry, enjoying the closeness of her. 'This may require stitches. If I can't stop the bleeding, we'll have to fetch the doctor.'

'I've got the money to return to Hermione.'

'And it looks like you and Margaret had it out. Did she bite you?'

'She went mad. I've never seen anything like it in my life.' Hugh shook his head. 'I think she needs a doctor.' He put his hand over Vera's and turned to face her. 'I hate to admit it, but she scared me. She would have killed me if she could.' He shivered. Vera squeezed his shoulder and kept tending to his ear. When she finished, she poured them both a generous dollop of brandy and sat down across from him.

'Tell me about your awful day. Why've you been crying?'

Vera nodded before she bowed her head. Her hair fell forward revealing the vulnerable skin and the knobby vertebrae at the back of her neck. A stillness overtook her. A knot of fear formed in

Hugh's stomach. He placed a gentle hand on her arm. 'Vera, please. Tell me. Let me help you.' His eyes ran over the gun, the cloth she used to clean it, finally coming to rest on the box of bullets.

'The police were here. My husband was involved with that poor girl who was murdered in Rivenby, the one who was in the newspapers. He was a suspect in her murder and the murder of her unborn child.'

'*Was* a suspect?'

Vera nodded. 'Apparently they've found evidence that exonerates him. They've been holding him in jail. Now he's being released. I'm to fetch him tomorrow morning.'

'Surely you're not going to let him come here.' Hugh heard the indignation in his voice and regretted it. He had no rights here, no business telling Vera what she could or couldn't do.

'I've no choice,' Vera said. 'And I know better than to make any major decision while I'm so upset. I'm to pick him up tomorrow morning.'

'We're in a mess, aren't we?' He whispered into her ear, taking in the earthy scent of her, so different from his wife who always reeked of money and deceit. They stayed like that, sitting in those uncomfortable chairs, leaning on each other for comfort and support. 'I've decided to stay here in Much Killham. I know we can never be more than friends, Vera. I don't care. I just want to be near you. Being friends doesn't bother me. Neither does being poor. We could give George my cottage and I could move in here,' Hugh said.

Vera pushed away and met his eyes. As the absurdity of Hugh's suggestion sunk in, Vera smiled. Suddenly she burst into laughter, uncontrollable and tinged with a hint of hysteria. Soon Hugh was laughing with her, rollicking laughter that caused tears of mirth to stream down his cheeks. The moment passed. They sat quiet in Vera's kitchen, the gun on the table before them, cleansed by their hysteria. Just as Hugh resolved to be content with Vera's friendship, she took his hand and led him to her bed.

Chapter 19

Using his brand-new Carl Zeiss binoculars, Alex watched the back of the cottage he shared with Margaret from his secluded hiding place in the woods. As he sat in the cover of darkness, he thought that he would pay a princely sum for an orange. He wondered when the war would end and thought about the ways men killed each other to resolve their differences and how stupid it all was. Alex knew he was risking his life running away from Michael Grenville, especially after failing to provide the stolen chalice. But Alex accepted the risks of walking away. If he could hide from his nemesis, if he could escape the bombs of London, a life of sweet freedom awaited him.

He zoomed in on the scene in the cottage, not surprised to discover Margaret Bettencourt waging a full-scale internal war of her own. Alex had watched her fight with her husband, had seen the poor man leave the house, blood gushing from his earlobe where Margaret had bitten him. The blood had seeped through the white fabric of Margaret's blouse, forming deep red peonies in the pristine silk. Now, as Margaret spun through the cottage like a tornado, throwing lamps, figurines and anything else she could get her hands on, he felt validated in his decision to turn her into the authorities. Margaret needed help. Alex had taken subtle steps to ensure she would get it.

Through his binoculars he could see her lips move as clearly as if he were in the room with her. He pitied Margaret, but hadn't known what to do as he watched her grow more and more unstable and erratic by the day. Certain she now posed a danger to herself and all those in her destructive path, Alex had formulated a plan.

Alex – much like Timmer – lived by a very rigid code of ethics. The code provided rules and boundaries in a business that functioned on lawlessness. In his line of work, straying from this code could mean capture by the police or death. Never had he thrown anyone to the wolves. Never had he attempted to manipulate or control another human being's life. Alex had an aunt who had similar behaviour patterns to Margaret. She was exciting and fun. But as Alex grew older, he overheard his parents whisper about the poor woman's mental condition, saddened when his uncle had her committed. After much deliberation, Alex had decided on a course of action intended to keep Margaret's brother safe and provide an opportunity for Margaret to get the psychiatric help she so desperately needed.

He watched through his binoculars as Margaret moved from their bedroom into the kitchen. Alex had left a very fine bottle of one-hundred-year-old brandy behind. She picked it up and started to splash some in a teacup, then had second thoughts and drank directly from the bottle. Cradling the bottle to her chest like a babe in arms, she danced around the tiny kitchen before she moved back to the bedroom and changed into her black trousers and sweater. Just as the sun went down, Margaret slipped out of the house. There had been many times Alex had witnessed Margaret slip out late at night and return exhausted and smelling of sweat in the early morning hours. He had no idea where she went or what she did while she was away. Would she go for her brother tonight? If so, he needed to hurry. He felt in his pocket for Lady Trevelyan's brooch. As soon as Margaret slipped out of the house and into the shadows, he scurried to the back door and let himself in.

***

Thomas watched as Cat lay on her back – her arm flung over her head, her mouth hanging open, snoring like a drunken sailor – and loved her all the more. Usually Thomas didn't mind Cat's night noises. As a matter of fact, he found them endearing. But the snoring, coupled with worries over his sister, had kept him awake. At 3 a.m., he had given up on sleep all together and had ended up spending the night in his study, sitting in the chair before the fire drinking endless cups of tea. Like a warrior waiting for battle, Thomas – usually a patient man – found the waiting enervating. Every now and again he would patrol the house and check the windows, triple checking everything was appropriately locked. He wished his sister would just come for him, so he could confront her and be done with it.

After the long night passed without incident, Thomas took a tray of tea and toast up to Cat. The autumn chill had settled into the bedroom. He tried to stay quiet as he stoked the fire, creating what appeared to be a cosy atmosphere.

'Good morning.' He felt Cat's eyes on him as he fussed around the bedroom they shared.

'You're worried,' she said. 'Is it about Margaret?'

'I suppose. In truth, I'll feel better once she's shown her face. At least then I'll know what I'm dealing with.' Thomas poured out tea for both of them before he sat in one of the chairs before the fire. 'And then there's Lucy Bardwell's murder and, of course, worries over Michael Grenville.'

'Are you questioning whether or not you should continue working for DCI Kent?'

Startled, Thomas met Cat's eyes. 'I swear, woman, you must be a witch.'

She came to him and snuggled on his lap, wrapping her arms around his neck. 'I'm not a witch, darling. I just know you. So much of your sense of worth is wrapped up in your ability to protect others, especially me.' She smiled. 'Wouldn't it be ironic if I wound up being the one to save you?'

He kissed her. 'You already have, love.'

She kissed his nose and stood. 'Tell me what you're going to do today?'

'See what I can do to help locate and neutralise Michael Grenville, after which I will turn my attention to finding out who killed Lucy Bardwell.'

Cat's face became serious for a moment. 'You will find out who killed her, won't you?'

'You know I can't make promises like that.'

'I also know you'll never forgive yourself if the case goes unsolved,' Cat said. 'I wonder if her brother has any of her diaries or letters. Young girls tend to keep those things. I know I did. Have you asked Ambrose?'

'No,' Thomas said. 'But I'll mention your suggestion to DCI Kent.'

'Don't tell him it was my idea. He'll dismiss it categorically.'

Thomas laughed. 'Good point. I must go. What will you do today?'

'Write letters. I'm going to plead with Lydia to come to us. You're still amenable to her staying here?'

'Of course.' Thomas kissed Cat's cheek and left her to it.

They didn't speak of the relentless bombing in London, but reminders of it showed up every day in the newspapers. The mail was slow now, and Cat had not heard from her Aunt Lydia – a successful artist who thwarted social convention for a more Bohemian lifestyle – in weeks. She was worried and had good reason to be. Not that they didn't have bombs in the North. They did. But they hadn't suffered like the Londoners. According to the newspapers, the bombing wasn't as relentless as it was a year

191

ago, when the Luftwaffe had done their best to decimate the City of London, along with all the major railways and shipping areas, but there was always the risk of bombs. Thomas was surprised Aunt Lydia had remained in London for as long as she had. Although she didn't express it, Thomas knew Cat feared for her aunt's safety. The idea of free-spirited Lydia Paxton mingling with the villagers of Rivenby put a smile on Thomas's face. She'd certainly give them something to talk about.

***

Exhaustion caught up with Thomas just as he arrived at work, where constables loitered, huddled in groups, talking earnestly. Some sat at desks and reviewed reports, somehow able to tune out the buzz of energy surrounding them. Some huddled around a large chalkboard studying the list of assignments.

Thomas found DCI Kent in his office, hunched over a big cup of dark tea. He stared at Thomas with puffy, red-rimmed eyes. 'Good morning, Tom.'

'Sir. What news of Michael Grenville?'

'We got him,' DCI Kent grumbled into his tea. 'Mrs Carlisle's assumption was correct. He came back in the middle of the night and was right surprised to see us there, let me tell you. Put up quite a fight. Broke one lad's nose. Took two men to subdue him. On the way to the car, he broke loose and took off running. They gave chase through the woods. The man who finally got him had to punch him hard enough to knock him out. We put him in a cell, and when he woke up he raised holy hell. Scotland Yard can have him. Good riddance, I say.'

'What? So soon? Don't we at least get to question him about Lucy Bardwell's killer?' In reality, Thomas wanted to give the man a thrashing for his interaction with Cat.

'Alibied. Had to let him go. It seems our illustrious Mr Grenville was locked up in a London nick at the time of Lucy Bardwell's murder. He's desperate, but he's not our murderer.' DCI Kent ran his fingers through his cropped hair.

'So what do we do next?'

'We start at the beginning. Re-interview the witnesses, revisit and re-evaluate the crime scene. I feel like I'm missing something, and I don't know what it is.'

'And Hinks?'

'Getting released this morning. His wife is coming to fetch him.' DCI Kent checked his watch. 'She should be here within the hour. Before she gets here, I'd like to meet with the men and make a plan.'

'With your permission, sir, I'd like to talk to Hinks, ask him for information about Lucy Bardwell we would not get otherwise. If she was seeing someone else, had another circle of friends, or any other secrets, he may know about them.'

'We'll let him go home, eat a meal and sleep in his own bed. Tell him he's got a twenty-four-hour rest period. We'll talk to him after that.'

'No disrespect, sir, but I would like to speak to him today before he goes home. He'll be eager to help so he can get out of here. We can conduct a more thorough interview in a day or two. But I'd like to get some background, if you don't mind. I'm afraid his surly attitude will return once he is out of our control. Knowing Hinks, he'll conjure up a good deal of anger at being locked up.'

DCI Kent stared at Thomas for a moment, before he nodded. 'Agreed. See to it.'

'Sir,' Thomas said. 'I need to tell you something.' He shut DCI Kent's office door and took the chair across from him. 'I have a sister.' He told DCI Kent about Margaret, leaving out the emotional pain about his parents and his own fruitless efforts to find her. When he was finished, he added, 'I felt you should know. She's probably going to come after me.'

'I cannot believe the way that Carlisle woman attracts trouble,' DCI Kent said. He walked to the window and stood with his back to Thomas.

'Cat doesn't have anything to do with this, sir. She didn't attract Margaret. I'm afraid that mess lies with me,' Thomas said.

DCI Kent turned to face him. 'Maybe not. But she didn't hesitate to bring your sister into her home, did she? Life with Mrs Carlisle is going to be interesting, Tom.'

'I think that's part of the attraction, if you don't mind my saying so.' Thomas gave DCI Kent a sheepish grin.

'Do you think your sister had anything to do with Lucy Bardwell's murder?'

'I don't know, sir,' Thomas said. 'I haven't seen her in decades. She was so violent when we were young, my parents had her committed. I don't know what type of woman she became.' Thomas thought about taking Cat away. But where would they go? There was nowhere to run. Thomas and Cat would have to face Margaret. Together, out of necessity, they would see this scenario through. 'If she comes after me, I may need to call for help. I hate to burden you with this, but I've Beck and the missus to think about.'

He was surprised when his superior officer turned to face him, a steely determination in his eyes. 'Of course you'll call for help. That's what we're here for.'

***

Hugh woke up with the sun. He reached for Vera, but the bed was empty, the place where she had lain rumpled and warm and smelling of her. Rolling into her pillow, he paid attention to this feeling, unsure how long it would last, and wanting to remember it. As he sat up, he reached for his bandaged ear, surprised to find the sticking plaster damp. Droplets of blood dotted his pillow. He ran his finger over the stain, a physical reminder of his time in Vera's bed. In all the years he had been married to Margaret, Hugh had never experienced anything like last night. He gave a pleasurable sigh.

Now he had to contend with the idea of George Hinks returning home. Hugh had been so surprised and enraptured by their love-making he had forgotten all about George Hinks. Vera had whispered she loved him right before she fell asleep, the sweet words echoing through his mind as she lay next to him. Their future was uncertain, Hugh acknowledged that, but he wouldn't abandon Vera. How convenient it would have been if George had indeed murdered that girl. How easily their problems would have been solved.

Hugh threw on his clothes and hurried down to the kitchen, where Vera bustled about, busying herself with breakfast. After pouring Hugh's tea, she cracked four eggs into a cast-iron frying pan, sliced four pieces of fresh bread and put them under the grill. Once that was finished, she set about slicing apples. 'There's cheese in the refrigerator. Would you get it?'

Hugh did as she asked, setting the block of cheese on the table before he took her in his arms. 'I don't like the idea of George in bed with you, especially after last night.'

'Don't worry, darling. George won't be sleeping with me.' She gave him a bright smile. 'Ever again.'

'What do you mean?' Hugh hoped against hope Vera had found the strength to toss aside her religious conviction and follow her heart. 'Are you going to leave him?'

'I don't want to speak of it now. Come sit.' Vera looked at him with soft eyes and touched his cheek before she put the toast in the rack and set it on the table. 'I've got fresh butter from Harley's farm. Usually we trade a jar of apples for a chunk of butter. Not anymore. I had to give four jars of apples this time and my butter portion was smaller. It's the rationing.'

'I'm afraid it will get worse before it gets better,' Hugh said. In the beginning, many predicted the war would be over quickly. Hugh had never agreed. Naive in many ways, Hugh had seen the worst of mankind in the trenches. He, along with many men of his ilk, had known that Germany would never rest easy after the Treaty of Versailles. This war would be a long one. Germany wouldn't go down easily. Hitler would never capitulate. Turning his mind to better things, he focused on Vera, the curve of her hips, the feel of her arms around his neck. Soon they were having their breakfast in silent companionship, like an old married couple.

'What will you do with the money?' Vera asked.

'Give it to the police and let them return it to Hermione. I'll need to tell them about Margaret.'

'Your blood has seeped through the sticking plaster. I'll put a fresh one on before we leave.' Vera stared at Hugh's injured ear. 'You should tell the police how she bit your ear, Hugh. It speaks to her state of mind.'

'I intend to.' After sopping up the last of eggs with his toast, Hugh pushed his plate aside, concerned all of a sudden for Vera. Her demeanour was a wee bit too chipper this morning. 'What is it? Something's wrong. I can tell.'

In one efficient motion she swept their plates from the table and plopped them into the sink full of sudsy water. 'Nothing. I'm just trying to cope as best I can.' She turned, her face serious now. On edge already, Hugh's heart leaped. 'I don't want George in this house, Hugh. I don't care if he rots.'

Hugh moved to her, trying to hold her, but she pushed him away. 'Don't. Please. Don't look at me with pity. I can't bear it.'

'I'm not looking at you with pity. You need my help. Surely there's something you can do. Does George have family? Could he stay in a hotel?'

'No, you dear man. That's not the answer. I've something else in mind.' She turned back to the sink and busied herself with the dishes. 'I've made other arrangements. You just need to trust me.'

Hugh left Vera long enough to return to his cottage, shave and put on his best suit. As they walked from Vera's kitchen to the garage, Hugh tried to hold Vera's hand. Distracted, she pushed it away and tossed him the car keys. They didn't speak during the drive. By the time they arrived in Rivenby, Vera's face had become so pale, her eyes so haunted, Hugh wondered if she was ill.

Grabbing her arm before she got out of the car, he said, 'You don't have to do this. I can go in there and tell him you don't want to see him. No one would blame you.'

'I have to face him.' Vera stared straight ahead, not meeting his eyes. 'This is my problem, Hugh. I've never been one to send another body to clean up my messes. No matter what happens, you should know I love you. I never stopped loving you. Seeing you again has changed my life.'

'Vera …' Hugh said. But Vera didn't hear his words. She was already out of the car.

When they entered the lobby area, Vera stepped away from Hugh and hurried over to a female constable. Imagining she was looking for the loo, Hugh didn't think twice when she turned to him and said, 'I'll be right back.'

Hugh watched as Vera walked away from him, her back rigid as a soldier on parade, clutching that blasted handbag as though it were a lifeline.

***

Thomas waited for George Hinks at the desk just outside DCI Kent's office. Situated in the back of the main room, the desk afforded a supervisory view of the constabulary but was well enough away to ensure privacy. DCI Kent had suggested Thomas use the desk while he conducted the morning briefing, and Thomas was glad of it. Aside from a slew of burglaries in surrounding villages, Lucy Bardwell's murder remained the prime focus of the Rivenby Constabulary. Thomas had spent six years in the Army and another twenty-plus years working for Sir Reginald Wright doing undercover work. During his long career, he had served under intelligent men who had achieved success where others surely would have failed. DCI Kent had earned Thomas's respect, along with the respect of his men, who listened intently to the morning briefing. Kent's words were a combination of praise for a job well done so far, and strategy for how to proceed in the future. Shoulders slumped and a collective sigh filled the room when DCI Kent said, 'Now we start over.'

A constable accompanied George Hinks as he stepped into the room, staying towards the back so as not to disturb the others. The time spent in police custody had not been kind to Mr Hinks. Gone was the surly mien and sneering mouth. Gaunt and unshaven, George Hinks's clothes – the same ones he had been wearing when they had taken him from his local pub – smelled of sweat and fear.

He sat down, gazing at Thomas with eyes that were bloodshot and swollen. 'You probably think I had this coming to me.'

'I'm not judging you, Hinks. But we need your help to figure out who killed Lucy. You knew her, probably better than most.'

'Thank you,' he said.

'For what?' Thomas asked.

'Reserving your judgement. I am not deserving of your goodwill. I treated you rotten. And I'm sorry for it. My poor wife. She's going to bear the brunt of this. My god, what a mess I've made.' He rubbed his face. 'I'll help you. I'll tell you anything you need to know.'

'Good,' Thomas said. He handed a list of names to George Hinks as he uncapped his fountain pen. 'Here's a list of all of Lucy Bardwell's friends. Can you think of anyone else we should talk to?'

George read the names and handed the list back to Thomas. 'None on this list. Those are just her mates from school. She had another group of friends, most of them newly relocated from London, her party crowd. She used to meet them at the dances in Hendleigh. A bit wild, but Lucy did like a good time.'

'Good time?'

'She liked to go to the dance clubs, sip from a flask, have a few laughs.'

'How often did you and Lucy spend time together? Did you have a set night you met? And where did you conduct your trysts?' Thomas asked.

Hinks's stomach rumbled. 'I haven't eaten much.'

Thomas ignored him.

'We met on Wednesdays.'

'Hinks, how did you stay away from home so much? Didn't your wife wonder where you where?'

'Vera and I haven't been close these past few years. I started spending most nights with an old Army friend.' He shrugged. 'She didn't seem to miss me.'

And you didn't seem to miss her. Thomas didn't give voice to his words.

'Lucy had money, so she would get us a hotel in Hendleigh.'

'And you would spend the night there?'

'Not me, no. Not the whole night. Lucy would sometimes. But she'd hurry back to Saint Monica's so she could sneak in of a morning. She liked Mrs Carlisle. I want you to know Lucy spoke very highly of her.'

'I'll pass that along. Tell me more about the friends from London. Do you know their names?'

'Not their names.' He fidgeted, as though he were deciding how much to tell Thomas.

'We need your full cooperation, Hinks. If you know something—'

'It's probably nothing. One night Lucy and I were supposed to meet – this was in the beginning before we had our Wednesdays regular like. I followed her and her friends to the dance club near the hotel where she would get our room. I watched her dance with one of the lads – a soldier on leave, I reckon – and when he made a pass at her, she slapped him good. Kicked him in the shin before she flounced off the dance floor. Grabbed her friends and left. She was a tough one, especially for someone so young.' He met Thomas's gaze. 'She didn't deserve to die.' His stomach rumbled again. 'I don't suppose you'd see your way to some tea and biscuits?'

Thomas looked around for a lad he could send to the canteen, but didn't want to take anyone from DCI Kent's briefing. 'I'll go. Wait here.'

Rumour had it the tea in the canteen was strong enough to put hair on your chest. Thomas had never availed himself so he couldn't speak to its quality one way or another. He was always amused at the cornucopia of baked goods, provided by the Women's Institute and a bevy of other citizens, who felt it incumbent upon them to keep the wheels of justice in Rivenby well stocked with baked goods. After loading up a plate for George Hinks, Thomas took the proffered cup of tea and headed back to his desk when he recognised a man talking to the desk sergeant.

'Excuse me,' Thomas said. 'I believe I saw you walking near my house the other day. I'd like to speak with you, if you could spare a moment.'

The man faced Thomas, eyed the plate piled high with biscuits and the cup of tea with a healthy dose of scepticism and said, 'Are you a policeman?'

'In a manner of speaking,' Thomas said.

The man scrutinised Thomas from top to bottom. Finally he gave a grunt of satisfaction. 'Very well. But when we're finished, I'd like to speak to a proper policeman, if you please. I've come to make a statement.'

The man followed Thomas through the back room to the desk where George Hinks sat. DCI Kent had stopped speaking to the group and was now huddled in the corner with three sergeants looking over a large map of the woods behind Saint Monica's. Thomas set the plate of biscuits and the tea in front of George Hinks. 'I'll leave you to eat in peace for a few minutes.'

Hinks nodded as he tucked into the biscuits.

'Come with me, sir,' Thomas said. He led the man away from Hinks to a quiet corner where they could speak without being heard. The man was tall and thin, with bright blue eyes and a weak chin. 'My name is Thomas Charles. I assist in investigations here at the constabulary.' Thomas held out his hand.

200

The man took it. 'Hugh Bettencourt.'

'I saw you near my home the other day. Do you remember?'

The man nodded.

'Did you by chance return a relic and leave it by the front door?'

'Yes, sir. I did.'

Thomas bit back his irritation. The man wasn't exactly forthcoming. 'Would you care to tell me why?'

'First of all, you should know that I had nothing to do with the theft. My wife stole it. I happened to follow her because I knew she was up to no good. We're divorcing, but that's not important. We came here from Scotland so she could collect some sort of inheritance. She was desperate for money, as I have none to give her and she needs to support herself. Shortly after we arrived, I discovered she had blackmailed a dear friend. I've got a letter to prove it. After I found the letter, I grew suspicious, thought she was up to no good. I followed her and saw her and her lover break into your house and steal that relic. Don't know why they buried it in the woods rather than take it with them. But I took it and gave it back to you.'

'So are you saying you just returned the chalice out of the goodness of your heart?' Thomas didn't bother to hide his scepticism.

'Not my choice of words. I feel responsible for my wife'. The man reached into his pocket and took out a packet of money, along with a folded piece of paper, worn thin at the creases. 'My wife discovered Martin had a mistress and used it to ruin him. There's a letter from Martin in there. I found it with Margaret's things. It proves she blackmailed him. If you see the money is returned to Martin's wife, I'd appreciate it. Somehow, I think returning it personally isn't appropriate.' Hugh wiped his eyes with the back of his sleeve.

Thomas read the letter twice. As he read, the strange events clicked into place, and he knew without question the man in front of him was Margaret's husband. 'I'm Margaret's brother. I've been told she came to Rivenby to find me.'

Hugh stared at Thomas, a look of his surprise in his tired eyes. 'Is it true then? Was she coming to you about an inheritance?'

Thomas sighed. 'I don't know. I haven't heard from her, nor have I seen her in years. Frankly, I don't even know what she looks like now. But I've money for her. When I sold our parents' home, I saved her half.'

'That's probably the first honest thing she's told me,' Hugh said.

'Do you have any idea where Margaret is now?'

'I do not. She's taken a cottage near the high street. I'm finished with her. I don't care if I never see her again, quite frankly. The last I time I saw her, she attacked me. Actually bit my ear.' Hugh pointed to his bandaged ear.

'I assume those scratches on your cheek are from her?'

'They are. She went mad. I'm—' He stopped speaking, and stared over Thomas's shoulder, wide-eyed. 'Vera. Good god. What are you doing?'

Thomas turned around to see Vera Hinks approaching her husband, an intent look on her pale face. Her right hand hung at her side. It held a gun.

'Kent,' Thomas shouted.

George Hinks didn't see his wife until she came to a stop behind him.

'Look at me, George.' Her voice was calm.

Hinks turned around to face his wife. As far as Thomas could tell, George Hinks hadn't yet noticed the gun.

'For once in your life, look at me. What do you see? Do you see a woman who has stood faithfully by you?'

She pointed the gun at his chest. George Hinks dropped the biscuit he was eating and put his hands up in surrender.

'Vera! What are you doing? I'm sorry. Oh, god. Please ...'

By the time Vera spoke, everyone in the vicinity noticed the gun. One brave constable tried to creep up to her, but DCI Kent held him back with a quiet shake of his head.

Vera pointed the gun, her hand surprisingly sure.

'I can't do this anymore, George. You expect me to stand by you, ever faithful while you chase women. I've suffered a lifetime of humiliation.' Vera looked at DCI Kent. 'Lucy Bardwell came to our home looking for you. She looked down her nose at me, talked to me as though I were your servant. Can you imagine the humiliation?' She turned her attention back to George. 'I gave her money and drove her back to Rivenby. The way she looked at me when she got out of the car … I just couldn't control myself. When she got out of the car and walked away, her back straight, her head held high, something snapped inside me. I followed her through the woods and—' Tears ran down Vera's face, but she kept the gun trained on George's heart, her hand steady and sure. 'She was so arrogant and sure of herself. It was as though I was possessed by the devil. I crept after her. She didn't even know I was there. When she stopped and pulled a pair of boots out of the bushes, I grabbed a rock and struck her.' Vera's confession resonated through the room, clear and true. 'I've sinned and will have to live with that. God help me, but I don't regret it one bit.'

Thomas slowly moved close to her.

'I'm finished. Finished being humiliated, finished with you.'

'I know, love. I've been rotten,' George Hinks said. He stood up and faced his wife, his hands still up in the air. 'I'll go away. You won't have to see me. I'll divorce you—'

'No. It's too late for that. We can't divorce.' Spittle flew as Vera hissed at her husband. 'And there will always be women. Men like you don't change. You'll meet someone new, tell her you love her, spend your nights with her. And when you're finished, when you've used her up so she no longer satisfies you, you'll come creeping home. I cannot take another second of this. Of you.'

'Vera, please. I'm begging you,' George said.

Thomas edged a little closer. Behind Vera, everyone stood frozen, as though unsure what to do.

Vera noticed Thomas. 'Don't come any closer. I'll shoot you.'

Out of the blue, Hugh Bettencourt sprung to action. He threw himself in front of George Hinks just as Vera fired.

Chapter 20

Pandemonium erupted. Policemen scattered everywhere. Some rushed to Hugh Bettencourt's lifeless body, others went to the phones, and still others ran out of the room, in search of a doctor. Thomas's ears rang. He couldn't hear a thing. This wasn't the first time someone had fired a gun near him. In a few moments, his hearing would return. Vera stood before Hugh's fallen body, her mouth hanging open. Her scream pierced the room, echoed off the walls. Dropping the gun, she fell to her knees beside Hugh. George Hinks went to his wife, trying to put a comforting arm around her. Vera ignored her husband. She pushed him aside and lay down on the cold, hard floor next to Hugh, resting her head on his chest, heedless of the pooling blood that seeped onto her clothes and her cheek.

Ignoring the incessant ringing in his ears, after-effects of the gunshot, Thomas moved towards Vera. Hugh Bettencourt stared at Thomas with lifeless eyes, a bloom of crimson spreading across his chest. Thomas didn't have to take the man's pulse to know he was dead.

Squatting down next to Vera, Thomas put a gentle hand on

her shoulder. Careful to keep his voice calm, he said, 'Come on, Mrs Hinks. You need to come with me now.' He sensed George Hinks behind him.

'She's my wife. I'll take care of her.'

'Did you know she had a gun?' DCI Kent said.

'The gun's mine. It was my service revolver. I kept it hidden in a shoebox. My wife's a good shot. Learned in the war. She doesn't talk about what she did, but I can tell you she knew her way around a gun.'

'Step aside, Mr Hinks,' DCI Kent said.

Together he and Thomas pulled Vera to her feet, trying not to grimace at the splatters of blood that covered her face. Crimson stains were scattered over her jumper, yet she didn't seem to notice. Her eyes had a dull, unseeing look. They lingered on Thomas before they went to her husband. When she spoke to him, her voice sounded rough.

'Stay away from me, George. I don't want you. Go home. Leave me be.'

'Vera, don't say anything. I'm going to get you a solicitor.'

Vera shook her head, locking her eyes onto Hugh. Her eyes filled with tears. They flowed unchecked down her pale checks, dripping off her chin and onto her clothes, mingling with Hugh Bettencourt's blood.

'Mrs Hinks, you need to step away from the body,' DCI Kent said. He spoke to a woman constable who appeared behind him. 'Get her into a holding cell, please. Photograph her with her clothes on before you give her something clean. I don't need to tell you her bloody clothes are evidence.'

'No, sir,' the WPC said.

'And don't leave her alone. Do you understand? I want an officer on a chair outside her cell until I say otherwise.'

'Yes, sir,' the WPC said. Thomas recognised the woman and remembered the calm and level-headed way in which she helped secure the crime scene after Lucy Bardwell's murder. She moved over to Vera Hinks and put a gentle arm around her shoulder. 'Come on, Mrs Hinks. It's time to step away.'

DCI Kent turned to another uniformed constable. 'Get a doctor to see to Mrs Hinks. After she's tended to, report back to me.'

Vera stared down at Hugh, tears streaming down her face.

'I'm so sorry, Hugh. Please forgive me.' She turned away from him and allowed herself to be led away.

'I need to make a phone call, arrange a solicitor,' George said. 'She's not in her right mind.'

'Of course, Mr Hinks. Use the phone in my office to call a solicitor. After that, you'll need to make a statement. I'll get a lad to take it down now. Once you've signed it you're free to leave.'

'Yes, sir.' George Hinks said. He was crying now.

'What do you want me to do, sir?' Thomas said.

'Write up a report of your conversation with Hinks, Thomas. You're a witness now, so you are officially off this investigation. Your statement should contain the circumstances regarding how the dead man wound up back here, and the events leading up to the shooting. Don't leave anything out. I'll assign a detective to the case. He'll want to interview you. Have the report on my desk first thing tomorrow morning. I'll trust you to write the report at home. After that, it's best if you take a few days off.'

'Very well,' Thomas said. He knew better than to argue.

'At least we know who killed Lucy Bardwell.' DCI Kent shook his head. 'We should have seen that. I should have seen that. Mrs Hinks was the most likely suspect, but I didn't give it a second thought.'

'It's hard to suspect a woman,' Thomas said.

'It is indeed,' DCI Kent said. 'I'm going to have a swallow of brandy before I telephone the Chief Superintendent. He'll probably have my job. God, I'm tired.'

'This isn't your fault, sir,' Thomas said.

'I know it's not,' DCI Kent said. 'It's no one's fault. It's a horrid, unfortunate set of circumstances.'

Once DCI Kent shut his office door, Thomas hurried home.

***

Cat sealed the last envelope, set it on the pile of outgoing post and stood up from Thomas's writing desk, relishing the sweet freedom that was now hers. Michael Grenville had been captured, and there was much to do before the wedding. She looked around the room she would share with Thomas after they were married, surprised to find she would be pleased to call this house home. Truth be told, home was where Thomas was. Who would have thought a woman of her age would get a second chance at happiness? Donning old trousers and comfortable walking shoes, she decided to go for a nice long walk. What better way to work through the anxiety of the past few days?

Half an hour later, the letters were posted and Cat was walking briskly on the path towards the moors, a canteen of water over her shoulder. As she walked, she thought about the logistics of Saint Monica's and the steps necessary to hand its management over to a proper board of directors. Papers would need to be drawn up, potential board members would have to be approached. Cat knew from experience many people didn't agree with Saint Monica's purpose. They argued women should stay married, submit to their husbands and be good wives. If their husbands beat them, it was probably their own fault. The very idea made her angry. With a little luck, she hoped to find six or eight people who would be as passionate about Saint Monica's as she was.

Emmeline Hinch-Billings would be the first candidate Cat approached. In addition to a managing board of directors, three or four trusted men would need to be enlisted to serve as a security detail. Cat paused on the trail, turning her face to the sun. As the warm light bathed her face, Cat pushed worries about

Saint Monica's away. Winter would be here soon. She and Thomas would be married. Smiling to herself, she took a sip of fresh water and headed along the trail, wishing she had brought her camera. There was something about the way the subdued autumn light bounced off the red and orange leaves that struck her artist's eye.

Hours later, Cat arrived back at the house, wiped her shoes on the mat outside the kitchen door, and let herself in. 'Hello?' Something wonderful simmered away on the stovetop, and two fresh loaves of bread sat on the worktable. The missus was nowhere to be seen.

'Hello?' Cat called out again.

'In the study. Help!' the missus yelled.

Cat broke into a run, skidding to a stop in her stockinged feet when she reached Thomas's study. Margaret sat behind the desk. Her hair had been styled and a sizable diamond on a delicate chain hung from around her neck. The blue-green wool dress she wore accentuated her eyes. Piles of papers lay scattered in front of her, as though Margaret had been rummaging through the drawers.

The missus stood off to the side, fidgeting with her hands, a worried look on her face. 'I tried to stop her, but she wouldn't—'

'Get us some tea, please,' Margaret ordered.

The missus looked at Cat for approval.

'Now,' Margaret said.

Cat gave the missus a slight shake of the head. To her credit, the missus stayed put. 'Where's Beck?'

'He's gone to fetch chicken wire.'

'That stupid old man?' Margaret inspected her cuticles. 'You think he can protect you?'

Cat's cheeks flushed red, a zig-zagged vein throbbed on her forehead. 'Get up from behind that desk before I forcefully remove you.'

Margaret chuckled. She leaned back in Thomas's chair and crossed her legs as she put her feet up on the desk. 'Aren't you the lady of the manor. You're so smug and self-righteous, acting like you want to save all the injured women, yet you're about to marry a bully yourself. Did you know my little brother used to beat me when we were children?'

Cat gasped and immediately regretted the display of emotion. 'Surprising, isn't it? He also used to watch me in the bathtub.'

This time the wild accusations didn't faze Cat. She didn't believe Margaret. 'What do you want?'

Margaret took her feet off the desk. 'I've come for what's rightfully mine.' With a gleeful laugh, she swept Thomas's papers onto the floor before she turned to the missus and said, 'Clean that up.'

'She's not going to take orders from you, Margaret.'

'You're not married yet, are you?'

'That's none of your business,' Cat said.

Margaret gave Cat a sardonic look. 'You realise as Thomas's next of kin, if he were to die, I would inherit all this.' Her eyes travelled around the room. 'Maybe I'll come back and kill him.'

The missus gasped.

In an instant Cat understood the relentless desire of protectiveness Thomas felt towards her. Margaret would never be allowed to harm Thomas, not if Cat could help it. She took two steps closer to Thomas's desk. Thomas's letter opener – a silver dagger given to him by a friend years ago – sat on top. Cat reached for it. Margaret snatched it away first, holding it in her hand, testing the sharpness of the blade, smiling when it cut her skin. When a tiny droplet of blood appeared on her finger, she wiped it on one of the papers. 'It's sharp. What were you going to do, stab me? Believe me, darling, you haven't got the guts.'

Oh, you are so wrong.

Ignoring the weapon, Cat moved around the back of the desk. Margaret rose. The two women stood nose to nose, an unspoken challenge between them, while the missus watched. When Cat grabbed Margaret's wrist and twisted, Margaret yelped and dropped the letter opener. Wrenching Margaret's arm tighter, she stepped close to Margaret and whispered in her ear. 'If you ever set foot in this house again, I'll kill you.'

A moment of fear flashed in Margaret's eye. Cat let go of her wrist. Margaret stepped away, rubbing the spot where Cat had grabbed her. 'You are a fool, Mrs Carlisle. Helping those women. None of them needed it. They took advantage of you. And you, living in that house, acting as though you're better than everyone else. I'm actually surprised you'd debase yourself by staying in my brother's bed without a wedding ring. Think of what your fellow villagers would say.'

'I'd tell them you were lying if you were to say that,' the missus said. 'Lived here my whole life, I have. They'd believe me over you, missy.'

'Hello, Margaret,' Thomas said.

As though someone flipped a switch, Margaret's expression changed, the aggressive confrontational woman replaced now by smiles and warmth.

'Tommy.' She rushed to her brother with her hands outstretched. 'I'm so pleased to see you.' When Margaret reached him, she wrapped her hands around his neck and pressed against him, as though he were her lover and she wanted to kiss him.

'Stop that.' Thomas pushed Margaret away and stepped closer to Cat. 'Are you all right?'

'Yes,' Cat whispered.

Thomas leaned into her, pretending to kiss her cheek. 'The police are on their way,' he whispered.

Cat smirked.

'Oh, so you've called the police? Whatever for, Tom? You know why I'm here. If you'll just give me my money, I'll be off.' Margaret sat back down behind the desk.

Thomas strode to Margaret. 'Get up,' he barked at her.

211

Cat wondered why Margaret so readily obeyed Thomas. Reaching in his pocket, he took out a ring of keys and unlocked the cabinet behind his desk, drawing out an envelope with Margaret's name scrawled across the front, along with what looked like a small picture, wrapped in brown paper and tied with string. 'That's one half of our parents' estate, the documentation concerning your share, plus interest. Take it.'

'What's this?' Margaret set the envelope on the desk as she unwrapped the string, revealing a small painting of sunflowers.

Thomas's hopeful smile as he watched his sister hold the painting nearly broke Cat's heart.

'You kept this all these years?' Margaret asked him, her voice full of wonder.

'I tried to find you, Margaret. For years. I hired investigators, the lot. Almost tracked you down in France, but alas, you slipped away. From me and from the police.'

Margaret looked at Thomas for a good long moment, staring at him with her head cocked like an eager spaniel, while Thomas let his guard down, exposing the sadness he felt at the loss of a sister who – at least as far as Cat could tell – had never loved him in the first place. Margaret sneered at Thomas as she ripped the painting in half and tossed the pieces on the floor.

'You're a fool, brother. I've no use for you or your sentiment.'

The surprise on Thomas's face, the disappointment, morphed into controlled anger. 'Very well. Take your money and get out of my house. You're to leave me and my family alone. I don't want to hear from you again.'

'Family? You haven't got a family.' She peeked in the envelope. 'This will do very nicely, for now.'

'No,' Thomas said. 'No more. I wasn't required to share that money with you, Margaret. But I did out of the goodness of my heart. I suggest you think twice before pushing me.'

'The goodness of your heart? My god, how I hate you.' Margaret's voice became shrill as she manoeuvred around the desk, positioning herself directly in line with the door. 'You're a bastard, Tom. Did you know that? Mummy and Daddy doted on you, favoured you like a spoiled child, even though Daddy wasn't your real father. Yes, dear brother, our mum was a whore. She coupled in the field with any worker who would have her. You can lay your head down at night knowing you're no more than the bastard child of a farmworker.'

Cat knew Thomas's emotions as well as her own. Taken aback by the exhaustion in his eyes, she watched as he reacted with surprise and then pity at his sister's scathing words.

'Our family was fine until you came along. Bastard child.'

The crunch of tyres on gravel interrupted Margaret's tirade.

Thomas said, 'Oh, good. The police are here. They received an anonymous tip about you, dear sister. Someone called and told them about some stolen diamonds. A brooch, I think they mentioned. Were you in Scotland recently?'

This time Margaret paused, her confidence faltering. 'A brooch? What are you talking about?'

'When I left the constabulary, the police were off to your cottage with a search warrant. They must have found something, stolen jewels, I reckon.'

Cat, Thomas and Margaret watched out the window as four constables got out of the car.

'She's doing a runner,' the missus called, as Margaret pushed Cat aside and ran out of the drawing room towards the back of the house, where the woods and a myriad of trails provided ample opportunity to escape.

'She'll get away,' Cat cried.

She and Thomas, with the missus at their heels, hurried after Margaret, who burst out the back door straight into the arms of a constable. For a moment she struggled, kicking and scratching like a cat. And then her body went limp. The resistance went away as she put her arms around the constable's neck and moulded herself to him. Cat saw the young man's cheeks grow red with embarrassment as he tried to wriggle out of Margaret's clinging grasp. When he finally broke free, the other constable grabbed her arm.

'Come now, lassie. Let's get you in the car.'

Margaret didn't resist. She went with them, docile and submissive, while the missus, Cat and Thomas watched.

'I need a cup of tea,' the missus said, after Margaret was safely tucked into the police car. 'We all do. I'll put the kettle on.' She headed into the kitchen, mumbling under her breath about mad women and the mess in Thomas's study.

'Did you really receive an anonymous tip?' Cat wove her arm through Thomas's as they walked back into the house.

'Yes. I think it was Stephen Templeton's driver. I'm betting he called in the anonymous tip to DCI Kent about the stolen diamonds. Since Margaret is my sister, DCI Kent thought it best I not be a part of the plan to catch her. Lucky I came home when I did.' He turned Cat so she faced him. 'Are you all right? She didn't try to harm you, did she?'

'She threatened to kill you.'

'Well, it's finished now. I'll arrange for a solicitor. At least now she can get some help. She belongs in an asylum.'

'I'm sorry, Thomas,' Cat said as they followed the missus back into the house.

'Whatever for?'

'You longed to reconnect with her.'

Thomas met Cat's eyes. 'For a moment part of me wished things were different. But I'm really not surprised about Margaret. If she wanted to have a relationship with me, she would have allowed herself to be found.' He kissed Cat's forehead. 'You're the only family I need, love.'

***

The next morning, Thomas spent a good hour at his desk writing up his statement regarding Vera Hinks's attempt to murder her

214

husband, and Hugh Bettencourt's resulting death. The heart-breaking consequences of George Hinks's infidelity would be the stuff of stories for decades to come, Thomas reckoned. Hugh Bettencourt's death was a tragedy, a lost opportunity to learn about Margaret's life. Nothing to be done about that. He had just signed his name to the statement, when DCI Kent's car pulled into the driveway.

'DCI Kent's here.' Cat came into the room, looking lovely and carrying their tea on a tray. She set the tray down and moved to the window. 'Something's wrong.'

'Why do you say that?'

'He's got that steely look on his face. His eyes are like ice. Something's happened. I can feel it.'

'It's probably the events of yesterday.'

'I suppose that would be enough to put anyone on edge. I'll go fetch extra cups.'

'Better let me speak to him alone,' Thomas said. Cat gave him a sweet smile, kissed his forehead and shut the door behind her.

DCI Kent didn't speak as Beck showed him and Sergeant Jeffers into the room. The Lucy Bardwell murder had taken its toll on the young sergeant. Thomas reckoned Jeffers had never seen a dead body. Not only had his new promotion put him in the thick of a murder investigation, it had exposed him – via Michael Grenville – to one of the most depraved criminals currently in operation. The poor lad looked as though he hadn't slept in days. The emotionless look on Kent's face told Thomas Cat's assumption had been correct. He folded his statement, placed it in an envelope and held it out to Jeffers.

'Here's my statement. Cat's gone to fetch tea.'

'Thank you.' DCI Kent responded. He nodded at his sergeant, who took the envelope and tucked it in his breast pocket.

'I take it there's been developments?' Thomas said.

'You could say that. Vera Hinks is dead. Lethal dose of sleeping powder.'

'Wasn't she under supervision by a female constable?'

'Apparently she took the overdose before she shot Hugh Bettencourt.'

'My god,' Thomas said, for lack of any other appropriate response.

'So I've got three deaths on my hands, two of them murders and one of them a suicide. And I know what you're going to say, Tom. It's not my fault. I know that. The Superintendent knows that.'

'It doesn't make it any better, does it,' Thomas said. 'What news of my sister?'

'She's been nothing but trouble. We found a stolen brooch among her possessions. Swears up and down she didn't steal it, even though we've got solid evidence she was in Scotland at the time it went missing. She all but confessed to blackmailing a man in Scotland named Martin Shoreham, but insists the brooch was planted by her lover. Sounds farfetched, I know, but she hasn't changed her story.'

'Should I arrange a solicitor for her?'

'No need,' DCI Kent said. 'Someone has already seen to it. Sir John Kettering, no less.'

'Sir John Kettering? How in the world did my sister manage to hire someone like him?'

'Arranged anonymously. Seems your sister has an influential friend or two.' DCI Kent nodded at Sergeant Jeffers, who bade Thomas goodbye as he left the room. When they were alone, DCI Kent said, 'This is for your ears only, Tom. I've received word that Michael Grenville is involved with a ring of men who are searching for art smuggled out of France. They are selling it back to the Germans for exorbitant prices. I've spoken to my superior and he's agreed your chalice can stay at the safe in the constabulary for the time being. Just because Grenville's behind bars doesn't mean someone else won't come for it.'

'Safe?'

'The building used to be a textile mill, as you may recall. The owner used to keep large sums of cash on hand. If you are in agreement, I'll have a few lads come up and help you transport the chalice in the evening, when it's quiet. We won't make a big fuss.'

'Thank you,' Thomas said.

'One more thing. My Superintendent has agreed to personally deliver the money Hugh Bettencourt brought to the police station to Hermione Shoreham. It seems her husband was a very influential man, who donated generously to various police charities.'

Thomas sighed. 'It's been a strange few weeks, hasn't it?'

'It has indeed,' DCI Kent said.

Chapter 21

Lydia arrived at Saint Monica's on an unseasonably warm and sunny day at the end of October. Eschewing her usual trousers and paint-splattered men's button-down shirt for a proper travelling suit, complete with hat, gloves and matching shoes, she showed up on Cat's doorstep with her artist's portfolio under one arm and a small travelling case in the other hand.

When the doorbell rang, Cat said, 'I'll get the door.' She hadn't heard from her aunt in ages. The last letter she received had been so heavily edited by the censors, Cat could hardly put a cohesive sentence together. She had no idea how Lydia or her home in Bloomsbury were faring in the nightly bombing raids. At first, she didn't recognise her Bohemian aunt, who rarely capitulated to social convention in her manner of dress or her attitude. When her mind absorbed the fact Aunt Lydia was standing before her, safe and sound, Cat nearly wept with relief.

'You look surprised. I take it you didn't get my letter?'

Cat burst out laughing and pulled Lydia into her arms. 'Come on, we're in the kitchen.'

Lydia surveyed Cat's trousers and messy hair.

'Looks like we've traded roles,' Lydia said. 'You're dressed like me. And as for this suit' – she looked down at her skirt and silk stockings – 'I hate it!'

'You look beautiful. Very proper.'

'That's the problem,' Lydia said. 'And you, darling niece, look like you've been cleaning house.'

'I have,' Cat said. 'I've much to tell you. But first you must come and meet Bede Turner. She's my housekeeper, friend and expert gardener. We've been scouring like maids today. I'll explain why after you've had tea. I'm hoping you've come to stay?'

'If you'll have me,' Lydia said. Her face grew serious. 'Hettie's gone. The bombs. They never found her body. Her house was reduced to rubble … It's horrible in London. When they stopped the buses, I knew I couldn't stay. I felt like I was just waiting to die.'

'Oh, Lyd,' Cat said. 'What about your paintings? Did you manage to stow them someplace safe?'

'I sold the lot to my publisher. Sounds a bit reckless, doesn't it? But keep in mind I could lose everything at any time. One bomb and all is lost. If you're lucky enough to survive, your property is in ruins. You should see the city. Anyway, I was glad to get the money. I'm going to be a country artist. At least until this bloody war is over.' She gave Cat a surprised look. 'I'm not too presumptuous assuming I can stay here?'

'Of course not.' They made their way into the kitchen, where they found Bede Turner sitting at the kitchen table with her feet propped up. 'Bede, this is my Aunt Lydia.'

Bede wiped her hands on her apron as she approached Lydia with her hand outstretched. 'How do you do, miss.'

'Tea?' Cat asked.

Lydia took off her gloves and tucked them into her purse. 'Something stronger?'

'Sure,' Cat said. She poured tea for both of them before dosing Lydia's with a generous pour of brandy.

Two hours later, the women were sitting in the drawing room, enjoying the afternoon sun. Lydia had kicked off her shoes and now sat on the sofa, her legs curled underneath her. Cat had opened a bottle of champagne – one of the last bottles she'd brought from London – and Bede, Lydia and Cat had toasted to Lydia's safe arrival and Cat's upcoming wedding. Bede had brought in a tray heaped with sandwiches and biscuits.

'So you turned this beautiful house into a shelter for mistreated women, but had to flee when one of the husbands found you?'

'Correct,' Cat said, refilling Lydia's champagne flute. 'And since I'll be moving in with Thomas in a few weeks, I am going to hand off the management to a proper board of directors. I'll be involved in a titular position, but I'm looking forward to a quiet life. I realised I haven't stopped since Benton's death. I'm tired.'

'Words of reason, darling niece,' Lydia said.

'I took on too much too fast,' Cat explained. 'Thomas and Bede warned me of the potential for danger, but I ignored them and ploughed on, certain I was doing the right thing.'

'What a surprise,' Lydia said.

'I know. I made a mistake. There will be other women who need my help. I want to keep Saint Monica's going, but I want it managed in a professional way. Thomas and I have a board of directors already in place. We're looking for one more member. I actually sent a letter to you about this, but I imagine you didn't receive it. I'm hoping you'll consider serving.'

'I'll think about it. This is a noble endeavour, darling. I'm impressed. You've actually used Benton's wealth in a positive way.' She gave Cat a sardonic look. 'And the irony isn't lost on me. Using your inheritance from Ben to fund this. I hope he's rolling in his grave. You look happy, Cat. Things are good with Thomas?'

Cat smiled. 'He's ready for us to be married. So am I. Once we're married, I'll be moving to Heart's Desire. We've a nice big room in readiness for you there.'

'What a hideous name for a house. Your happiness does my heart good, darling.'

'I'm truly content, Lydia. After Ben, I just never thought I would get a second chance.'

Lydia grabbed Cat's hand. 'You had your chance, darling. I'm just glad you took it.'

Chapter 22

Cat and Thomas married in November, on the cold Saturday before Bonfire Night. Stephen Templeton arranged for their marriage to be held at Saint Anne's, the church where Cat's parents were buried. The church had been made redundant years ago, but Stephen Templeton had called in a favour, so Cat and Thomas could be married in the beautiful sanctuary, with its mosaic floors and stained-glass window. They had to make do without electricity or gas to heat the building, but they didn't mind. The ceremony was held with close friends as witnesses, Emmeline Hinch-Billings and her husband Phillip, Beck and the missus, Lydia, Bede Turner, and DCI Kent. Everyone bundled up and huddled together as Cat and Thomas exchanged their vows by candlelight.

Cat's first wedding to Benton Carlisle, so long ago, had been a nerve-wracking, joyless affair. She remembered standing before an immense crowd of strangers, nervous and unsure of herself, in a state of wonder that a man like Benton Carlisle would have chosen her as his wife. He could have had anyone and was often photographed with a glamorous film star or a beautiful heiress on his arm, with the caption *the most eligible bachelor in England* emblazoned beneath. Cat was young and naive at the time of her first wedding. On tenterhooks the entire day, Cat felt certain everyone watched her and judged her. She was too worried about the opinions of others to enjoy her own celebration. Not today. Not with Thomas.

While Stephen Templeton recited the ancient words from the Book of Common Prayer, Cat swore she saw a lone tear slowly roll down Thomas's cheek. When she met his eyes and made her sacred vow to him, she felt the invisible cord that bound them together.

Cat's ward, Annie Havers, who was training to be a nurse, couldn't get away as originally planned. But she gave Cat and Thomas her blessing when Cat told her there would be a proper wedding feast at Heart's Desire during Christmas, to be organised by Bede Turner and the missus. Cat thanked the heavens the two women got along so well. Today, thanks to Bede Turner's clever bartering with ration books and the missus's seemingly endless supply of butter, they would feast on a decadent cake the likes of which Cat hadn't tasted since 1939.

Given the regular admonitions by the newspapers and wireless services not to engage in unnecessary travel during wartime, Cat and Thomas decided to spend their wedding night alone at Heart's Desire. Beck and the missus were going directly to Beck's brother's house for a few days. The missus had prepared ample food and had given specific instructions on how to heat up the various meals. Cat was looking forward to being alone with Thomas. Although he never let on, the incident with Margaret had troubled him deeply. Even though he was in a joyful mood and smiled and laughed as he usually did, Cat felt her husband's undercurrent of sadness. Only time would cure his hurt.

The wedding party had just left the church, amid much laughter and teasing, when Sergeant Jeffers got out of a police saloon parked across the lane and walked up to DCI Kent, a serious look on his face.

Jeffers nodded at Thomas and Cat. 'Congratulations.'

'What in the world are you doing here, Jeffers?' asked Kent. 'Isn't this your weekend off?'

'It was supposed to be. The wife and I were going to visit her sister,' Jeffers said. 'But the Superintendent called me and told me to fetch you.' Jeffers directed his gaze at DCI Kent. 'He wouldn't tell me why he wanted us to report, he just told me to fetch you and was rather insistent that we come right away.'

'Very well.' DCI Kent turned to Thomas and Catherine. 'I'm sorry to miss out on that cake.'

'We'll save you some,' Cat said.

'Congratulations, Thomas.' The two men shook hands. 'You two are very good together.'

Aren't we just, Cat thought as Thomas took her hand and led her towards their friends.

***

Cat and Thomas dropped Lydia back at Saint Monica's and made it back to Heart's Desire by early afternoon. The house seemed empty without Beck and the missus to greet them and cold without a continual fire going during the day.

'I'll tend to the fire,' Thomas said. He didn't wait for Cat's answer, just hurried into his study. Although not the biggest room in the house, they had taken to spending most of their time there, lounging before the fire in the comfortable chairs, yet giving Thomas the freedom to work at his desk, should the need arise.

'Wait.' Cat grabbed his hand before he hurried off. 'What's the matter? You've been looking over your shoulder since Sergeant Jeffers showed up at our wedding.'

Thomas stepped around Cat and locked the front door, double checking it held fast. 'I'm sorry, love. Something's not right. I've got that feeling again.'

'What feeling?'

'Like we're being watched.'

224

At Thomas's words, Cat shivered. She felt it too. 'No. We're not doing this on our wedding night. Let's go through the house together, check the windows and doors are locked. Once that's finished, let's try and forget about it.' She put her arms around his waist and leaned against him. 'We can open that bottle of champagne the missus left chilling for us. After that, we'll get out of these clothes.'

Thomas smiled at her. 'I love it when you take charge, Mrs Charles.'

Cat bowed. 'I'm pleased that you appreciate my strong personality.'

Thomas chuckled as he and Cat set out to secure the house.

***

When the clock struck midnight Cat woke up, entangled in Thomas's arms on the thick rug in front of the study fireplace. Her arm was numb from sleeping on it, but she was content. The fire had gone out, the chilly air a reminder that winter would arrive soon. The empty champagne bottle and two plates that held the crumbs of the ham sandwiches they had eaten sat next to their empty glasses. Thomas lay on his side, his mouth open, snoring softly, his arm draped over Cat. She stood, covered Thomas with a throw and padded naked up the stairs. *It's cold enough to snow*, Cat thought. Once in the bedroom, she lit the fire the missus had laid earlier, waiting for the flames to take hold, and throwing another two logs on before she drew herself a bath. She soaked until the water ran cold, surprised that Thomas didn't join her. Surely he'd woken up when he heard the water running. Reaching for her warmest dressing gown, she headed back down to the study to wake him, knowing tomorrow his back would be sore from sleeping on the hard floor.

Back downstairs, Cat's eyes were drawn to the open window and the freezing night air that filled the room. *Why did Thomas open the window?* For a moment Cat envisioned the Luftwaffe above, seeing the dim light of the coals on the fireplace and dropping a bomb on them. When her eyes adjusted to the dark, she saw the man who stood before Thomas's desk, with his back facing her, a steaming cup of tea sitting on the table, eating the wedding cake she had saved for DCI Kent. She would have recognised him anywhere.

Michael Grenville. Making himself very comfortable in her home. The desk chair had been moved over to the fireplace. Thomas sat in it, naked, his arms and legs bound, a gag in his mouth. Her stomach clenched in fear as her brain absorbed the scene before her. By some stroke of luck, she didn't cry out. Cat should have flinched seeing Thomas so utterly dominated, but the anger rose from her stomach, like acrid bile, a bitter taste that blossomed in her mouth, enraging her all the more. Forcing herself to remain calm, she stilled her breath and backed out of the doorway, standing in the hall by the front door, just out of sight. She had the advantage. Michael Grenville wasn't yet aware of her presence. Her eyes wandered to a bust of Alexander Hamilton, which sat on the sideboard to Cat's left. In five steps she could take it in hand. Six steps to Grenville. One sweeping motion, one bash on the head and Grenville would be dead. Killing him would be so easy.

Thomas met Cat's eyes and gave a slight shake of the head. He winked at her, as though being bound and gagged was an everyday occurrence. *Does he have some plan?*

She turned and ran up the stairs, quiet as a mouse and light as a feather, thanking the gods, the goddesses, and everything in between that she and Thomas had an upstairs telephone extension on the dial system.

'Rivenby Constabulary,' an anonymous voice said on the other line.

'This is Catherine Carlisle – Charles. Catherine Charles. I'm with Thomas Charles. At Heart's Desire. Michael Grenville is here. Please send help.'

'Sorry, ma'am. Can you speak up? Seems we have a bad connection.'

'No. I cannot speak up. Send the police. Help—'

'Nice try.' The voice whispered in her ear. Like a striking viper, Michael Grenville wrenched the phone out of her grasp, grabbed a large chunk of her hair and dragged her downstairs to the study, where he threw her on the couch.

'You and I are going to have a little talk,' Michael Grenville said. 'You're going to tell me what you've done with my wife.'

'You don't want her back,' said Cat. 'You want her money. What kind of a woman would want to stay with you, enslaved and living in squalor while you do whatever it is you do all day.' She stood and moved towards Michael Grenville like she had when he confronted her in the garden. 'Get out of my house, Mr Grenville. We've nothing to say to you.'

He stood up, tipped his head back and laughed.

'Your breath is odious,' Cat said. 'Do you ever clean your teeth?'

The sting of a slap took Cat by surprise, but she didn't flinch, didn't look away. 'You don't scare me, Mr Grenville. I don't kowtow to bullies.'

Grenville moved to Thomas and tore the gag from his mouth. 'Tell her to cooperate.'

Thomas's voice was husky from being gagged. 'Don't tell him anything. He's going to kill us anyway. When he finds his wife, he'll kill her, too. Or find someone else to do it.'

Grenville punched Thomas twice in the face. The second punch knocked Thomas out. His head flopped forward, blood dripping from his nose. Grenville grabbed Thomas by the hair and forced his head up. Sneering at Cat, he said, 'How's that, you little bitch? You'll talk now, won't you? I've killed other men with these fists. Believe me when I tell you that I'll kill him. Save him. Tell me where my wife is.'

Cat didn't think, didn't evaluate her response or consider the consequences of her actions. She catapulted off the sofa and launched herself at Michael Grenville. She scratched and clawed and pummelled. Despite the quick fury of her attack, Grenville was not only stronger, but he possessed the skills of an experienced, dirty-playing street fighter. He pushed her away so hard she nearly stumbled to the ground. They stood facing each other. Scratch marks rose across Grenville's cheeks. His eyes blazed with fury.

'I'm going to beat your husband some more. When you're ready to tell me where Alice is, I'll stop.' He spoke the words without anguish or emotion. He spoke as if killing a man with his bare hands were an everyday occurrence.

When he turned his back on Cat, she launched herself at him once again, this time jumping on his back, wrapping her legs around his waist and grabbing his neck in a strangle hold, squeezing for all her might. For the briefest moment, she felt the strength drain out of him. He wobbled on his feet. She squeezed harder. In a surprising show of strength, Grenville grunted before he backed into the wall, slamming Cat against it hard enough to knock the wind out her. When she let go and fell to the floor, Grenville hurried back to Thomas. Unable to breathe, unable to move, Cat watched as Grenville clenched his fists, taking his time as he approached Thomas, who still remained unconscious. She opened her mouth to cry out just as the front door splintered open, and Sergeant Jeffers, along with a slew of constables burst into the room.

***

An hour later, DCI Kent, Sergeant Jeffers and Cat stood outside the closed door of the study, waiting while the doctor examined Thomas. He had drifted in and out of consciousness, and it was all Cat could do to not break down the door to get to him.

'You did a good turn, Jeffers,' DCI Kent said.

'Thank you, sir.'

DCI Kent turned to Cat. 'We heard Grenville had escaped. He told his cellmate he was headed to Rivenby. Scotland Yard didn't believe him. Thought it was just a ruse to get them looking in the wrong place. He's got a vast criminal network in the south. But Jeffers was onto him. Thought he'd come here looking for his wife.'

'Thank you, Sergeant Jeffers,' Cat said. She wiped her tears with the back of her hand and pulled her dressing gown tight around her.

'Sorry about your front door,' Sergeant Jeffers said.

'That's all right. Front doors are fixable.' Cat accepted a hand-kerchief from DCI Kent and wiped her eyes. 'Grenville was going to kill him. And enjoy doing it.'

'He'll be all right, Mrs Charles. You'll see,' Sergeant Jeffers said.

'Grenville will go to prison now, Mrs Charles. He's wanted in connection with three other deaths, and we've evidence of his smuggling operation.' DCI Kent said. 'This time he won't escape.'

The door opened and the doctor came out, closing the study door behind him. He gave Cat a kind look. 'He's concussed, but he should heal. He needs absolute rest. I cannot impress upon this enough. He must stay in bed for the next couple of days, after that very little activity. I'll arrange a nurse, as he needs to be carefully monitored.' The doctor turned to DCI Kent and Sergeant Jeffers. 'If you gentlemen will help me get him upstairs, once he's in bed, I'll sedate him.'

'Thank you,' Cat said.

Cat stayed out of the way while Thomas put his arms around Sergeant Jeffers and DCI Kent. With some effort, they managed to get him upstairs and into bed.

After everyone had left and Thomas was tucked in bed, asleep from the sedation the doctor administered, Cat stood in the study, amid Michael Grenville's destruction. In the chaos, Thomas's inkwell and favourite fountain pen had been knocked off the desk. The nib of the fountain pen was ruined. The inkwell had spilled and it now lay in a pool of blue on the rug. Cat shook her head. It would take all day to clean up the mess. She didn't have the heart to leave it for the missus.

She thought of the women who by necessity were forced to live with brutes like Michael Grenville. Thank goodness Alice had got away. Cat allowed herself to feel a brief moment of pride. This work would never end, but the satisfaction of making even a small difference was worth the risk.

Cat shut the door of the study just as the sun came up. She'd clean the evidence of Michael Grenville's destruction tomorrow.

Chapter 23

Christmas Eve, 1941

Saint Monica's glittered with the Christmas candles Emmeline Hinch-Billings had spread through the hallway. The smell of biscuits and cakes in the oven permeated the house. Lydia had woven garlands around the sweeping bannister, and by some unknown set of circumstances, Lydia and Emmeline had managed to find a piano in need of a new home. It now rested in the corner, fitting perfectly near the stairs. The newly founded Board of Directors of Saint Monica's were circled around it, along with Ambrose Bardwell and the three men he'd hired to serve as a security detail. Emmeline did a fine job of playing Christmas carols, while Lydia, whose voice was entirely off key, sang the loudest.

It was official. Cat had formed a board of directors and had handed the running of Saint Monica's off to a more competent and less emotionally invested group of people, handpicked by her. Soon Cat and Thomas would meet Annie's train and return to Heart's Desire to celebrate their first Christmas as a married couple.

Things were changing for England and for the world. It didn't take long after the Japanese bombed a naval base in Hawaii for the Americans to enter the war. Churchill and Roosevelt were working together, and a sense of hope and optimism hung in the air. They still lived with the worry of bombs, rationing and curfews. But there was no denying that the tide was turning.

'Champagne?' Thomas handed Cat a flute of bubbling golden liquid. She sipped and leaned into him.

'This is delicious.'

'Enjoy it. We've only two more bottles left.'

Cat clinked glasses with her husband.

'Happy Christmas, Mrs Charles,' he said.

Cat stood on her tiptoes and gave Thomas a quick kiss. Arm in arm, they stepped towards the group as Emmeline played the opening notes of 'Silent Night'.

Acknowledgements

I've dreamed of writing novels and entertaining readers with my stories since childhood. As my love of reading developed over the years, British mysteries quickly became my go-to source of entertainment and writing inspiration. The Cat Carlisle Series is an homage to the mysteries that have inspired me so deeply.

As with all my books, many people helped me stay the course and write the best story possible. My beta readers in the US and the UK caught my silly mistakes and inconsistencies. Big thanks to Courtney Swan, Kim Laird, Gloria Bagwell-Rowland, Janet Robinson, Angela Baxter, and Cheryl Henriksen. Annie Whitehead made herself available to chase down strange questions about train travel and other miscellaneous details about the Northern England in the 1940s. Heartfelt thanks to Abi Fenton for pushing me to grow as a writer and dig deep for a more meaningful story.

And finally, a big thanks to all of you who have read and reviewed my books. I appreciate you so much!

Keep reading for an excerpt from
The Silent Woman ...

Prologue

Berlin, May 1936

It rained the day the Gestapo came.

Dieter Reinsinger didn't mind the rain. He liked the sound of the drops on the tight fabric of his umbrella as he walked from his office on Wilhelmstrasse to the flat he shared with his sister Leni and her husband Michael on Nollendorfstrasse. The trip took him the good part of an hour, but he walked to and from work every day, come rain or shine. He passed the familiar apartments and plazas, nodding at the familiar faces with a smile.

Dieter liked his routine. He passed Mrs Kleiman's bakery, and longed for the *pfannkuchen* that used to tempt passers-by from the display window. He remembered Mrs Kleiman's kind ways, as she would beckon him into the shop, where she would sit with him and share a plate of the jelly doughnuts and the strong coffee that she brewed especially to his liking. She was a kind woman, who had lost her husband and only son in the war.

In January the Reich took over the bakery, replacing gentle Mrs Kleiman with a ham-fisted fraulein with a surly attitude and no skill in the kitchen whatsoever. *No use complaining over things that cannot be fixed*, Dieter chided himself. He found he no longer had a taste for *pfannkuchen*.

By the time he turned onto his block, his sodden trouser legs clung to his calves. He didn't care. He thought of the hot coffee he would have when he got home, followed by the vegetable soup that Leni had started that morning. Dieter ignored the changes taking place around him. If he just kept to himself, he could rationalise the gangs of soldiers that patrolled the streets, taking pleasure in the fear they induced. He could ignore the lack of fresh butter, soap, sugar, and coffee. He could ignore the clenching in his belly every time he saw the pictures of Adolf Hitler, which hung in every shop, home, café, and business in Berlin. If he could carry on as usual, Dieter could convince himself that things were just as they used to be.

He turned onto his block and stopped short when he saw the black Mercedes parked at the kerb in front of his apartment. The lobby door was open. The pavement around the apartment deserted. He knew this day would come – how could it not? He just didn't know it would come so soon. The Mercedes was running, the windscreen wipers swooshing back and forth. Without thinking, Dieter shut his umbrella and tucked himself into the sheltered doorway of the apartment building across the street. He peered through the pale rain and bided his time. Soon he would be rid of Michael Blackwell. Soon he and Leni could get back to living their quiet life. Leni would thank him in the end. How could she not?

Dieter was a loyal German. He had enlisted in the *Deutsches Heer* – the Germany Army – as an 18-year-old boy. He had fought in the trenches and had lived to tell about it. He came home a hardened man – grateful to still have his arms and legs attached – ready to settle down to a simple life. Dieter didn't want a wife. He didn't like women much. He didn't care much for sex, and he had Leni to care for the house. All Dieter needed was a comfortable chair at the end of the day and food for his belly. He wanted nothing else.

Leni was five years younger than Dieter. She'd celebrated her fortieth birthday in March, but to Dieter she would always be a child. While Dieter was steadfast and hardworking, Leni was wild and flighty. When she was younger she had thought she would try to be a dancer, but quickly found that she lacked the required discipline. After dancing, she turned to painting and poured her passion into her work for a year. The walls of the flat were covered with canvases filled with splatters of vivid paint. She used her considerable charm to connive a showing at a small gallery, but her work wasn't well received.

Leni claimed that no one understood her. She tossed her paint-brushes and supplies in the rubbish bin and moved on to writing. Writing was a good preoccupation for Leni. Now she called herself a writer, but rarely sat down to work. She had a desk tucked into one of the corners of the apartment, complete with a sterling fountain pen and inkwell, a gift from Dieter, who held a secret hope that his restless sister had found her calling.

Now Michael Blackwell commandeered the writing desk, the silver pen, and the damned inkwell. Just like he commandeered everything else.

For a long time, Leni kept her relationship with Michael Blackwell a secret. Dieter noticed small changes: the ink well in a different spot on Leni's writing desk and the bottle of ink actually being used. The stack of linen writing paper depleted. Had Leni started writing in earnest? Something had infused her spirit with a new effervescence. Her cheeks had a new glow to them. Leni floated around the apartment. She hummed as she cooked. Dieter assumed that his sister – like him – had discovered passion in a vocation. She bought new dresses and took special care with her appearance. When Dieter asked how she had paid for them, she told him she had been economical with the housekeeping money.

For the first time ever, the household ran smoothly. Meals were produced on time, laundry was folded and put away, and the house sparkled. Dieter should have been suspicious. He wasn't.

He discovered them in bed together on a beautiful September day when a client had cancelled an appointment and Dieter had decided to go home early. He looked forward to sitting in his chair in front of the window, while Leni brought him lunch and a stein filled with thick dark beer on a tray. These thoughts of home and hearth were in his mind when he let himself into the flat and heard the moan – soft as a heartbeat – coming from Leni's room. Thinking that she had fallen and hurt herself, Dieter burst into the bedroom, only to discover his sister naked in the bed, her limbs entwined with the long muscular legs of Michael Blackwell.

'Good god,' Michael said as he rolled off Leni and covered them both under the eiderdown. Dieter hated Michael Blackwell then, hated the way he shielded his sister, as if Leni needed protection from her own brother. Dieter bit back the scream that threatened and with great effort forced himself to unfurl his hands, which he was surprised to discover had clenched into tight fists. He swallowed the anger, taking it back into his gut where it could fester.

Leni sat up, the golden sun from the window forming a halo around her body as she held the blanket over her breasts. 'Dieter, darling,' she giggled. 'I'd like you to meet my husband.' Dieter took the giggle as a taunting insult. It sent his mind spinning. For the first time in his life, he wanted to throttle his sister.

At least Michael Blackwell had the sense to look sheepish. 'I'd shake your hand, but I'm afraid …'

'We'll explain everything,' Leni said. 'Let us get dressed. Michael said he'd treat us to a special dinner. We must celebrate!'

Dieter had turned on his heel and left the flat. He didn't return until late that evening, expecting Leni to be alone, hurt, or even angry with him. He expected her to come running to the door when he let himself in and beg his forgiveness. But Leni wasn't alone. She and Michael were waiting for Dieter, sitting on the couch. Leni pouted. Michael insisted the three of them talk it out and come to an understanding. 'Your sister loves you, Dieter. Don't make her choose between us.'

Michael took charge – as he was wont to do. Leni explained that she loved Michael, and that they had been seeing each other for months, right under Dieter's nose. Dieter imagined the two of them, naked, loving each other, while he slaved at the office to put food on the table.

'You could have told me, Leni,' he said to his sister. 'I've never kept anything from you.'

'You would have forbidden me to see him,' Leni said. She had taken Michael's hand. 'And I would have defied you.'

She was right. He would have forbidden the relationship. As for Leni's defiance, Dieter could forgive his foolish sister that trespass. Michael Blackwell would pay the penance for Leni's sins. After all, he was to blame for them.

Leni left them to discuss the situation man to man. Dieter found himself telling Michael about their parents' deaths and the life he and Leni shared. Michael told Dieter that he was a journalist in England and was in Germany to research a book. *So that's where the ink and paper have been going,* Dieter thought. When he realised that for the past few months Michael and Leni had been spending their days here, in the flat that he paid for, Dieter hated Michael Blackwell even more. But he didn't show it.

Michael brought out a fine bottle of brandy. The two men stayed up all night, talking about their lives, plans for the future, and the ever-looming war. When the sun crept up in the morning sky, they stood and shook hands. Dieter decided he could pretend to like this man. He'd do it for Leni's sake.

241

'I love your sister, Dieter. I hope to be friends with you,' Michael said.

Dieter wanted to slap him. Instead he forced a smile. 'I'm happy for you.'

'Do you mind if we stay here until we find a flat of our own?'

'Of course. Why move? I'd be happy if you both would live here in the house. I'll give you my bedroom. It's bigger and has a better view. I'm never home anyway.'

Michael nodded. 'I'd pay our share, of course. I'll discuss it with Leni.'

Leni agreed to stay in the flat, happy that her new husband and her brother had become friends.

Months went by. The three of them fell into a routine. Each morning, Leni would make both men breakfast. They would sit together and share a meal, after which Dieter would leave for the office. Dieter had no idea what Michael Blackwell got up to during the day. Michael didn't discuss his personal activities with Dieter. Dieter didn't ask about them.

He spent more and more time in his room after dinner, leaving Leni and Michael in the living room of the flat. He told himself he didn't care, until he noticed subtle changes taking place. They would talk in whispers, but when Dieter entered the room, they stopped speaking and stared at him with blank smiles on their faces.

It was about this time when Dieter noticed a change in his neighbours. They used to look at him and smile. Now they wouldn't look him in the eye, and some had taken to crossing the street when he came near. They no longer stopped to ask after his health or discuss the utter lack of decent coffee or meat. His neighbours were afraid of him. Leni and Michael were up to something, or Michael was up to something and Leni was blindly following along.

During this time, Dieter noticed a man milling outside the

flat when he left for his walk to the office. He recognised him, as he had been there the day before, standing in the doorway in the apartment building across the street. Fear clenched Dieter's gut, cramping his bowels. He forced himself to breathe, to keep his eyes focused straight ahead and continue on as though nothing were amiss. He knew a Gestapo agent when he saw one. He heard the rumours of Hitler's secret police. Dieter was a good German. He kept his eyes on the ground and his mouth shut.

Once he arrived at his office, he hurried up to his desk and peered out the window onto the street below. Nothing. So they weren't following him. Of course they weren't following him. Why would they? It didn't take Dieter long to figure out that Michael Blackwell had aroused the Gestapo's interest. He had to protect Leni. He vowed to find out what Michael was up to.

His opportunity came on a Saturday in April, when Leni and Michael had plans to be out for the day. They claimed they were going on a picnic, but Dieter was certain they were lying when he discovered the picnic hamper on the shelf in the kitchen. He wasn't surprised. His sister was a liar now. It wasn't her fault. He blamed Michael Blackwell. He had smiled and wished them a pleasant day. After that, he moved to the window and waited until they exited the apartment, arm in arm, and headed away on their outing. When they were safely out of sight, Dieter bolted the door and conducted a thorough, methodical search.

He went through all of the books in the flat, thumbing through them before putting them back exactly as he found them. Nothing. He rifled drawers, looked under mattresses, went through pockets. Still nothing. Desperate now, he removed everything from the wardrobe where Michael and Leni hung their clothes. Only after everything was removed did Dieter see the wooden crate on the floor, tucked into the back behind Michael's tennis racket. He took it out and lifted the lid, to reveal neat stacks of brochures, the front of which depicted a castle and a charming German village. The cover read, *Lernen Sie Das Schone Deutschland*: Learn About Beautiful Germany. Puzzled, Dieter took one of the brochures, opened it, read the first sentence, and cried out.

Inside the brochure was a detailed narrative of the conditions under Hitler's regime. The writer didn't hold back. The brochure told of an alleged terror campaign of murder, mass arrests, execution, and an utter suspension of civil rights. There was a map of all the camps, which – at least according to this brochure – held over one hundred thousand or more Communists, Social Democrats, and trade unionists. The last page was a plea for help, a battle cry calling for Hitler and his entire regime to be overthrown.

Dieter's hand shook. Fear made his mouth go dry. They would all be taken to the basement at Prinz Albrecht Strasse for interrogation and torture. If they survived, they would be sent to one of the camps. A bullet to the back of the head would be a mercy. Sweat broke out on Dieter's face; drops of it formed between his shoulder blades. He swallowed the lump that formed in the back of his throat, as the fear morphed into blind, infuriating anger and exploded in a black cloud of rage directed at Michael Blackwell.

How dare he expose Leni to this type of danger? Dieter needed to protect his sister. He stuffed the brochures back in the crate, put the lid on it, and pushed the box back into the recesses of the wardrobe. There was only one thing for Dieter to do.

Dear Reader,

We hope you enjoyed reading this book. If you did, we'd be so appreciative if you left a review. It really helps us and the author to bring more books like this to you.

Here at HQ Digital we are dedicated to publishing fiction that will keep you turning the pages into the early hours. Don't want to miss a thing? To find out more about our books, promotions, discover exclusive content and enter competitions you can keep in touch in the following ways:

JOIN OUR COMMUNITY:

Sign up to our new email newsletter: hyperurl.co/hqnewsletter

Read our new blog www.hqstories.co.uk

🐦 : https://twitter.com/HQDigitalUK

📘 : www.facebook.com/HQStories

BUDDING WRITER?

We're also looking for authors to join the HQ Digital family!
Please submit your manuscript to:

www.hqstories.co.uk/want-to-write-for-us/

Thanks for reading, from the HQ Digital team

If you enjoyed *House of Lies*, then why not try another gripping mystery from HQ Digital?